*The*

*Two-Headed*

*Calf*

BOOKS BY SANDRA BIRDSELL

Novels

*The Missing Child* (1989)
*The Chrome Suite* (1992)

Short Fiction

*Night Travellers* (1982) and *Ladies of the House* (1984),
reissued in one volume entitled *Agassiz Stories* (1987)
*The Two-Headed Calf* (1997)

# SANDRA BIRDSELL

## *The Two-Headed Calf*

**Canadian Cataloguing in Publication Data**

Birdsell, Sandra, 1942-
    The two-headed calf

ISBN 0-7710-1454-6

I. Title.

PS8553.I76T86 1997   C813'.54   C97-930052-5
PR9199.3.B57T86   1997

The publishers acknowledge the support of the Canada Council and the Ontario Arts Council for their publishing program.

Book design by Kong Njo
Typesetting by MacTrix DTP

Printed and bound in Canada

McClelland & Stewart Inc.
*The Canadian Publishers*
481 University Avenue
Toronto, Ontario
M5G 2E9

1  2  3  4  5  6    02  01  00  99  98  97

For Betty Dyck

# Contents

# I Used to Play Bass in a Band

❧❧

I was out after dark when Roland arrived. I was salvaging clematis vines that had become intertwined with fleabane, amazed as always at how the wilderness of the prairie is only as far as the back gate and marches in at the slightest whiff of carelessness. Roland wanted, he said, to fill me in on what changes had taken place in the neighbourhood while I'd been away. Roland was one of the few who had grown up in the Wolseley district and now, in his mid-sixties, played the role of historian and custodian, overseeing the struggle of the community between gentrification and stagnation.

He climbed wearily up the stairs and I followed, thinking that he'd grown seedier, that his pants bagged at the knees and seat more than usual. I wondered if living on the West Coast had given me a muted watercolour way of seeing things, because Winnipeg, my street, and Roland seemed blunt and excessively ordinary. From between the houses came a shout, singing, and the clink of empty beer bottles being carried to the Sherbrook Hotel to be redeemed for full ones.

"The night run begins," I said. "That hasn't changed."

"Should throw a match to it," Roland said, his standard refrain at the end of his sling of grievances about the hotel.

It was the first place newly released inmates from Stony headed for, he complained. It had become a kind of think-tank and resource centre for ex-convicts and people whose lives had stopped. There was a new guy in the neighbourhood, he said, who looked as if his face had been used for an ashtray. But it wasn't so much his appearance, he said, as it was that his pan-handling was so aggressive. Shouting "faggot!" when Roland refused to dole out coins.

I hid my grin. I had lit a citronella candle and it flickered between our chairs. Otherwise, we were in darkness.

Roland is the kind of person you dislike yourself for needing. His skin has sallowed from cigarette smoke and creased from an overindulgence in caustic commentaries on the people who pass by his real-estate agency on Maryland. "Another christly boggan," he says, meaning a person who, on moving day, will likely transport his belongings from one rooming house to another in a grocery cart. He's coined the word "boggan" from "toboggan." It's his code word for native people who have come down from the north. Of my tenant he'd once said, "She's one of those autistic types, but employed." Because I'm a writer, and not a painter or a musician or an actor, I am therefore, in Roland's opinion, not "autistic."

I had planned during the flight home from Vancouver how I would go about reclaiming my space. What colours I would paint the walls after I had pitched out or scrubbed away evidence of the tenant. I hadn't met the woman who had rented my house. A double-bass player, new to the Winnipeg Symphony, Roland had told me on the telephone. Normally, he wouldn't touch rentals, he'd said. I was the exception. She'd come from San Francisco. She had found it difficult getting used to flannel bedsheets in the winter. They made her feel like a barbarian, she had told Roland. As if she were sleeping between fur pelts, her body slathered with seal oil to prevent her skin from cracking and flaking off in our dry winter air. She'd gone out and bought humidifiers for her piano. The woman also gave music lessons, and the only concession to her needs was that Roland had had to store my couch and a chair to make room for her grand piano. I had expected the walls to be streaked from moisture but they weren't. And when I came across three boxes of corn starch and identical packages of raisins and pasta, all opened and partly used, I decided I would have liked the tenant, and my desire to redecorate subsided. She'd been a harried overachiever, I guessed, or else a dreamer, which probably amounts to the same thing.

Shortly after, as if an imp had been waiting in the rafters for me to return and on a cue had opened a trapdoor, all my past came tumbling down around my head and shoulders in multi-coloured chunks. Safeway bags full of photographs slid from a shelf in an upstairs closet where, in desperation, I had flung them before I'd left.

I stood looking down at the photographs scattered across the floor, at the toothless gaps in the eager grins of my three children, at how their features became rearranged as they made their onward trek to adulthood; startling or subtle changes. At the cat I had inherited with my house when I bought it: a ginger tabby that kept returning to me. One of my sisters said she needed a mouser, and so she took it to her farm beyond the city's perimeter, and, a week later, it leapt over my back gate and sauntered through the garden. At first I thought it was a phantom come to haunt me. The next time, it hitched a ride with my sister into the city. She caught sight of it in the rear-view mirror, springing over the tailgate as she stopped for the first traffic light. A day later a shadow passed across the kitchen window. The cat, peering in at me.

I saw photographs of Christmas gatherings at my mother's home, my sisters' hair colouring changing yearly from red to blonde, to frosted combinations of brunette. Their men, steadily balding and greying.

And I saw myself, sitting in front of my mother's house on a kitchen chair on a particular spring day along with several members of my family. Have you heard from your children, lately? my sisters had asked. All of us, gathering at our mother's to exchange progress reports on the children we had launched. Theirs, to houses in the same city and even neighbourhoods; mine, for some suspect reason, had gone farther afield. I told them that, on one hand, I was glad Christina was gone. At least there wouldn't be any more stray cats, the needy people she had kept bringing home. On the other hand, I missed her. I still do. My youngest child is away in Japan. Within a month of getting there, she began writing angry and accusing letters about the *Enola Gay*, as if I had something to do with that. This will not happen when I rule the world, Christina writes to me. In the photograph, I sit with my hands in my lap, palms turned up. I had nothing to conceal.

Instead of reclaiming my house, as I had intended, I spent

the first days home sorting and categorizing the photographs. Eleven identical albums, their spines dated and subjects listed, now line a shelf in the living room for my children to invent histories to puzzle over.

"And then there's Terry," Roland sang under his breath as a rider on a bicycle passed through the light of a street lamp in the lane beyond. "That's new," he said. I saw a flash of long coppery hair. Roland was about to say more when the young man, straddling his bicycle, walked backwards into view. He stopped beside boxes piled against a garage across the lane. There had been a garage sale earlier in the day and the leftovers had already attracted a lot of attention. Roland called a greeting and then explained that the kid had begun to drop into his agency. He can talk your ear off, he warned.

Terry peered into the yard. "Marion?" he said.

I forgot to say that my tenant's name was Marion Turnbell. Terry walked free of his bicycle and leaned it against the fence. He entered the gate and passed by the yard light, and his shadow split in two, became a grey spectre moving across the garage, a chunk of darkness on the lawn. As he came up the walk, he realized I wasn't Marion and he stopped, his shoulders dropping in obvious disappointment.

Roland introduced us. "Yeah," he said, without looking at me. "So Marion's gone, eh?"

I went into the house to get some iced tea and, when I returned, Terry had got over his disappointment, it seemed, because his face was lit up with animation as he talked. "I checked out your lead?" he was saying, as I came out onto the deck. Without glancing at me, he took a glass of tea from the tray as though it had his name on it.

"Medi Equip?" he said. "Yeah. Went down there, like you told me. They had a job, all right. They wanted me to work in a spray booth?" he said, insulted. "No ventilation. Can you imagine? Just masks? So I told them, forget it. No way. Thanks, Roland, but I'm not putting my body on the line. Not for the minimum, that's for sure."

His breathless run-on way of talking, his young voice scooping up at the end of each sentence in a question, had a disarming quality; I recognized the wooing call of the vulnerable in it. Against my new spirit of non-involvement, I was intrigued by his appearance. The jaunty tilt of his khaki beret, the stylish paisley scarf knotted at the waist of his jeans, the scuffed western boots. He was like the street, I thought, a combination of the people who lived in the neighbourhood.

The neighbourhood: what was once Winnipeg's granola belt in the '60s. Where professional people rub shoulders with the indigent and most of the city's artists and writers, living in tall or sprawling turn-of-the-century wood houses set along broad streets arched over by elm trees. Streets that are blessed by the trees, survivors of the Dutch elm disease and the largest number of mature elm to be found anywhere in North America.

There was a suggestion of fragility in Terry's thin body that worked against an audacious, screw-the-world kind of message on his T-shirt. A fragility that Christina would have glommed on to. His vulnerability made the message sound more like a plea than a roar.

Terry jostled a handful of nuts he'd scooped from a bowl on the table. Give them an inch, I thought, and they'll take the whole refrigerator. Move in upstairs. Stick up their posters. Rack up a long-distance telephone bill.

He turned to me, suddenly. "Your soffits are rotting," he said, still not looking directly at me. "If you don't get them fixed, you'll wind up with water damage. Ceilings. On the second floor," he said. "Actually, I was going to give Marion this to give to you." He took a pamphlet from his knapsack and handed it to me. It was an advertisement for a line of roofing products.

"I'm not in the business," he said, in answer to a question he thought I was going to ask.

"You're not in any business," Roland said sarcastically. "Some people wouldn't mind working for the minimum. A job's a job."

"I should be happy for the opportunity to get cancer of the liver?" Terry said. "Work with isocyanates? No way. Good line of products," he said to me, meaning the pamphlet. He looked at me for the first time. He gave nothing away with his eyes. "They cost more. But your house is worth looking after," he said. Like most houses in the neighbourhood, he told me, it had character.

"So, you live in the neighbourhood, then?" I asked.

He blinked with annoyance, and then shifted in his chair, as though to put himself back into an amiable frame of mind. "Did you know that was once a livery stable?" he asked, and nodded in the direction of the garage across the lane where the leftovers of the garage sale had been set out. "Far out," he said, as though the idea of it was amazing. He'd made a steeple with his long fingers, had slumped down into the chair, and his long legs had splayed out across the deck. He sighed, studying the sky. People walked by the house in the front street, their voices and laughter echoing.

"Trilobites," he said, moments later. "Used to burn coal, eh? All along here?" He hitched upright in the chair and swept his arm, a dramatic gesture, across the sky. "Trilobites in the sky."

Several nights ago I had gone walking and passed by a young woman who stopped me, and with a dreamy, serene smile, she'd pointed to the sky and said, "The cats are out tonight. They're flying in the sky. Be careful."

I wondered if something had slipped past me. A mood, or a suspension of laws. I remembered the sudden appearance of angels in shops and stores in Vancouver; in Winnipeg, too, I'd discovered. Lawn ornaments, stationery, flowerpots, angels peered out from among flowers in a flower bed. There were angels in the bath. Trilobites in the sky.

Terry rummaged through his knapsack and came up with a book. It was a guide to rocks and minerals, the kind often sold in museum gift shops. He set it down on the table and Roland scooped it up and began leafing through it. "Interested in geology?" he asked. He'd had a rock collection when he was a kid, he said.

"Paleontology," Terry said. He seemed to study me. "You're a writer, right?" he said. And then he said, "I can't believe how many books you've got. Upstairs, especially. Tons. Have you actually read all of them?"

I couldn't have been more shocked than if he'd said that he'd found my bed to be lumpy and uncomfortable. It occurred to me that I should have had the locks changed.

He didn't wait for an answer but leaned towards me, his face intent on mine, earnest. "You know that picture you have? The one hanging in the front hall? *Starry Night*?"

My throat tightened and I couldn't answer. I glanced at Roland. He kept a straight face, but I could feel him enjoying this.

"I'd like to paint like that," Terry said. "But not stars. I'd fill the sky with trilobites, instead. Trilobites swimming in a tropical rainforest." He became like a tent collapsing in on itself as he dropped back into his chair. "Yes," he said to himself, satisfied, as though he had already painted the picture and hung it.

"So, turns out Terry's autistic," Roland said from the corner of his mouth.

"Artistic," I snapped. I was surprised by the heat in my face. Months after Christina had left I ran away from the silence. I had leapt at the chance to house-and-dog-sit in Vancouver while a friend went to work on a television series in Nova Scotia. Even though I had entertained people in his house, I never imagined anyone but the tenant being in mine; and I fought the impulse to go inside, to try to see myself in it, what failures it had exposed or any straining for style.

"I'd love to paint," Terry said. "I'd like to do that, and music. I used to play bass in a band."

I almost laughed. Good title for a story, I thought, wryly, remembering heavy metal thrashing against the stone foundation of my house. Whenever ignoramuses come riding in their boom-boxes to hijack the peace of the neighbourhood, I am reminded of the viciousness of the basement band. The footwork and back-stabbing that passed for band practice while Christina sat on the stairs watching, directing traffic, trying to keep what was exploding in her hands.

A motorcycle whined as it sped by in the street, its rider gearing down for the lights at Maryland, and I thought about Christina, then. How, when she was four years old, I awoke one morning to find her standing beside the bed with a suitcase. She'd been waiting, she said, for me to wake up so she could say goodbye. She was sorry she had to leave me, and hoped I wouldn't cry. She'd been waiting to say goodbye ever since. The trick to keeping her put, I eventually realized, would be to let her bring the world home. Thus the cats, the dogs, the band. I remember, one particular night, her turning the corner on her motorcycle into the back lane. The sound of her bike's motor would change when it passed by the solid fronts of garages, the slats of a cedar fence, the pleasant growl of it rising into the corridor of sky above the lane; a sky pink with the glow of lights from the city's centre and slung with dark wires.

I had been out working that summer night, too, still in grungy shorts, knees patched with soil as I rose from the flower bed to watch her pull into the driveway. She had a passenger, a young man whose blond hair flowed from his helmet and skimmed the tops of his shoulders. Behind them, a green van braked to a stop and stood idling. Then its battered doors swung open and two young men leapt from it, shouting "All right!" to Christina and her rider, as though some mission had just been accomplished. When they saw me, they became silent.

"Garage is empty, isn't it?" Christina said, after she had introduced me to her passenger. Glenn: a large mouth wobbling in a tremulous smile; eyes, washed-out blue, appealing. Michael, Jason, and Glenn, Christina said, brothers. Earth, fire, and water, I thought. They needed a place to store their furniture for a short time. She winked, and said she'd fill me in later.

"Okay, guys, move your butts," she yelled, a fake bossiness that had failed to hold the basement band together. A voice that animals wind themselves around. When they had unloaded, she went into the house to pop corn and make banana shakes; had slipped raw eggs and wheat germ into them, she told me later.

They had sat around the table on the deck that first night, subdued, but barely containing their energy, I thought, by the way a knee would bounce, by the constant rearranging of themselves in their chairs. Michael was the youngest. He was also the tallest and had dark red hair that lay in tight curls like a cap, close to his head. Jason was in the middle, and the smallest, strung taut, energetic, fingers tapping out a rhythm on the chair's arm. Their mother had dubbed him "Ivan the Terrible," Glenn said, with a nervous laugh and without explaining why. Glenn had several earrings in each ear, and wore a pink silk shirt that settled like a cloud around his narrow body. His long hair had obviously been bleached platinum. They looked costumed, rather than dressed; understudies, waiting to be called into their roles.

Glenn was the storyteller, I would learn; he recalled his brothers' high jinks, resurrected their rambunctious collective past, gave a picture of three freewheeling and unruly terrors that made Michael and Jason chortle and hug themselves during the telling of it, and glance at me for affirmation that they had been unique. Bad little runts, Roland had said later. Lorraine, Lorraine, he said to me, shaking his head. Now there's a lost cause if I ever saw one. An accident about to happen.

Were they students? I wanted to know. They looked younger than Christina but, except for Michael, they were older, I later learned. Michael, it seemed, was still in high school but it was doubtful he'd be returning in the fall. About this, they appeared vague and noncommittal. They'd just been to L.A., Glenn said, his voice raw-sounding, as though he had allergies, and when they returned they had found their mother's furniture tossed out onto the lawn outside the apartment.

"I'll fill you in later," Christina said, as she came from the house and took charge.

I excused myself, said I thought I could hear the telephone ringing, and went inside. The explosion of sound was immediate as the door closed behind me, bravado, jittery laughter, taunts; emotions turning on a dime, songs chanted simultaneously and accompanied by Jason, an adroit mimic of an electric guitar or drum.

When they left I went out into the garage, knowing that Christina was waiting to fill me in. They had piled boxes on top of pieces of a brown velvet sectional couch and a kidney-shaped coffee table. A burlap swag lamp hung from the rafters. There were various tables and small lamps. A child's captain's bed leaned against a wall. They had kept their mattresses, Christina explained, and were going to camp out on them in the back of their van. Kmart or Woolco furniture, I thought. A hopeful arrangement. And what about the mother? I wondered, but didn't ask.

"So, what was in Los Angeles?"

"A wake," Christina said, turning to me, her eyes glittering, wet. "A damned wake." Their mother had died suddenly of pneumonia, a strange infection. They had taken the money from her life-insurance policy and gone to Los Angeles on a kind of wake, not thinking to pay the rent.

It had been a small policy, apparently. They had bought a bottle of Jack Daniel's and then first-class air tickets to Los Angeles where they had taken a stretch limo from the airport to visit the homes of the stars. They became overwhelmed at what they had done, by the sight of palm trees and Spanish-looking haciendas, the walls and gates that enclosed neighbourhoods, being questioned by security police cruising the streets. No image on a theatre or television screen had prepared them for the turquoise and what seemed to be foreign sky. It made them feel as ineffectual as refugees, and when they saw their frightened pale-skinned faces in store windows, they knew they were a rag-tag bunch. They had taken a suite in a hotel then, and stayed inside, ordering room service and videos of rock bands until their money ran out five days later.

"And their father?" I asked. I longed for an adult to take charge.

The father had left the picture years ago, she said, and his body had been found frozen, one winter, in a field beside a highway.

I felt wary, discomfited. Christina had once brought home a young man who was severely asthmatic. And when she'd tired of him, I spent hours on the telephone while he wrung himself dry of tears. Days later, I was still bloated with his misery. There had been others. I have never doubted Christina's determination, but I knew too well the capriciousness of a young heart.

I remembered a child I had once met, on a day at a beach when I was pregnant with Christina. A three-year-old girl in a pink sun suit with wispy blonde hair, a twist of a curl at the nape of her neck. She had plodded with unwavering determination between the water and sand, gathering shells and pressing them into sand cakes; it was as though it was a job she had to do because she was a child and it was what the other children were doing. Both parents had recently been killed in a car accident on the way home from a dance, her guardian, an aunt, had confided in a hushed, almost reverent tone. We had sat, the two of us, strangers, watching the child's stolid efforts to be a child and wincing inwardly at the wisdom in her face, an aware-ness she held that the world was an untrustworthy place. As my husband circled the lake in his boat, my two children flashed by, their bodies white pillars of light skimming across the surface of the water on skis. I put my arms around Christina; held my belly to shield my child from the sound of the boat's engine, the possibility of future collisions.

There's a kind of holiness about children who have lost their parents on a road to Rwanda, or become victims of despera-tion in a place like Romania; a room full of orphans sitting around a table speaking their how-I-lost-my-parents stories into a television camera, others, spooning food into their mouths, chewing and swallowing as though they are normal, everyday children, and not part angel.

Christina said that Glenn felt it was his responsibility to keep his brothers together as a family.

"In the back of a van?" I said.

She shrugged and raked her fingers through her buzz cut. She hated how the smell of the bar where she worked clung to her hair, and so she kept it short. But she liked bartending. You meet people with real problems, she'd explained. Real people, real problems. Meeting real people had not turned into a vocation as I had once feared, but had become summer employment after Christina decided to go to university.

The best way to change the world, she says, is to rule it.

"Until they can get their act together," Christina said. "I said we'd store their stuff until then."

"Well, okay," I said, as I locked the garage door. Hearing myself say, well, okay, as though I'd had a choice. Hearing myself say, as long as you look after it. As long as it stays off the couch.

"Thanks, Unit." She kissed me, and as a cool breeze swept between the houses from one street to another, I felt the shape of her mouth lingering on my cheek. I saw spores, and tufts of white wind-blown seeds, seeds parachuting into my flower beds about to take root.

Cats are flying in the sky. Trilobites have left the water and, upstairs, angels float in my bathtub.

Weeks later, the elm trees were stripped of leaves which were scuttling down the street, the air chilly with the idea of winter. When I stepped onto the verandah to get the morning newspaper, I heard footsteps on the stairs behind me, turned and saw Glenn coming down from the second floor, naked to the waist, his hair a frowzy tangle. He smiled apologetically at my surprise at seeing him there. "Howdy," he said, softly. "Christina wants to sleep in. She said you'd show me to the coffee-maker."


"You have mail," I told Christina on the telephone. I had called her at the apartment the brothers had rented, where Christina spent most of her time. I almost had to shout to make myself heard. Whenever I called, their voices, on edge and energized by the blatant sound of rock music, made me think they were in the middle of a party.

She yelled into the background and the music died. "Mike's vacuuming. You still coming?" she asked. And could she have the recipe for my noodle dish?

I offered to bring the ingredients. Grey clouds bunched above a house, looking like freezing rain, or first snowfall. Sometimes the ceiling beneath Christina's room would creak and I would think for a moment she was up there.

The guys were working for a house painter, supper was on them, Christina said. It was compensation for the lasagna and pots of lentil soup, scalloped potatoes and shepherd's pie, sloppy joes, recipes from my mother's cookbook; what is referred to now as comfort food. Glenn was going to take some videos back to the store and she wanted to send him with a list of groceries, she said.

"It's from Japan," I said. "You've got a letter from Osaka."

I heard her start, and then she said, "Really?" Holding onto the tail of the word as she wandered off into her thoughts.

"Want me to open it?" This was our routine. I asked permission and she usually gave it.

"Don't bother," she said, offhand. She supposed it was likely junk mail. I could bring it with me.

"Junk mail from Japan?"

"Just bring it," she said. "And don't say anything."

She'd already spent five years on her Arts degree and so, when she decided to take a breather from studying, we fought. She was only one course short of completion. I had tried to put my foot down, but I remembered our nocturnal dance when she was a child, me with a foot on the bottom step, threatening. Me with my foot on the second step an hour later, threatening, and so on, until I gave up and she stayed awake, calling down for a doll, a snack, or just to hear her father's or my voice telling her to go to sleep, as if it was a place you could get to by walking, or will. Only once did I go past the middle step on the stairs. A kind of rage had caught up to me. A rage that I had been given a child who didn't seem to need more than four hours of sleep, who wouldn't fall asleep until early morning. I tore up the stairs. I heard myself yelling. I was going to thrash her senseless, I said.

Make her go to sleep. She sat in her crib, black curls winding up from her ears like corkscrews, hands raised, palms pushing out as if to block my coming. Okay, she said, eyes fearful, but her voice calm, reasoning, okay, okay. All right. Go ahead. Spank me, she almost demanded, and then her voice quavered as she said, "but would you do it softly, softly, please?"

You can see what kind of child I was dealing with. And so when the brothers rented an apartment and Christina moved in to keep house for them, I didn't venture past the second step.

Their apartment was a newer one, a corner apartment at the top of the building. Eight floors up. I had dropped Christina off at the door several times but had never gone inside. I sat in the car looking up at their window, my heart thumping with the parties I had imagined, drugs and arguments, bodies flying over the balcony railing. I took comfort in a measly tree, scrawny and nude, thinking that its branches might break a fall.

I had not been prepared for the airiness of bare white walls, light glancing off tables, the light in Glenn's eyes as they followed Christina around the room, holding her, a coveting in them. We dined on perogies she had made from scratch, she said, in a matter-of-fact way that insinuated I was not to be surprised. The bowl brimmed with what looked like gooey envelopes oozing cheddar and potato, encrusted with bacon bits and chives. She had not made the noodle dish as planned because Glenn had ordered perogies, Jason had wanted hash browns, and Mike an unheated can of ravioli. They were accustomed to eating one thing at a meal. She was getting them used to the idea of food groups. Glenn laughed when she said that, a tiny spurt of joy coming from his narrow chest, and went on to tell how Michael had once faked choking so they could chuck their broccoli out the window when their mother's back was turned. I got a picture of their mother as a flywheel they had strained away from but which had held them, these erratic satellites, in place. I imagined the flywheel falling apart and them being flung outwards, backwards, into the dark. I wished for earth mothers, for women with large breasts to come to their rescue; women other than myself or my daughter.

"Look," Christina said afterwards, and opened the closet door. She had brought me into the bedroom to show me something. Hanging in the closet were pink and yellow Angora vests, a grey pleated skirt, blouses and shirt-waist dresses that all looked the same. She held up a pair of white cowboy boots with fringes and studded with red and blue stones. "My mom's dancing shoes," Glenn said from the doorway. Then Christina showed me the box, a small wooden box with photographs of the three boys, school photographs like the ones I had of my own children. Among them, several black-and-white snapshots of a man lying on a blanket and holding a child up at arm's length. There were several others of the father and the boys and only one of the mother, an out-of-focus black-and-white of a young woman with a gap in her teeth, smiling. There were also bits of costume jewellery in the box, chunky beaded earrings and pins.

"Take it," Glenn said, closing the box and setting it into Christina's hands. "I want you to have it." My daughter's satisfied glow, when he said that, made me afraid that bartending might wind up becoming her full-time occupation after all.

"I brought your mail," I told her. "The letter from Japan?" I was relieved when her face clouded with confusion.

"It's just something I sent away for ages ago," she said. "Information, that's all."

That evening when I stepped in the door, the telephone was ringing. It was Christina, her voice an anguished whisper. She'd received a job offer to teach English in Osaka. "Oh God, what am I going to do?" she moaned, and then said she was going to have to finish off that one course, and fast, and I knew that the present had already become the past, even before she had left it.

When she went away I expected winds in the night, windows rattling, waking to a swirling blizzard and biting cold. Accusations of betrayal that I would need to deflect. I had not expected their silence, a telephone disconnected, or to find the little wooden box on Christina's bed, and beside it a note asking me to return it to Glenn.

I saw the brothers one wet day, spring, when ice floes rushed beneath bridges on swift currents. The boys were like skinny dark spiders, dressed all in black, walking beyond me on the opposite side of the street, pushing grocery carts filled with garbage bags through the slushy snow, and getting bogged down. Boggans, I thought. Moving day. When I called to them, they shouted to me across the street, "Hi, Mom! How're you doing? We're great! We're doing just great," they shouted, one after the other. I crossed the street to greet them. The work they'd had was seasonal, they said, and had finished. They'd had to leave their apartment only a month after Christina left and move into a friend's basement room. But the friend's parents were too uptight, apparently, and so they were checking out a rooming-house nearby, advertised in the paper. Jason had been offered a gig with a band, they said, all he needed was a set of drums.

I imagined that they had left the brown velvet sectional couch behind in someone's basement room, that chairs rotted in a backyard, lamps jutted up from garbage cans, that they must have had to shed their mother's life, piece by piece.

It had become too much for them to carry, too much for what had become lives without any rooms. I came to think of the box sitting on Christina's bedside table as an urn, holding the remains of a vanished family.

"Do you think Vincent van Gogh was crazy?" Terry asked Roland.

Roland shrugged, said there was talk now of Menière's disease. The artist had been plagued by noise in his ears.

"Call it what you want," Terry said. "If it helps. What van Gogh had was a different state of consciousness. That's why he painted."

"Yes," Roland said, and laughed. "Drunk, as opposed to sober."

Lorraine, Lorraine, Roland had said to me, those boys don't need you. They don't even want rescuing. They're too far gone into their lifestyle to ever be rescued.

My arms ached from spading the garden and suddenly I wanted to go inside.

Terry's face grew strained as he appealed for Roland's patience. "Hey, no. Listen," he said, his voice a pleading whine. I gathered he was accustomed to being dismissed. "Why do you think there's so many crazy people in the world?" I realized he had played the trick of a question to get attention, as he went on to answer it. "Because so-called crazy people don't conform to the common idea of what is reality," he said. Satisfied, he crossed his arms against his chest and rocked gently.

"Which is what?" I asked. I wanted to walk him through this, make him finish and go away.

"The reality determined by the first scientists," he said. "The cause-and-effect guys?" He tapped his forehead. "Tunnel thinking. We've adopted a caveman theory of what is sense and what is nonsense," he said. "Van Gogh had an alternate sense of reality. Probably all artists do."

"You too, I suppose," Roland said.

Terry laughed. "What would you think if I told you I could actually see trilobites in the sky? You'd get nervous, right? And I might wind up with a chemically induced sense of your reality. There's no way I'm cutting off my ear, man."

"Time to hit the road," Roland said, seeing my yawn. He tapped Terry on the knee with the *Rocks and Minerals Guide*, held it out for him to take and put into his knapsack.

"It's yours," Terry said. "Marion lent it to me."

I took it from him, and thanked him.

"Yeah," he said. He waited, wanting me to say more, I knew. And so I said in my two-faced voice, as Christina would call it, "Well, wherever Marion is, I'm sure she's sorry she didn't get to say goodbye."

"Yeah," he said. "Marion was great."

We stood on the sidewalk in front of the house. Terry said he wanted to go down into the Village to check out the buskers. In the glare of the streetlight, he looked undernourished and too pale.

"Talk about your alternate state of reality," Roland said, as Terry joined the flow of traffic, the music, and other cyclists. He explained he'd begun to notice Terry in spring. From time to time, he had been sleeping in the bus shelter on the corner and, he suspected, along the river-bank now that it was warmer. "Try and give a fellow a break, and he doesn't want it. The fool," Roland said, because he was frustrated by a less than perfect world and didn't know who else to be angry with.

I sat in bed after Roland had gone, propping a photo album against my knees, turning its pages towards the lamp. In the photograph where I am sitting outside at my mother's on a kitchen chair with my hands turned up in my lap, I am wearing dark glasses because I had been crying. The picture was taken only last spring. It was only weeks after I had seen Michael, Jason, and Glenn on the street, and spring had grown calmer and warm by then, and tulips stood like red-tipped arrows against the white siding of my mother's house. I had driven out to her home in the country, exchanged reports on the progress of our children with my sisters while the memory of Jason's recent funeral pressed behind my eyes.

Glenn had called me on a Sunday morning, early. "Mom?" he said. His voice sounded as though he was calling from a tunnel, and not a telephone booth. "Those pictures?"

Glenn wanted to know if Christina had kept the photographs he'd given to her. He needed one of Jason, he said. For the funeral. As he told me about Jason's accident, it was as though he was talking about something he'd read in a newspaper. The skid marks, the estimated speed of the vehicle, head and internal injures. Evidence of alcohol consumption. Jason had wrapped the van around a telephone pole on Corydon Avenue. Glenn coughed, and the line went silent for a few moments. They'd had an argument, he said, his voice gone nasal. Jason had taken off, angry. "But the thing is," Glenn said, sounding puzzled and wounded. "The thing is, Mom, about his jacket." Apparently Jason had just got a pogey cheque and had bought a leather jacket. They found it several blocks from the scene of the accident folded neatly inside the bag with the store's name on it, set against a tree on a boulevard.

There was a note, Glenn said, saying Michael should have it.

I stood in line with the mourners at the funeral chapel, waiting my turn to pass by the casket to view the photograph of Jason set on top of it. I had been given instructions to give it to a tall blonde female bartender where Christina used to work, but I had sent the wooden box over by cab. I saw Glenn and Michael behind a curtain on a glass-fronted room. They were surrounded by a select group of mourners, all young. Later, in the sunlight, I saw their costumes — the animal prints and silks, white and black leather, chains and studded neck-pieces, crosses dangling from ears and a nose — the way they clasped hands, moving together as though one. In the daylight, they looked uncertain as to what grief was and how they might display it. The brothers' faces appeared airbrushed, skin flaw-less beneath a coating of pancake makeup, mouths shiny with gloss, eyelids the colour of iridescent peacock feathers. They and the other mourners had the look of actors in a rock video waiting for a director to choreograph their movements, waiting for someone to tell them what they were feeling.

I followed the crowd through the cemetery, among head-stones and other burials already happening. We stopped. There was an uncertainty, panicky murmurs, and then an abrupt turning away. It was the wrong grave site, I overheard, and fol-lowed, as the crowd of MuchMusic mourners doubled back to the right one. Michael carried a huge ghetto-blaster on his shoulder the whole time, and as the coffin was lowered onto the straps above the grave, he set it down. A minister's voice droned in prayer, closed, and then said the brothers wanted to play Jason's favourite song. Michael switched on the player. Music wafted up, strange, oriental-sounding; a band on downers, half-asleep and playing in slow time. Then I realized with a sick stomach that it wasn't the music, but the player. The batteries in the player were going dead. People glanced at each other, uneasy. Michael stood among them, tall, looking straight ahead, as though nothing unusual was happening, as though what was interesting was the airplane gliding in above the city. Glenn flicked his head and his platinum hair fanned out across his white leather back.

I am writing an essay about literacy, I had explained to Glenn one day as he stood looking over my shoulder at my computer screen. It's the International Year of Literacy, I had said. I confessed that I had always wanted the pleasure of teaching someone to read. "Why don't you teach Jason?" he asked. Well, yes, I said, surprised. I should. He smiled his wide and wobbly smile, and his washed-out blue eyes shone. He left the room, both of us knowing that I didn't wish for it enough, and, with his smile, he had forgiven me.

The wavering song ground on, and on, and their grieving seemed a mockery. They had dreamed a ceremony, and wound up with farce. I had the urge to laugh and, at the same time, to cry. Turn it off, I begged them silently. But they let it play on, until the batteries were finished.

The brothers walked to a limousine with tangled-haired girls clinging to their arms. There was going to be a party, I heard, and the young people surged towards the parking lot. Within minutes it was empty.

Late in the night, I called Christina.

"That never would have happened if I'd been there," she said, wanting me to think she meant she would have made certain the batteries in the player were working. But I had caught the note of regret in her voice. These things happen, I said. I didn't tell her about the jacket, because that, too, was an accident she could not have prevented.

I closed the last photo album and gathered them up, all eleven of the identical volumes scattered around me on the bed, their spines telling what episode of my family's chronicle lies inside them. I heard a noise outside then. It's the small things happening in the night that alert me, not the sound of a party, but footsteps echoing in the lane, the creak of a gate. I heard the sound of stealth. I turned off the bedside lamp and went to the window to investigate. I saw a bright halo of coppery hair, Terry, shirtless now, rummaging through the remains of the garage sale. I saw the outline of his ribs beneath his shallow chest. He'd found a book and cradled it in his hands, turning its pages. The cat came back, I thought. It's okay for you, Marion, you could just up and leave. But I've got to live here.

And then I thought, what harm? What could go wrong in just lending him books? Lorraine, Lorraine, this one's not even a christly boggan. At least this one can read, I thought. And anyway, every band needs a bass player, I thought. A heart, throbbing.

# The Midnight Hour

❧

Christina prefers the direct approach. She would like to go into her mother's room, drop a book on the floor to wake her and say, For your information: I'm going suntanning in Assiniboine Park with Pam and Lisa. Not ask, just tell. But she knows what complications can arise from being face to face, and so she'll leave a note instead. *Dear Unit. Have gone to the park to suntan with Pam and Lisa,* she writes. She began calling her parents "my parental unit" when recently it became certain they were going to split up. They never caught the irony in it, never really listened to how she said it. Going to the park, Lorraine would say, you mean hang around, don't you? And so Christina picks up the felt marker and adds, *and to hang around.*

She flips a cassette into her Walkman, puts the earphones on, and sticks the note under a butterfly magnet on the refrigerator door just as Yo-Yo Ma begins bowing his cello. Lorraine is suspicious of Pam and Lisa. "They don't look me in the eye," she says. What do their parents do? Christina doesn't know because Grant Park isn't like junior high where everyone complains constantly about parents' bitching and curfews. At Grant Park the kids talk about being grounded for a week as though it's a reward and joke about ruining their parents' social lives. Pam and Lisa write notes to each other about complications of break-through bleeding on the pill and yeast infections. Never about parents.

Will you please reason with the other half of my parental unit? Christina asked her father last night when he telephoned to wish her a happy birthday. She couldn't understand why wanting to go to the park was such a big deal. She was pleased that he remembered her birthday and then wondered if Georgina had reminded him. He asked what she wanted. He was going to the lake for the weekend, he said, and was sorry, his bum had been smack against the wall all week, and he hadn't got anywhere near a shopping mall. His gift would be a tad late. That's okay, Christina told him. She understood, she said, and reached for her flip-flop to squash a spider crawling up the wall towards the window and its nest of webs clotted with husks of insects.

— So, is everything okay?

— I've grown out of my jeans. I need new ones.

— Okay.

— I'm thinking about getting my hair streaked?

— How's your mother?

— Okay.

— How much do you think that would cost? Jeans and hair?

— About a hundred and fifty.

— I can't promise.

— Pam's dad? He works for Air Canada?

— Who's Pam?

— He's taking Pam to Hawaii for Christmas if her marks are good.

Christina heard one of Georgina's boys shouting in the background and Georgina's shrill reply. She heard her father sigh.

— I'll see what I can do, Chris. But no promises.

— Calvin committed suicide.

— Who?

— My friend Calvin. With his dad's gun.


Yo-Yo Ma isn't bad, Christina thinks as she spoons yoghurt into a bowl and sprinkles it with Harvest Crunch. She thinks the sound of the cello is deep, a purple sound. It makes her think of the suicide note her friend Calvin left behind in the bathroom sink and, beside it, a picture of Jennifer. He sat on the toilet to do it, had hooked his toe into the trigger and, like the man she'd seen in a movie, a man who failed to make boot-camp training, all Calvin's memories, every idea he'd ever had, splashed against the wall behind him. Here, take a listen to this, Christina wants to tell Lorraine. Listen to this music and tell me what it makes you think about. But Lorraine is still sleeping, repairing her mind, she calls it, because it's like pulling teeth from her brain, she says about the script she's presently working on.

Once Christina thought that nothing would ever happen to her, that she was doomed to a boring life, embedded like a bug in amber, at age thirteen. Since they'd moved to the four-plex, what passed for excitement happened only once. A transformer blew up on the telephone pole outside their building and the boom of it had woken her from a deep sleep. She stood on her bed looking out the window and saw the air arcing with white light as recoiling wires spurted electricity, lashing against the fence and threatening to incinerate Lorraine's swimming pool. Still in her nightgown, Christina had run out to save it, had dragged the plastic pool across the yard and through the back door into the kitchen.

"You silly fool," Lorraine said, crying and grabbing her in a hug. "You could have been electrocuted," she said, making, as usual, a big issue out of a small one.

"Your mother has this imagination," her father said. "You know." Yes, she knows too well how the smallest misdemeanour becomes a full-scale production in her mother's mind that ends with Christina winding up behind bars in prison. She suspects her mother had stood at the door, watching her rescue the pool, writing the obituary, choosing music for the funeral service at the same time.

But she's fifteen today and it seems that, lately, too much happens. The mouse mattresses every month, for example. The irritating wad of sanitary napkins between the legs. And her height. She's shot up six inches in a year, and the marks of the growth spurt climb up the kitchen door in ink smudges they'll have to paint over when Lorraine, if ever, saves enough money so they can move. She's noticed, too, how the world seems to be going faster. Masses of people wander in deserts, starving; airports are exploding. She has stopped watching the news. "It's wrong," she told Lorraine, "how they're trying to make me face up to things that aren't my fault." She refuses to watch starving children, their swollen bellies, and not enough common sense to brush away the flies crawling across their dumb eyes. "We're poor, too," she said. Their house went to the divorce settlement, to pay off credit cards, car loans, bad debts. She has to bang the side of the television to stop its picture from rolling. She chose for her Social Studies newspaper project the topic of rock stars involved in car accidents, instead of Ethiopia. A one-armed drummer is tragic, too, she thinks.

She hears the droning of an electric can opener in the suite above and then cat's claws clicking against the floor. She can't get used to the sound of people going about their lives beside her and above her. She needs to concentrate, to think before she goes to the park. What did Diamond Dave say? "I used to have a drug problem, but now I can afford it." Diamond Dave again: "I had to quit jogging because the ice cubes kept falling out of the glass." She stayed up late last night copying the quotes into her journal after she and Lorraine had returned from the failed birthday dinner. She went down into her room and put Billy Idol on loud so she wouldn't hear the television or think about her mother huddled in front of it, mascara ground to a black smudge beneath her eyes. Lorraine, reaching across Christina in the parking lot outside the four-plex for the glove compartment, tossing the gift-wrapped cassette of Billy Idol into her lap.

— Why do I even bother to try?

— Just tell me what I did.

— Happy birthday, sweet fifteen.

— What did I do?

— I'm going inside. Lock your door.

— We don't communicate.

— What you mean is, I don't agree with everything you say.

Christina went downstairs, propped pillows against the wall and copied the Diamond Dave quotes in her journal. Then she lay on the floor and listened to Billy Idol as the street light slanted down into her basement room illuminating the poster of Baryshnikov. She had gone to see *White Nights* three times. She wanted to see the dancer suspended in air and try to discover how he did it. Around the ballet dancer, the Mötley Crüe grimaced at her, made funny faces, devil's horns with their fingers. She cradled a pillow and thought about her father and his bum always being against the wall. She imagined his boat sinking and herself, cutting through the water, kicking down into its depths and grabbing for her father, dragging him to the surface.

Footsteps thump against the ceiling in the kitchen and a dish thuds against it, bounces twice. Christina pulls the earphones out and listens. Chris? You're not going to the park and that's that. The absence of her mother's voice makes the room feel dead, like the sudden silence when the television is turned off, the picture collapsing into itself. She pushes aside the bowl of yoghurt, full suddenly and craving a cigarette. The wallpaper does it to me, she told Lorraine. Its positive ugliness makes her itch to smoke. What do you think? Lorraine said, pulling Christina through the rooms of the suite, trying to make her feel as though finding it was a gift from God. I think ugly. Forget the wallpaper, she said. It's temporary. Their stay will be for only as long as it takes her to get enough money for a down payment on another house. Christina doesn't want another house. She wants the old one back. Lorraine hung travel posters over the wallpaper, and now lime-green and orange flowers bleed through matadors sticking bulls, a tropical forest rimming a crescent of white beach.

Lorraine's cigarettes aren't in their usual place on the refrigerator. Smoking in bed, she'll kill us one of these days, Christina thinks, as she inches her mother's door open. She sees her tucked up in one corner of the futon, a pillow jammed against her stomach and dark head curled into her chest. Christina listens to the soft puff of her mother's breathing, the squeak of bedsprings as the tenant in the apartment above rolls over in bed. Sometimes Christina comes upstairs in the night to go to the bathroom, and finds Lorraine seated at the kitchen table in the dark, smoking. Waiting, Christina knows, for the couple upstairs to be finished making love. She saw the squiggly line drawings in her mother's journal when she left it lying open beside the bed. Lines that formed a woman's face, wild hair, tears squirting from the eyes and all over the page; and nipples, dark, accentuated, as though she'd pressed hard on the pencil when she drew them, and the shape of an open vulva.

They'd had a window booth at Grapes for the birthday supper the night before, had watched the traffic rolling by on Route 90; ate Mediterranean salads, barely speaking. Lorraine absent, worrying because they had not been satisfied with the most recent draft of her script. "They" being the people who pay the rent, she explained. She ate as though starved, tearing apart huge shrimps with her fingers. She had pulled the blue butterfly clips from her hair and it drooped around her face, making her look wilted.

"So, ladies, which one of you is fifteen today?" the waiter asked.

Lorraine laughed. "I wonder," she said, and fiddled with the sand dollar hanging from her neck.

As the waiter reached across the table for her plate, Christina felt him staring at her breasts. She looked up and saw Lorraine watching, faint surprise rising in her eyes that became dread as she frowned and ground her cigarette out in the ashtray, as though she was in danger of starting a forest fire, performing a complicated task that demanded her complete attention. "Cheeky twit," she said after he had left. "I don't think we should come here any more." After that, their conversation, while more animated, had gone downhill.

— I'm thinking about going on the pill.

— What, in god's name, for?

— There's this guy at school? He looks like Diamond Dave.

— So?

— So I think I'm going to have sex with him.

— And?

— I thought you might want to know.

— Why can't you just sneak around like your sister did?

— You want me to lie, then?

— Let's just say that I don't want a blueprint of your future sexual activity. And I don't think much of your new friends. And your schoolwork is going down the tube. An incomplete in your Social Studies newspaper project. Chris. Just what is this about, anyway?

— They give it away, you know. I can go on the pill without your consent.

— You'll put on weight. Become bloated. Your breasts will be sore and swollen. Get even larger.

A clutter of magazines, a half-eaten cheese sandwich, pages of notes, an overflowing ashtray litter the floor around Lorraine's futon. Christina stoops, about to slide a cigarette from its package.

Lorraine's legs scissor through the blankets. "You're not

going to the park," she says. She flings her pillow aside and rises onto an elbow and the strap of her nightgown slides down a shoulder, to her upper arm, its skin dimpled beneath a deep tan.

"I hate that place," Lorraine says, meaning Assiniboine Park. "Bunch of creeps hanging around, flashing their noodles."

"It's Sunday. There's nothing else to do." Christina is gratified by the wince of guilt in Lorraine's dark eyes. Though they have the right to use the cabin at the lake, they haven't gone once in two summers.

"At least I can talk to Pam and Lisa." She shuffles through the pile of magazines with her foot. Lorraine's journal lies on top, opened to a column of figures, her attempt to predict how much she needs to sock away for income tax. Every several pages of notes stop for figures with different titles: WHAT I NEED. INCOME HOPED FOR. EXPENDITURES.

"You'd kill me if my room looked like this."

Lorraine groans, flops back onto the bed, pulls a floral sheet over her head. The smell of coconut cream rises, thick, too heavy, like the lard aftertaste of the icing on mass-produced birthday cakes. "Oh, Chris." A sigh, and the sheet puffs out around her mouth. "Now what?"

"I'm pregnant."

The sheet collapses around Lorraine's face as she inhales deeply.

"What if I was? What would you do?"

Lorraine rolls over, faces the wall, pretends to be asleep.

"I could get mother's allowance, you know. Raise it myself. At least it wouldn't be so boring around here."

Still Lorraine feigns sleep.

Christina has clear memories of walking upstairs to her bedroom in their house, and feeling as though her feet never touched the steps. She rides past the house on her bicycle often to check for changes. New curtains. A cedar deck. If the evergreen seedling she brought home from a field trip has grown. She saw a young couple walk up the front sidewalk holding hands. She wonders if the air inside the house has cleared. Believes someone should invent a spray bomb, like a new-car scent, that covers spillage, emotions erupting, hostility. She wonders if the new owners found her name. She had got a wood-burning set one Christmas and had burned her name into the hardwood floor under her bed.

Where they live now is called a four-plex, and better than an apartment because it has a yard, Lorraine says. Christina hasn't told her that she's found messages written on water pipes near the ceiling in her bedroom. F.A. LOVES B.D. L.A. IS A DYKE. She thought the misspelling made the person sound pathetic. She'd found the word HELP! And sometimes she thinks she hears the word whispered. Once the building was a home for girls, the landlord said. On nights when she can't fall asleep it's because she feels she's being watched. In this new room, she dreamed of being a baby. Of seeing herself curled in a strange mist, and receding, falling backwards and becoming smaller, a curled pink shrimp about to disappear, until she kicked out at it, yelled away her own disappearance.

"Well, if you won't have a baby," she tells Lorraine, "then I will."

"I don't even have a boyfriend, for god's sake."

"No wonder." Christina slams the bedroom door behind her. She stands in the kitchen, fists clenched against the window, against a knot in her throat. Lorraine is not going to ruin this day.

"You're not going to the park," Lorraine says through the door. Then Christina hears her mother's step against the floor. "And I'll thank you to stay out of my cancer sticks."

Through the kitchen window Christina sees the wind lift paper and whisk it about the knees of a boy crossing the parking lot beside McDonald's. The glare of sunlight is reflected in the windows of the restaurant. Across from it, Grant Park High squats in a broad field. Inside it all year, boys back girls into lockers, trap them with wiry arms laid across their shoulders. When someone backs Christina into a locker and says, How about you and me fucking? she punches him, and says, Sorry, but I'm totally devoted to the man I love. Sometimes she wishes this were true, but she has doubts. She's seen what can happen when Pam and Lisa became totally devoted over and over and wind up being totally miserable.

She saw Calvin's brains, like flecks of porridge, all over the photograph of Jennifer.

"I'm quitting school," Christina says as Lorraine enters the kitchen.

"Oh, Chris," Lorraine says, as she struggles with the zipper on her shorts. "You're crying again. It must be that time of month."

"I can't stand it."

"It'll pass," Lorraine says, and pats Christina lightly on the buttocks as though she is still five years old and just swallowed a penny.

She wheels her bicycle out into the blast of hot air that makes the day smell used and already spent. A styrofoam container cupping splashes of relish and ketchup tumbles across the yard and nestles against the leg of Lorraine's chaise longue. Dishes clatter in the sink as Lorraine rushes about in shorts and halter, trying to make up for the hours of lost sunlight. The window slides open.

"Make sure you stay away from the bushes, and be home no later than five."

"I'll try." The words are covered by the sudden drone of an air conditioner. Lorraine caved in too easily, Christina thinks, as she bounces the bicycle down the steps. She'd got up her strength to batter down a door and it opened just as she put her shoulder to it.

Damned garbage again, Christina thinks, as the bike's wheel meets a plastic Zellers bag on the bottom step. But as she reaches for it, she knows from the look of it, how the bag's opening is tucked under neatly, that it's been set there. She sees the hurried dash of her name on an envelope inside it.

The birthday card has a picture of a mirror and large XXXOOO'S ETC. written in lipstick across it and red letters below that say, "Especially the etc." "A little something for someone sweet." Her father's tight printing adds to the card's message. Inside the bag is a round tin of assorted toffee. A hurried, last-minute gift, she thinks, while Georgina shopped for steak and barbecue sauce. She slits the plastic seal and pries off the lid. Just what she needs; mondo fat, she thinks. She sifts through the candy, enjoys the slippery feel of the cellophane-wrapped swirls. Her favourite. She remembers the sheet of Mackintosh's toffee, her father putting it in the freezer until it was as hard as glass, then smashing it with a hammer and pressing crumbs of it with his finger onto her tongue. The wind blows too hot against her neck. Forget it, she thinks, she won't go to the park. I've changed my mind, she'll tell Lorraine. Instead, she'll sit in the dark coolness of her room, Randy

Rhoads and Nikki Sixx watching as she tries on clothing, ties scarves around her breasts, draws hearts on her cheeks, and then she will practise her ballet, will stretch and bend into the sound of Yo-Yo Ma's cello.

"What in god's name did you spill in the kitchen?" Lorraine calls from the window. "I'm sticking to the floor."

She's been watching, Christina realizes. She puts the tin of candy into her knapsack and wheels across the yard. Lorraine watching. Lorraine telephoning on the hour whenever she has to go out at night, checking, listening carefully to Christina's answers to determine if anything has changed.


Christina pedals down the wide street bordering Assiniboine Park, Yo-Yo Ma working hard on her ears. She passes by graceful stone houses, lawn sprinklers twisting out rainbows. She doesn't know why she likes the music, because sometimes it's confusing. The cello has so many sounds, it seems to work around the melody, to hide its message. And then suddenly, the melody pushes through the confusion, clear, easy to follow. She was with Pam and Lisa in Eaton's when they stole the tapes. Pam, more certain of herself, took her time and got exactly what she wanted. Lisa, too obvious with her purple hair, grabbed the first tape she came to. This is it: the Elgar Cello Concerto, Opus 85. Yo-Yo Ma playing the cello.

"I hate that place," Lorraine said about the park, because once she'd been flashed there. She tried to act casual, Lorraine, up on her feet demonstrating the man's shuffle, how he swung his walking-stick, and each time she told the story she added a detail, a white moustache, patent-leather shoes, a red handkerchief in his blazer pocket, but always ended by saying, "And his pathetic little dink, dangling from his unzipped pants, like a piece of old leather." Building something that will likely appear somewhere, later. Making a big issue out of nothing. As Christina enters the park's stone gates, she feels the welcome of cooler air, anticipates how the trees beside the river harbour deep shadows.

&#x294B;&#x294A;

"'I'm a very family-oriented person. I have personally been responsible for starting about seven families this year,'" Christina says, quoting Diamond Dave.

"He's an animal!" Lisa shrieks. Her knees uncurl as she falls backwards onto the blanket. Her hair, purple and maroon flames, licks at the grass.

"That's an old one," Pam says.

Lisa rises to her knees, arms raised as she stretches, and a whistle rises up from a car passing by. The two girls were already stripped to their bathing suits when Christina finally found them in a clearing below the Pavilion. Her black T-shirt sucks up the heat of the sun and sticks to her back, but she won't take it off. You can see through my bathing suit when it's wet, she explained. But we're not going anywhere near water, Pam said with a flicker of annoyance. Christina envies their short bodies. She can't find jeans that fit. Her problem, Lorraine says, is an extra-long torso. And her bathing suit isn't long enough, either. She hangs out over it on top, and bulges out below.

Lisa runs fingers through her hair, shakes it loose across her shoulders. "I think Tod's still mad at me," she says, collapsing suddenly. "He still hangs up when I call."

"What did you expect?" Pam says.

"He's too serious. Thinks he owns me."

"Like Calvin and Jennifer," Christina says. For weeks they picked it apart. Jennifer should have waited to dump Calvin until things got better for him at home; that his parents are wrong to blame her, cruel even. It's not fair, they reassured Jennifer, and invited her to sit with them at their table at McDonald's, the one they usually occupied during study periods. Until Calvin shot himself, Pam and Lisa didn't know Jennifer existed, Christina thinks, as she makes a pillow of her knapsack and lies down.

A yellow Frisbee arcs across the sky, through the jangle of music playing from car radios. She watches a man; tall, his hair shines orange in the sunlight as he chases after it. There is something close to loser about a person who plays Frisbee alone, she thinks. She thought she would feel different when she turned fifteen, but here she is still wearing Lorraine's knobby knees and must lie on her stomach to hide them. Her face is in the process of deciding who she will look like, Lorraine said. It takes time. Right now, her nose is her father's. Strong, her mother says, a handsome nose that she will grow into. Unfortunately, she also has inherited her father's caterpillar eyebrows. The park swims with heat and the man playing Frisbee becomes a spot of colour wavering against a watery wall.

When Christina wakes up, the girls are gone. She watches as the ribbons of a kite sway above the trees. The hoarse toot of a miniature train signals its entry into the tunnel. Beyond, children yank at parents' hands, drawing them towards the sound.

— Oh look! See the tunnel, the tunnel! We're going into the tunnel now.

— Here it comes! Here comes the tunnel, Chris. Duck!

An island of trees emerged, a deer in the underbrush reared its head, watching them pass through a forest of muskeg and the sprinkling of pink and blue wild asters alongside the tracks. Her father's hand gripped hers, tight, squeezing, he more excited than she.

— Oh, Chris! Here it comes! Here comes the tunnel!

A girl runs towards Christina, hair streaming and, pulling her face taut, becomes a moving picture stopped in frame, action suspended, and her eyes are blank and flat. It seems to Christina that the light changed. It became flat, too, and she feels she's turning pages in a book, looking at a picture of a girl playing in a park, and that she's the only one who is real.

She can't go home yet. It isn't quite five o'clock. Lorraine will be cooling off in the wading pool, towel, suntan lotion, diet-drink cans, the columns of figures lying on the lounge chair. And she will pry with questions as though she suspects oncoming illness. Christina sits cross-legged, cradling the tin of candy, when she spots Lisa, her hair, the iridescent flare of colour, as the girl runs backwards down a grassy incline, hands flailing at the air.

Then she sees Pam emerge from the shadows of an ivy trestle beside the Pavilion. She strides across the open field with a certain hard knowledge in her punchy, determined movement. Then she turns and beckons, and a man with orange hair, wearing a red vest, steps out from the ivy trestle. It's the man who played Frisbee with himself, Christina realizes, as Lisa scoops up a yellow Frisbee, and sprints towards her. She drops onto the blanket beside Christina, chest heaving and collar-bone slick with perspiration. "You are not going to believe this guy. He is so incredibly gorgeous. I can't stand it."

Pam begins stuffing towels and cosmetics into a bag. "We went for a walk," she says, avoiding her gaze. "We didn't think you'd want us to wake you."

Black beads swing against the man's chest as he stands at the edge of the blanket, his body blocking out the sun. "Who's she?"

"Christina," Pam says, "this is Darren."

"So, it's Christina. Listen, when I said you should come and see my room, I hadn't planned on a party."

"I have to go," Christina tells them. She pulls on her jeans, turns away as she sucks in her stomach and yanks at the zipper. Damned jeans. She will call her father, put the pressure on Georgina every day until he comes through. She will go home, turn on the television, and let the world blow up.

Darren whistles. "Holy, an Amazon. No, wait," Darren says as Christina turns, a fist balled. "I like Amazons." He grins and cracks his knuckles. Gold crosses dangle from his ears. "I guess I am having a party," he says. "You dudes like monkey's lunch?" The tattoo of a woman's face ripples on his forearm. She has a red star in the middle of her forehead, hair whipped by the wind. The tattoo, his hair, the gold crosses in the ears look familiar.

"What's monkey's lunch?" Lisa wants to know.

"You've never heard of monkey's lunch?"

"And so what?" Pam snaps.

He bangs his fist against his forehead. "Lordy. Bunch of Ethiopians coming to my party." He smiles suddenly, as though the pain they'd caused is gone. "It's okay," he says. "I'm used to it."

"Definitely strange," Pam says as they wheel their bicycles behind him. He strides, his red vest flapping. "But interesting."

"You coming?" they ask Christina.

Lorraine will be waiting, her small frame coiled and humming with pent-up energy.

Darren turns and, leaping up, grabs a tree branch and swings down in front of her. "Of course she's coming."

He punches the air as he walks, lips moving constantly, as though he's plugged into music, Christina thinks.

He lives in a house on one of the streets that border the park, in a tall stone house with diamond-shaped bevelled glass in its windows. Like the houses she and Lorraine sometimes cruise past, Lorraine hoping to catch glimpses of rooms, see how the other side lives, she says.

"You rich or something?" Lisa asks.

"Don't give him the satisfaction," Pam mutters.

They pass through a stone archway to the back of the house. Christina feels as though it's night and she is home alone, listening for a knock at the door, feeling the danger of opening it, the danger compelling her forward.

They climb up cedar stairs to a second-floor deck with white canvas chairs and a table with a yellow umbrella. Christina thinks of Lorraine draped over the edges of the wading pool, her body lying in six inches of water, misting her body with water in a Windex bottle.

"Shoes," Darren says and points to their feet.

"This is getting boring," Pam says, but takes off her runners.

Keys jangle as he unlocks the door. "You're breathing on me," he says to Pam.

Christina follows them into a room that's completely blue.

Plush blue carpet brushes against her bare feet. A blue couch rests against a wall, its plump cushions creaseless as in a furniture advertisement. The only thing in the room not blue is a refrigerator.

Darren walks to the wall, spreads his arms, and sliding doors open; on the other side, more blue.

"There was a sale on paint," Pam says.

"Far out," Lisa says as she steps into the bedroom. The bed flashes with navy blue satin sheets. On each side of it are upholstered platforms in crushed velvet, on one, a television set and VCR. Pam pokes the bed. It undulates with water.

"I did it myself," Darren says. "The couch is custom-built."

"I never would have guessed," Pam says.

Darren fake-punches her on the chin. "And I'll bet your hole is lined with glass," he says.

Lisa giggles nervously.

"I've only got two rules," Darren says. "No tampons in the toilet, and don't pop zits on the mirror. Can't have any of those little white spots, can we?"

"A preppy in disguise," Pam says, as she circles the room. Except for a raised platform and speakers mounted above it, one end of the room is completely bare. A row of stuffed animals lines a wall along the floor and she stops and nudges them with her foot.

Darren enters carrying a tray with glasses, thick brown cream jiggling against their sides. "Over there," he says. They are to sit on the floor, along with the rest of the animals, he says. As he kneels beside Christina, she feels his breath on her neck. "It's your birthday?" he asks, and holds up the birthday card.

"You were in my knapsack."

"Okay, that's it. We're out of here," Pam says.

"Wait," Darren says. He springs to his feet. "I had to check. You could be terrorists, for all I know."

"I didn't know it was your birthday," Lisa says.

"It's no big deal."

"You're wrong," Darren tells her. "It is a big deal. A very big deal. I'll be right back."

Brown cream rims Lisa's mouth and she licks it away. "It's not a milkshake, that's for sure. Definitely not."

"Weirder and weirder," Pam says, as the light in the room begins to dim and a faint circle of light grows on the wall above the platform, becoming wide, sharp, and bright. Pulsing staccato music taps against Christina's breastbone. The rhythmic slide of a snare drum and cymbal dies to a guitar that rises suddenly, screaming up the scale. Darren leaps into the spotlight and punches the air with a black gloved hand. He becomes Billy Idol singing to Christina. What had set her free and brought her to him? In the midnight hour, he sang, as though he knew that she had been down in her basement room for two years watching the grass grow outside the window. She wants more, too, like him. She wants more than Lorraine, more than a basement view, a tin of toffee, watching the world blow up on TV. She wants to know, most of all, what it is she wants. Not knowing gives her heart-cramps.

"It's not really him," Pam shouts. "He's lip-syncing."

"Who cares?" Lisa says. She gets up and begins swaying and clapping to the beat.

Christina's arms grow heavy, and it seems that a weight sits on top of her head, presses her into the floor, keeps her fixed on Darren's contorted face, and what she thinks are tears rolling in his eyes. The song ends, but he is into another one immediately, and then another, his energy frantic, unfaltering, until, finally, just when Christina thinks her head will cave in, the show ends. He drops to his knees, presses his forehead into the blue shag. Christina gropes for the wall, slides her hands along it until she finds the bathroom door.

"You're great," Lisa says.

Behind Christina, the bedroom fills with light and she sees her face in the bathroom mirror. She runs water into the sink, scoops its coolness against her cheeks. When she looks up she sees him in the mirror, his orange spiky head bending towards her.

"Happy birthday," he says.

She grabs him, and presses her cheek into his hot one. "I know what you feel," she tells him.

His crab-like arms become a vice, squeezing her, flattening her breasts against his ribs. "And what do I feel?" he asks.

"Like there's too many radios playing at the same time, all on different stations."

Darren takes her hand and sets it against the lump in his jeans. "What would you say if I jumped you?"

"She'd say, no thanks." Pam stands in the doorway, her hand searching for the light switch. Fluorescent lights bounce off the mirror and wall tiles.

"Get lost," Darren says. Perspiration trails down his face, leaving pale tracks through his deep tan. Christina sees the tinge of blue whiskers. She pushes him away. She notices that his hair is thinning on top and she sees through it to the black roots at his pink scalp.

"You okay?" Pam asks.

"Okay." Christina's eyes meet Pam's hand at the switch. "Look," she says. The switch is the shape of an erect penis; red, ridiculous-looking.

Pam's face cracks open with laughter. "I am going to wet my pants," she says, and, taking Christina by the wrist, leads her from the bathroom. "Let's get out of here."

But they don't leave. Pam dances around the room, jeering and laughing, and Christina follows. The two of them leap onto the bed, wind themselves in satin sheets and dance. *With a rebel yell*, they chant, *we want more, more, more*. Lisa joins in, and the stuffed animals bounce off the blue walls. Then Christina remembers her knapsack. "Food fight," she says, and as they had seen in a video of an old movie, and had once begun to do in McDonald's, they grab handfuls of toffee, pelt one another. Darren stands in the bathroom doorway, white-faced, stricken.

"My room," he says. "Get out of here, you animals. You're ruining my fucking room."


She has only two gears left on her bicycle, high and low, and the muscles in her legs knot as she pedals up an incline in the street. "Fucking room, I'll bet," Pam said. "He couldn't get it up, I'll bet." There is something about Pam she doesn't like, Christina thinks, as Pam and Lisa pedal across an open parking lot and disappear behind an apartment building. But she isn't sure what it is. She coasts down the street, passes through blocks of shadows cast by the sun hanging low behind the houses. Yo-Yo Ma's music makes her think of a wolf, now. In one of those wilderness films, a wolf standing on an outcrop of rock, howling at the moon.

And then the music is full and charged, like a suicide note that is romantic and terrible, but sad, too, because the person is gone and can't have the satisfaction of knowing that people have cried. Or know that their writing has been analyzed, words remembered forever. It's not fair, she thinks, that you have to die before people pay that kind of attention. She looks for Calvin in the streets. Long hair, black Johnny Walker T-shirt, looking like a hundred others at Grant Park High. Slippery skin, because all he ate was French fries. Once he bummed a cigarette from her. If she'd known, she would have given him the whole package.

On the cover of the cassette there is a picture of Yo-Yo Ma. He is a small person who curls around the cello as he plays, eyes closed in concentration behind glasses, the music the only living thing for the moment. Like Lorraine, keening over Christina's bed most mornings. "Christina, Christina, honey. Are you awake? Christina, wake up, please. You'll be late. Good morning, Christina, honey bun."

When she wheels her bicycle into the yard, she sees Lorraine's chaise longue resting against the stair railing, folded up and chained to it. The wading pool is upended against the wall beneath the kitchen window. She smells the smoky remains of barbecues on the balconies of the high-rises towering above their four-plex on three sides. A mixture of spicy sauce and singed meat. Someone strums awkwardly at a guitar. Lorraine's shadow passes the kitchen window and, moments later, the back door flies open.

"Chris? That you?" She's still in shorts and halter, and its strap droops, reveals a wedge of untanned flesh set against the gentle curve of her sun-freckled breast. "You're late. Good job. That's the thanks I get, eh?"

Christina smells coconut as she passes Lorraine in the doorway.

"Well? What have you got to say?" Lorraine follows Christina into the kitchen. Pink candles circle a cake, a circle of light centred on the table that she's spread with a white cloth. Christina frees her arms, lets the knapsack drop to the floor, and for a moment, for the moment it takes to absorb the presence of the cake, its lit candles, she wants to grab Lorraine, to wind her arms about her mother's neck and cradle her head against her.

"Well?" Lorraine waits, hands at her hips. "So that's the thanks I get. First time I let you go, and look what happens."

Christina thinks that if you didn't know Lorraine as well as she does, you could be fooled and taken in by her eyes. They are always bright, huge discs of light with questions in them, or filled with the reflections of the people she talks to, reflections of their sadness, or happiness, reflections of the programs she watches on television. But if you look further, to her mouth, for instance, you will see a dryness at the corners of her lips, a withering that could be taken for meanness. But it's more a drying up from caring than from meanness, Christina thinks.

"The minute I get home, you're on my case."

"I have the right."

"And if I were you, I wouldn't wear short shorts."

"Really."

"I wouldn't. You've got cellulite on the backs of your legs."

"Take a hike, kiddo. Was that nice?" Lorraine's voice follows Christina down the stairs. "We need to talk, you and I."

"Be up in ten," Christina says, thinking, Hah, you mean you'll do the talking and I'll do the listening.

*June 22*, Christina writes in her journal as, overhead, Lorraine slams cupboard drawers and cutlery clinks down into place on the table. She would like to write a poem, something for Calvin, call it Opus 85. But instead she writes, *Life is dull and boring and sometimes I think that if Lorraine doesn't get off my case, I'm going to take off. I have places to go,* she writes, because she suspects that Lorraine reads her journal.

"Sorry to report, Unit, no flasher in the bushes," Christina says as she comes up the stairs. May as well help, she thinks, or else have to put up with Lorraine the martyr.

"It's not them I worry about," Lorraine says, as Christina enters the kitchen.

Changed into her jeans, Christina notices. Good.

"Or white-slave traders, either."

"There's a movie on, later," Christina says.

"I'll make popcorn," Lorraine says.

"Should I open up the hide-a-bed? Okay?"

"Okay," Lorraine says. "Happy birthday, honey."

Their lips touch, a quiver of hope passes between them.

# A Necessary Treason

❧

"Lovers are meeting in the gazebo," Sadie told Janice. She called to see if Janice would still be coming out on Saturday as planned. The lilacs were crowding out a false spirea; she thought it might fare better if Janice moved it to the back-yard. The word "lovers," an anachronism dropping into the day, dangled on a string between them. Janice had never heard her mother use the word "lovers" before. To most, the word called up a tenderness, an act of generosity. Not mockery or derision, as Sadie's tone implied. I'll show you when you come, her mother said about the gazebo and lovers. She didn't want to waste long-distance time.

"I'm bringing my friend Neil," Janice told her.

"Oh."

Questions, suspicions galloped through Sadie's simple response, Janice knew. It was a source of humour among her sisters, how, when they were girls still at home and Sadie did the laundry, she snooped through their underwear for unusual stains. If they entertained a boyfriend and she had to be away, she felt the beds for heat the moment she returned. If they spent an overnight visit now with their husbands, or their brothers came with their wives, they expected she would search for telltale chalky spots in their bed linen. Scratch and sniff, that's Mom, they joke. Unlike her sisters, Janice has never found this amusing, rather she puzzles over what might have made Sadie like that. There are reasons for it. She certainly would like to know what.

One of Janice's sisters told Sadie she thought Janice was seeing someone. When Sadie asked, Janice said Neil and I are just friends. And you're full of baloney if you think I believe that, her mother's eyes told her. Men and women can't be just friends. She said this in a scoffing tone, as though she had caught Janice trying to pull one over on her. Why is it, Janice asked her three sisters, that here we are, all over forty, and still, whenever we get together, our main topic of conversation is our mother? What do you suppose happened to give Sadie a heart disposed to suspicion? she asked them.

౿ౚ

Janice is in a reflective mood as she and Neil drive out on number 75 to Sparling. It's strange, Janice tells Neil, how she's been making the one-hour drive back and forth between Winnipeg and Sparling for years and only just noticed that the city stops abruptly in the south end at Rue des Trappists. It's as though a curtain parts, she says, and there it is. Sky and land for miles. In the distance a mauve fan of trees conceals the horizon, and looks like a wash of watercolour, a mirage. She is in the mood for drawing lines, making connections between A and C. Ghosts stopped the city from spreading, she imagines. A cabal of ghosts – of the First Nations people, for instance, whose cooking fires once clotted the trees along the Red River with smoke. Settlers, too, and the Mennonites, people of her mother's culture, the first of them landing in the late 1800s. Neil's ancestors came over with that first lot, the ones who had settled along the American border in villages, and named them after the places they had left in Ukraine. Her mother's family followed later, in the mid-1920s after they had lost everything.

As Janice talks she competes for Neil's attention with music playing from the car's tape deck, Marianne Faithfull singing about a sports car and wind in her hair. About women at the age of thirty-seven who have never been to Paris. A voice filled with melancholy. It's Neil's tape. His favourite, at present. His preference ricochets from jazz to country and western to Mahler, depending on what he is reading or thinking about. Currently he was interested in women. He told her this on the third time they had met, lunch at Impressions, a small cafe down the street from the Angel gift shop where she works. She had walked into Impressions one day and there he was. He'd been a regular there years earlier, with Pat, his wife. Then they had gone north to Churchill to teach. He returned to Winnipeg alone, a published poet and substitute teacher. He wanted to understand, he told her, how women feel walking around inside their bodies.

Does he expect her to turn herself inside out for him? Janice wonders, and as the bittersweet music ends in a passionate leap off a cliff, the sound of it stays inside her chest.

Curtains on Sadie's front window slide closed as Janice and Neil pull up the gravel slope of her driveway. Neil is Janice's insurance that Sadie will be on her best behaviour today. Neil's presence, and gifts: walking shoes she will deliver on behalf of the sisters; a book she found in St. Jacobs while on a buying trip in Ontario. A book of photographs of people her mother might remember; the village where Sadie grew up in Ukraine. She's been watching for us, Janice says, and feels the weight of responsibility to present the gift of walking shoes. The sisters will telephone later and want to know how it went. She's going to break her neck, the shoes she wears, one of the sisters said on the telephone, voicing their most recent concern: their mother's penchant for high-heeled shoes. Although Sadie has always worn heels they have only just noticed. "A woman of eighty years! She'll wind up falling. Broken hip and game over," they worried.

It seems the more Janice and the sisters discuss Sadie, the telephone lines humming between their houses in the city, the more resentful they become. It irritates them how Sadie goes on and on about the end of the world, for instance. It's all she wants to talk about. It grates because of the effort they put into giving her cushy and worry-free golden years. What's so darn bad about Sadie's life that all she ever looks forward to is being taken to heaven by a returning Christ? They had met over lunch to sort through material swatches, paint chips that would go well in Sadie's family room. They had replaced the flooring in the kitchen, painted and wallpapered and put in new appliances. They had installed a tub-surround in the bathroom and finished the walls in peach-coloured ceramic tiles. Sadie is the last of a dying breed, they said. Not one of them will be able to afford to sit like a queen on a chair during their retirement age and not lift a finger. They have a right, they believe, to be enraged by the idea of their mother traipsing about her house, up and down stairs, for god's sake, wearing pointy-toed high-heeled shoes. Who is she trying to impress? they wonder.

The front door opens and Sadie makes an appearance on the front step. That's what she does, Janice thinks. Sadie is always making an appearance. Since the diagnosis of a heart condition five years ago, she has become a compelling presence. She has her own chair now, its legs shortened so her feet rest comfortably on the floor, and, when the sisters come visiting, they set the chair under the arch between the living and dining rooms so she can follow their movements through the house. "Oh, for Pete's sake," Sadie complains when they sit her down on it and take over in the kitchen. "Being catered to. And in my own house." It's as though a natural law has been suspended. But Sadie enjoys, nevertheless, her new freedom from responsibilities, the miracle of being weightless. Since her heart condition, Sadie has become a bright spot of co-ordinated colour. Sometimes she wears understated mauve or pink. At others, such as today, she's a vivid bird in a red and white dress that Janice hasn't seen before.

Janice gathers from Sadie's impatient wave that she's been waiting, perhaps all week, to say something, and knows that the gift of the shoes and book will need to be worked in later on during their visit.

"Lovers are meeting in my gazebo," Sadie says, in the same way she might announce her house had been burglarized, enjoying the drama and being affronted by it at the same time.

"Yes, so you said on the telephone."

"Oh, did I tell you already?" Sadie asks, flooded instantly with embarrassment.

She fears senility, Alzheimer's, Janice knows. Her hair is a soft puff of white brushing against Janice's face, lips an undefined smudge of pink gloss, a light touch on Janice's mouth. Sadie is like the peonies, Janice thinks, all open and spent and falling across the sidewalk. She squeezes her mother's shoulder in a hug. Her careful planning to ensure her mother's best behaviour no longer seems important. Clouds, flimsy and white as Sadie's hair, rush across the sky.

"Oh, your friend," Sadie says, as though she has only just noticed Neil.

"I have four daughters," she tells him after they are introduced. "And not one of them married a Mennonite." She is not claiming an elder's proclivity for outspokenness. This is Sadie, the way she's always been.

"You didn't marry a Mennonite," Janice reminds her.

"Well, yes. But that was me," Sadie says. I was special, her tone implies. Different from my sisters and daughters. Superior, because she had been misunderstood in her youth, unconventional; the way the black sheep of families often come to view themselves later on in life. Too intelligent for their own good.

"Now, what about those lovers?" Janice says.

"Things are being moved."

Sadie takes them through the vegetable garden, detailing other evidence. As they pass through orderly rows of vegetation, Janice half-listens. She fears insects. As she walks, she feels the nerves in her body buzz with a warning to be alert. She fears beetles on the potatoes, slugs, earthworms, crickets, ladybugs, ants, and, worse, spiders.

The gazebo door has been left open more than once, Sadie tells them. Once she found a strand of red wool snagged on the door frame. "I hear the lovers talking at night when I'm in bed." Sadie says the word "lovers" as though she is listening to herself say it. Wants to hear what it sounds like coming from her mouth. Today she appears amused by the idea of it rather than put off, Janice thinks; and thanks god she brought Neil.

Across the back lane a door closes, and a balding man gets into a car parked beside a garage and backs it into the alley.

"That's Mr. Bishop." Sadie's voice is a sharp whisper. "He's the new principal at the high school and people are already complaining," she says as he drives off down the lane.

Sadie had hammered nails into the gazebo door frame and looped strands of wire around them as a kind of lock. Janice sees a ragged piece of cardboard taped to the screen beside the door. The letters KEEP OUT on it in red crayon. Sadie steps inside the gazebo and points to the grass and several crushed cigarette butts. "Export 'A,' " she says. "And some of them have lipstick. Not only that," she says, "the lawn chairs aren't in their usual positions."

"Aha, the evidence," Neil says, and squats to play detective. "I wonder why they would be smoking here, when the chairs are over there?"

"Because they weren't sitting." Sadie walks, tracing an outline of a narrow strip of flattened grass. "They moved the chairs over there so they could lie down."

Smug, Janice thinks. "Missionary position, obviously," she says softly, and laughs while her eyes search the gazebo's screens, the two-by-four supports, for insects.

"What did you say?" Sadie's hearing is always more acute for the indirect than the direct.

"There's sure nothing wrong with your eyesight," Neil says. "I would have missed that."

"I may be old but I'm not stupid." Sadie's chin juts forward, a haughty stance. "They probably think because I'm old they can walk all over me."

Neil laughs and collects the lawn chairs, swinging them into place beside a low table. His laughter makes Janice forget about the gazebo harbouring insects. When she meets Neil for lunch on Saturdays, she prefers to sit beside him, the better to study him unnoticed. She wants to see how sunlight in the windows brings out the silver in his grey hair. She wonders what it would be like to make love with a man with a Low German accent. Silky wild poppies bob against the side of the garage like splotches of red paint among the froth of Queen Anne's lace. Sadie's garden comes up year after year, thicker and brighter. Clumps of purple and white alyssum push up through broken paving stones on the garden path.

Janice slides a potted plant aside to make room on a wooden bench, and a grey film of mould beneath it reminds her of spiders. There may be one, several, she thinks, hidden in the plant's foliage, crouching in a nook or cranny of the gazebo. She imagines spider legs testing strings, feeling for the vibration of their voices in its web. If she confessed to a fear of flying, open spaces, or even of dogs, she would meet with less derision. But Janice's bugaboo, as her father, Zeke, had called it, carries the same stigma as bedwetting. She thinks of a spider dropping from the ceiling and tries not to cringe. When she looks up she realizes that Sadie has been watching. Sadie's fine white hair, back-lit by the sun, looks incandescent. Her lips part as she smiles, revealing the edge of her teeth, bright with saliva.

"I sprayed," Sadie says, and for a moment Janice thinks she said, "I prayed."

"Don't worry." Sadie's smile says she's willing to play the mother who sweeps up after bad dreams. It says, The Lord is helping me to be more understanding of your silly affliction. She smooths creases from her dress, crosses her legs, and immediately the tip of her shoe moves in tight little circles.

Janice studies Sadie: new off-white pumps, shinbone pressing against opaque white hosiery. She becomes aware of her own grass-stained joggers, the oversize sweatshirt she wears, the thigh of her jeans scribbled with ballpoint-pen doodling. She smells her mother's cologne, sweet and bright.

"In Russia," Sadie says to Neil, "we always sat out in the summer. In an arbour, not a gazebo. It wasn't like this. It was covered in grapevines and my father built benches all along the sides, for sitting. The leaves made it feel so cool, even on the hottest days. Your grandparents must've had one, too."

She's disappointed when he says he doesn't know. His parents were born in this country, he says.

"Then you don't know suffering." It's both a complaint and an accusation.

"My mother's family lived near the city of Zaporozhye, Ukraine," Janice says, embarrassed by her mother's petulance.

"In Russia," Sadie interjects vehemently. "Not in the Ukraine. We knew it as Russia." She was thirteen when they left, she tells him.

"So you must remember a lot, then," Neil says.

Yes, Janice thinks. More than the usual, it was a beautiful place. So green. Milder winters than here. She wants to hear about the houses with tile roofs, barns attached and yards enclosed by saw-toothed picket fences. Which house was yours? she wants to know. The photographs in the book suggest Sadie came from a place of severely defined margins, as strict-looking as the elderly aunts she remembers vaguely. Their expressions, her father said, always made him think they had just sucked a lemon. They sang "Nearer My God to Thee," but acted as though it was a terrible calamity when someone grew ill and therefore in danger of actually getting closer to the Almighty. Neil is the only person Janice has been able to talk to about Sadie. She can tell him, "My mother has an apocalyptic eye," and he understands why. My mother sees portents of fire storms and avenging angels in a bank of night clouds on the horizon. My mother can find deep meaning in the arrangement of fly specks on a wall. And everything points to the return of Christ, of course.

She wants to leave the world alive, Neil once said. It could be that she's afraid to die. That's common among Christians. That's probably why Mennonites are pacifists. That's why they're ambulance chasers, want to be at the scene of every world accident. They're fixated by death and dying.

Janice hadn't thought of that.

"I remember the arbour," Sadie says to Neil. "Quite clearly."

"And what else?" Janice asks, as though she is only mildly interested; bait to entice a difficult child into wanting to perform.

"I think I should water this." Sadie pokes her finger into the soil of an aloe plant on the table beside her chair. "Well, let me see," she says. "Our fence was broken. I remember that. There were boards missing and I used to crawl through the hole instead of going through the gate. My father didn't like that."

She grows aware of Janice's waiting silence. "Why are you so anxious to know, anyway?"

"You know what I think you should do?" Neil interrupts, leaning towards Sadie, his voice conspiratorial. "I think you should find out who in town smokes Export 'A.'"

"I already know who," Sadie crows triumphantly. "Mr. Bishop. I was putting the garbage out and he was washing his car. 'Mrs. Palmer,' he said. 'You shouldn't be doing that. That's far too heavy for you to be carrying.' Well, who's going to do it? I told him. He said, 'I'll do it. You let me come over on garbage day and I'll take your garbage to the lane.' The idea. Now I'm supposed to get permission to carry my own garbage? I watch for him now before I go out. I make sure he's not around. He smokes Export 'A.' I saw the package in his shirt pocket; and his wife is never home. He said as much. She's a court reporter and travels and he comes home from work to a rowdy house. Full of teenagers and loud music and no supper. I feel sorry for him," Sadie says.

Her words, fuelled by the imagining of crimes committed in her gazebo unspoken for too long a time, break loose.

Janice raises her eyebrows at Neil. Spare me, she signals.

"A man goes looking if a woman isn't home. I don't approve of adultery, but I understand. And he's too easygoing with the kids at school, too. He wants to take a whole class to France in summer for French immersion. The pastor said last Sunday how it's foretold in the Bible that people will no longer know how to love one another. What love is. The breakdown of the family has come to this, and it's the children who are paying now."

Janice hears accusation in her mother's words. So far, she is the only one in the family divorced. Her marriage lies smashed to smithereens at the bottom of a dry well and needy children call from across Canada late at night and all she can do is doodle on the thigh of her jeans and listen and cross her fingers.

"I've got an idea," Neil says, interrupting Sadie's monologue. "I think you should charge them."

"Charge who?" Sadie asks, surprised at being stopped mid-stream.

"The lovers. Charge them for using your gazebo. Put up a sign." He writes the letters in the air. "Fee for use of gazebo. Ten dollars an hour."

Sadie's hand flies up to her mouth, a hand knotted with enlarged knuckles and lumpy veins, but the laughter she wants to hold back escapes, a young sound, sexy, Janice thinks. Sadie's grey eyes shine with a beguiling coquetry and a hooded slyness, directed at Neil. She understands suddenly the reason for her mother's white stockings, the red dress she hasn't seen before, the mouth smeared with lip gloss. Sadie is thinking about lovers.

"There's some orange Tang in the cupboard," Sadie says, recovering her composure. "Would you like some?"

"I could go for that," Neil says, rubbing his palms together in anticipation.

"Why don't you get it?" Sadie tells Janice.

Janice rushes off across the garden. Where did my mother learn to flirt? she wonders as she strides past a metal trough that rests against the house beneath a rain spout. She doesn't see the bugs skating among leaves floating on the surface of the water. It's goofy, she thinks, laughable. Coming from an eighty-year-old woman.

She walks softly, almost stealthily, about the kitchen, opens cupboard doors tentatively, as though looking for clues. She feels as if she is riffling through Sadie's underwear drawer and not just looking for sugar. The shelves are crammed with a lifetime collection of cooking spices, teas, soup mixes, and powdered drink crystals. Sadie can recognize the sound of every drawer in the kitchen. No, not that one, she would often call from another room, I keep the plastic bags in the second drawer, not that one. This is the person Janice thinks she knows and expects. Sadie, a blur of movement, or head stuck inside the oven or refrigerator, rushing between the stove and the table. Or a younger Sadie, as fierce as a Boston bulldog with a killer hold on an argument, not letting go until you caved in from exhaustion. Sadie, her dress knotted around her knees, chasing a screaming Janice through the garden and wrestling her to the ground. "See?" Sadie, holding up a grasshopper that had jumped down the neck of Janice's T-shirt. "You see how dangerous a bug is?" she says and squashes it between her fingers. This is Sadie. Not this metamorphosis a failing heart has produced. A fashion statement, with a bureau full of collagen- and placenta-enriched creams.

Sadie is alone now in the gazebo. She can hear water running in the house and, as she sees movement at the kitchen window, she realizes Janice is at the sink letting the water run for a bit to rid it of the initial metallic taste. Janice, as though sensing she is being watched, raises her head, and, for moments before she turns away, her face is framed by the window, her features made indistinguishable by distance. People have always said, of all Sadie's daughters Janice most resembles her, but Sadie fails to see it. She fails to see any of herself or her side of the family in any of her children. She watches as Neil walks through the garden to the car where he has gone to get something that he said he wanted to show her. He reminds Sadie of a distant cousin, a person given to teasing, allowing her to lose her temper, pummel him in mock fury with her fists.

She wonders what she might have lost by pushing away a person of her own kind.

ɔ⌒⌐

Sadie follows her sisters and aunts, who walk without speaking, single file. Eight women in light-coloured or white dresses of a soft fabric that allows the shape of a hip, a thigh — coming forward, retreating. It is a summer day, 1928, the sun is setting, and she walks along a path leading to a park beside a river. In the falling light they're all mauve, their dresses and skin; the grass dark, a blue-green. At the end of the day they bathe, the youngest to the oldest, in a galvanized tub set among trees behind a house. There are chairs arranged around it and blankets hung over the backs for privacy. The house stands on a light rise behind them as they make their way to the river, its windows bronze with the setting sun. Looking like a house on fire, Sadie thinks. They wash their hair with rainwater from a trough near the side of the house, a rinse of vinegar to make it shine. They plait and wind their hair about their heads, wear it like silver or blonde tiaras, then they dress in their coolest good-for-Sunday dresses.

They file down the dusty path clasping their songbooks, a path that gives way to deep grass and then a clearing among burr oak, with ash and maple trees growing thickly along the river. It's not a walnut grove, but it will do. Sadie's father, brother to the aunts, and her mother, are already there, waiting. Canvas folding chairs which he made for the purpose of meeting are arranged in a half-circle.

Sadie rests her head against her chair, songbook open on her lap. On the surface she has the look of a child politely bored by the adults around her. But she is fuming over not being able to say what she is thinking. It was their practice in the old country to bathe at the end of the day, climb up to a walnut grove planted on the side of a valley above their village, and gather for song. Sadie objects to continuing the practice. No one else does it, why should they? But her father insists. They have too much to forget, too much to be glad about. They require the steadying influence of ritual.

It's time, the aunts say, to put the little songbird into a house. Sadie is too temperamental, moody. This is Sadie, they say. Remember when she was a child, how she refused to sing for them unless they paid her two kopecks? This is the biter, the foot stamper. The child who hid the minute there was work to be done. Sadie's blood is too hot, her mind too quick, and she has big eyes for anything new. And so the aunts suggest to her parents that they write to a distant relative in a neighbouring town and ask them to send Hans, the grandson of a clockmaker, on a bus for a visit.

Sadie's father leads the song and the women's voices blend with his smoothly, their singing sweet and sad and with a tremor of lost hope, or with the steadiness of resignation. It isn't his fault that events catapulted them into this place, that he's much too old to learn the language and find employment, and that the women face work as farmhands or maids to the wealthy in the distant city until their passage fares and their parents' and aunts' houses are paid for. But not Sadie. The second youngest will be better off safely married, because she is Sadie. An older sister has brought with her a piece of crocheting that will go into her tomorrow chest and she works at it almost feverishly, her eyelashes fluttering. She left behind a first love. Two of the aunts have said farewell at the graves of husbands, a child. They are old at thirty. Their cherished hopes will always remain prayers only.

When Hans had come to visit last month, the aunts set two chairs in the garden and retreated to their brother's house where they could sit in the shadow of its extended roof and watch the couple unnoticed.

He worked for his father, Hans told Sadie. There wasn't enough business in clock and watch repair to keep him and his brothers busy, and so his brothers were going to normal school to become teachers. He didn't have the patience for teaching, he knew. So he wanted to build onto his father's store and sell furniture and household items. Sadie had watched him from the front garden as he'd come down the lane to the house, having walked the half-mile from town where the bus dropped him off. He'd slung his jacket across his shoulder and she liked that. She also liked the way his face flared with pleasure at the mention of her name, when, from the oldest to the youngest, she and her sisters had been introduced. Liked it too that when she laughed his ears turned red.

He terribly much wanted to buy a car, he told Sadie. It was hot and perspiration beaded his lip. Flies buzzed around the compost heap at the back of the garden and the air smelled faintly of decaying vegetation. His tight-fitting shirt strained across his stomach, revealing white skin and a feathering of gold hair. Sadie wanted to poke him, to feel if he was soft or muscular. Then she thought it would be nice to slide a finger between his shirt buttons and tickle him, gently, and she felt her breasts swell. They were small, high breasts, and she had only just come to appreciate them. She began to roll up a pink ribbon hanging from her waist. Then she let the ribbon fall and began turning it up again. She felt his gaze, his yearning. It seemed to her that her hands had become delicate and lovely, and that as she rolled up the ribbon, they spoke to him.

If he had a car, would she go riding with him? he asked her. You want to take me for a spin? Sadie said, and laughed, not knowing yet that she was beautiful. She'd heard the word "spin" already, one day when she went to buy milk. There had been two men, leaning against a car, caps pushed to the backs of their heads. "Hey, cutie. Want me to take you for a spin?" one of them said. She knew he had spoken to her like that because they thought she was just a little German girl. A dummy immigrant who could be fooled easily.

Sadie's youngest sister, Betty, came through the garden towards them. She'd been sent with glasses of tea. Sadie felt the space between their chairs widen and she remembered that the aunts sat hidden in the shadows, watching.

Betty stood in front of Hans, colouring as she offered him a glass of tea. Sadie thought suddenly that Betty had grown taller. She realized with a shock that it was Hans who had grown shorter. It had rained during the night and the ground in the garden was soft and, while they were talking, the legs of his chair had sunk slowly, minute by minute, into the damp earth. As Betty returned to the house, Hans sipped at his tea, crossed and uncrossed his legs, trying to get comfortable.

He lived at the back of his father's watch-repair shop because a window had been broken once and thieves tried to get in. He said he thought he would enlarge the living quarters, once he had added on to the business. Sadie wanted him to get up. To pull his chair legs free. To make a joke of it. As the legs sank deeper into the earth, he gave up on crossing his legs and his knees jutted up in front of him, level with his chest. She noticed his fingers wrapped around the glass, that they were pudgy and too blunt to work inside a clock. A muscle jerked in his face as he talked. She realized, too, that his stomach was fat and he had a bracelet of fat around his wrists. She clamped her hand against her mouth to try to hold back the laughter.

What's funny, Hans wanted to know, looking directly at her for the first time.

"You," Sadie told him. "Chubby cheeks," she said, and pinched one, surprising herself. She didn't know where this boldness came from. "You're such a fatty," she said. Once she said the word, she couldn't stop. She turned it into a song she had heard neighbourhood children singing.

"Fatty, fatty, two by four, can't get through the kitchen door," she chanted as she moved farther and farther away from him through the garden.

The sisters and aunts harmonize as they sing "Amen" at the end of the hymn. Sadie's father begins to recite the Lord's Prayer. She half closes her eyes, watches a man and two children disappear on a path that winds down to the edge of the river. Her attention is drawn to her sister's crocheting. Her fingers deftly loop and twist yarn while her eyes remain shut, lips moving in silent recitation. A chest heaves, a sigh escapes.

They all struggle not to remember what happened in the old country, Sadie knows. Their night terrors are assuaged with weak tea and honey. Forgiving trespassers means not remembering. Or remaining silent if they do remember. And they do remember, Sadie knows, the aunts and her older sisters; she knows this from their whispered conversations breaking off suddenly. She remembers, too, the sound of fists against a door in the night, raucous laughter, a breathless panic that brought them all from their beds to flee across open fields at night. Sadie suspects her aunts and older sisters have come to know desperate things that she doesn't. She suspects that they resent her for this.

They have forgotten how to dream, Sadie believes. As the women bow their heads and pray, Our Father, Our Father, Sadie sits on a chair, legs crossed, loving the look of her shapely foot, the slenderness of her ankle as she twists it around and around. She knows that if she's ever going to be able to dream, treason will be necessary.

~

Ice cubes wash against the sides of a glass pitcher as Janice steps out onto the stairs leading to the broken path through her mother's garden. Insects zigzag across the surface of water in the trough resting against the house. She skirts the water trough and is almost past it when a movement at its base catches her attention. An animal crouches on the grass, looking up at her. Like her, it's startled. It turns its worried-looking little face up to hers and their eyes meet. It blinks and scurries into a hole under the trough. No tail, Janice notes. Or else a small one and curled against its body.

"It was about the size of a small cat." She squats, showing Neil where the animal disappeared. Sadie hovers, wanting and not wanting to see the damp hole.

"I've been getting water almost every day and I've never seen anything," Sadie says. It's as though she holds Janice responsible for the appearance of the animal.

That's because you haven't spent your entire life being on guard, Janice thinks. "It looked straight at me. It was roundish and sort of hunkered close to the ground." She was always the first to spot a mouse, toads in the cucumber vines.

"I hope it didn't have a white stripe down its back," Neil says. "I wouldn't want to poke around if that's the case."

Sadie's laughter is tight, sardonic.

"I think it had a snout."

"Maybe a muskrat. The river's close enough," Neil says.

"Your dad would know," Sadie says. "He was good with animals," she tells Neil.

When Janice enters the gazebo, she sees the book of photographs lying on the ground in front of Sadie's chair. "I didn't think you'd mind," Neil says as their eyes meet. I do mind, she tells him with her eyes.

"Look," Sadie says, as she takes the book and sets it on her lap. "Look at what I found." She flips through it and holds it open at a double-page photograph of four young women. "My father's sisters. Lydia, Tien, Aganetha, and Marusya." She points at each as she names them. "It was taken the year I was born."

The women pose in front of a photographer's scrim. One reclines on a chaise longue, her flowing skirts arranged in a casual-looking swirl. Another sits beside her with a book lying open in the folds of her skirt while another leans across the back of the chaise longue as though reading from the book's pages. The fourth sister stands away from them at a pedestal set among ferns; her waist-length hair glints with light as it ripples across her back. They are round-faced and full-lipped and have fair complexions that Sadie's children inherited. They look like Tsarinas, Janice thinks, all dressed in white, faces brimming with youth, untroubled or perhaps ignorant of the events unfolding around them.

They're not the faces Janice remembers seeing at various family gatherings when her grandparents were still alive. Faces gone pulpy with an obsequious piety. Women whose imaginations seemed limited to simple daisy-chain patterns they forever embroidered along the edges of tea towels and dresser scarves. Inevitable gifts at Christmas, birthdays, and weddings.

"We used to have that picture in our photo album. When my mother died, they just cleaned the place right out. One of my sisters must have taken it. I don't care. What on earth would I do with it, anyway?" Sadie wants, Janice knows, for her to protest. To say it's a crying shame. How they had stripped Sadie of her past because she married out of her culture and religion.

"Look what else I found." Sadie opens the book at the photograph Janice puzzled over. *Rosenthal. Winter 1910.* The photograph is a study of textures, wood houses and pebbly-looking tile rooftops surrounded by white picket fences.

"There's my house. There's the hole in the fence." Sadie's face shines.

Janice realizes that, until then, Sadie has likely doubted her memory of the broken fence.

"I used to climb through that hole. I went through it the day the men came to our house. My mother was sick in bed and they stood over her. I'll never forget it. One of them had a small whip that he twitched, back and forth, in front of my mother's face. I can still see the look on his face. Mean. I ran out of the house and crawled through that hole, there." Her fingers dab at a fuzzy grey spot.

This is the first Janice has heard about a man and a whip. "You must have been terrified," Neil says.

"I went to my grandfather's house. I don't remember if I was scared, but they said I could barely talk. Which was unusual for me, not to have anything to say. They joked about it afterwards."

"So those men, they would have been who?" Janice asks.

"They called themselves anarchists," Sadie says to Neil, as though it was he and not Janice who had asked the question. "The peasants. My father used to say they didn't know the meaning of the word. They were hungry and they had heard someone had brought my mother a jar of jam because she was sick. They thought she was hiding it under her pillow." She becomes pensive, looks down at her hands folded against the photograph. She sighs. "Yes, well. We were taught not to dwell on hard times, you see. And we didn't."

Sadie looks at them as though she's forgotten where she is in the story and then becomes huffy with resolution. "It's not like now. People on TV every day. On the news, crying the blues over something or other. I have never cried." She says this last thing as though it has only just come to her. "Not even when Zeke died," she tells Neil, her eyes bright. "I never cried then, either." She sounds, Janice thinks, like a kid boasting about having perfect attendance at school. If that's something they would boast about now. She wonders.

A car approaches in the lane and they hear the sound of an

automatic garage-door opening. "It's Mr. Bishop," Sadie whispers. His car sweeps past them and then up and into the garage. The smell of exhaust hangs in the air. "It must be nice to be a teacher. He gets all the holidays off and summer too."

Janice glances at Neil, who sometimes teaches language arts at the junior-high level. The rest of the time he's an enforcer, he says. He brings an aluminum baseball bat to set beside his desk for emphasis. He used to make his own soup stock, he's told her. It's best to bake the bones in a hot oven first. That way, you got less fat and a darker stock. While he likes the uncomplicated lifestyle that comes from living in one room, he misses not being able to fuss in a kitchen, he said. He would like to borrow her kitchen, some time.

"Maybe that's his problem," Sadie says. "Maybe that man has got too much free time. Like King David, staying home instead of going to war. Lying in bed and spying on Bathsheba bathing. Look what that started."

Neil laughs. He rests his elbow against his thigh and his fingers curl around his cheek, creasing his skin. Janice likes his hands, the bit of potting soil usually caught in the cuticles.

He senses her studying him. "A little furry black animal, eh?"

Janice looks across the spikes of blue and purple delphinium, the exorbitant daisies, vivid orange and yellow clumps thriving among them a shock to the eye. She imagines the animal crouched in its hollow. That it has lived there for years and knows all the sounds of the house, the rattle of air in the ducts in the walls, Sadie singing in the bath, "Jesus, saviour, pilot me over the rough and stormy sea." Hears their voices in the gazebo as it hunkers in its moist earth cave.

"Show me where you want that bush moved," Janice says. The

sudden longing to feel Neil's body against hers, the weight and heat of it, catches her by surprise.

Janice swings the garden fork down from its hook in the garage and sets it into the wheelbarrow. As she bumps along the driveway she remembers the walking shoes and stops to get them from the car. Neil wanted to help. He insisted. She said no. She wants to do this alone.

After the bush is moved, Janice, with a forced exuberance, presents the gift of the walking shoes.

"But when in heaven's name will I wear them?" Sadie asks, perplexed.

Sadie's initial surprise and then strained enthusiasm over the gift of shoes peters out to barely concealed petulance. She holds them up on her hands as though they're mittens.

"Around the house. Wear them when you go to get the mail. Everyone is into more comfortable foot gear." Janice repeats herself and knows she's beginning to sound defensive.

They are the normal, everyday foot fashion of middle-aged women, such as herself. She says she doesn't think twice about wearing them everywhere. And elderly women, too, she concludes. The early-morning mall-walkers promoting healthy hearts and slowing bone loss. Just the other day, Janice tells Sadie, she had been in the Bay and saw several women shopping. They wore silk floral-print dresses with detachable crocheted collars and Reeboks, Adidas, Naturalizers on their feet.

"I hate anything crocheted," Sadie says. "And I'm too short to wear floral. That's one thing I've learned about myself. That's why I prefer a heel. I need the extra height."

What does she see in the mirror, Janice wonders, that an extra inch of height matters?

Sadie sets the shoes down, plants them firmly. "You girls. They always go to far too much expense and bother," she confides to Neil. "There's no point in spending so much money on an old woman like me. I keep telling them that. But do they listen? No, they do not." Her knuckles shine as she grips the chair's armrests. She presses her back into its webbing, rigid with determination to put as much distance as possible between herself and the topic of walking shoes.

"Make sure you thank your sisters for me. I always appreciate what you girls do for me." The tip of her pump draws circles in the air.

She'll never wear them, Janice thinks. They'll sit in her closet, forever.

"Why don't you try them on?"

"I will, dear. Later."

"I want to see if they fit."

"The box says size five. I don't see why they wouldn't fit." Her foot draws smaller and tighter circles.

"They cost a hundred bucks. The least you can do is try them on."

Sadie flinches. Janice feels Neil staring at her, his surprise that she raised her voice.

Sadie uncrosses her leg and hooks the toe of her foot into the heel of the other shoe, prying it loose. "I have such awful bunions," she says with a small laugh. She stands and looks down at her feet, at the bluish skin, mottled purple with broken veins. Misshapen clumps of flesh and bone. Not the foot of Cinderella, Janice thinks. Sadie grimaces at the sight of them and quickly wedges her feet into the walking shoes. "They're soft," she says. "Like a bath towel inside." The laces flop like pink rabbit ears across the tongue. "Don't you think they're too wide?"

"You need wide for your bunions." Janice almost grins at the absurd look of them. Pink and white pancakes. "Why not walk around a bit. Get the feel of them."

Sadie is about to comply when the back gate opens. They watch as Mr. Bishop comes through the garden to the gazebo.

"I wonder what he wants?" Sadie sits, plucks at the folds in her dress and smooths it across her thighs. She crosses her leg but then, remembering the shoes, tucks her feet under the chair.

Mr. Bishop stands outside the gazebo door. "I saw you out here earlier."

Sadie invites him in. "This is one of my daughters," she says. "And this is Neil Rempel."

Janice thinks how infrequently Sadie actually uses their names. You girls, she says, or the boys, when she refers to any of her three sons. You people.

"Janice," she introduces herself. The man's palm is hot against hers.

"I see your daughters out here quite often. They always seem to be giving you a hand. That's quite something, these days."

"And how is Mrs. Bishop?" Sadie asks. "Is she away working?" She turns her face up to him; the pink smear of her mouth opens in a smile. She raises a hand, as though offering it to him, that he might bend over and kiss it.

"I've been trying to convince my mother that she should switch to walking shoes," Janice tells him. "But I haven't been having much luck, I'm afraid."

"Oh, let's have a look," Mr. Bishop says. He puts his hands on his thighs as he bends to peer at Sadie's feet. "Well, now, those should be pretty comfy," he says in a loud, cheerful voice. A parent who believes enthusiasm is the key to bullying a stubborn child into submission.

"Nobody in Sparling wears them. I'll stick out like a sore thumb." Sadie sees through his ploy and the contempt in her voice is overt.

"Well, now, that's not so. My wife, Grace, has a pair."

"How come I never see her wearing them?"

"She does. When we go for our walk." He unfolds a wad of tissues from his shirt pocket and the label of his cigarette package appears behind the thin cotton. "It's just that we go walking at night," he says, "and so you don't see her. Actually, that's why I came over. I saw the sign posted on the gazebo and I thought I should explain. We like to have a smoke after our walk and the mosquitoes have been beggars. Grace and I, we've been using your gazebo."

"For smoking?" Sadie asks, incredulous.

"We should have checked with you first." He rushes in to fill the ensuing silence. "But it's fairly late when we go out. I was sure you wouldn't mind, and now I see that I was mistaken. And so I think an apology is in order."

Sadie's eyes stray to the spot of flattened grass. "With your wife?"

"We don't like to expose our kids to second-hand smoke."

"And you need to move the chairs for smoking?"

He blushes and backs towards the gazebo door. "I'm sure you must remember what it's like having kids underfoot all the time. Grace and I need to talk," he says, "without all the big ears around."

"Talk, I'm sure," Sadie says as he retreats. Seething with resentment, she kicks the shoes from her feet and slips back into her pumps.

"Talk. Well, if he wants to talk, why doesn't he sit in the car? That's what your dad and I had to do."

"Some couples do it in airplanes," Neil says to Janice with a wink. "They call it joining the Mile High club. I guess it adds a bit of spice to life."

Sadie stares at him but says nothing.

"Well," Sadie says after a moment, as though she has decided to put aside what had been running through her mind. Then her jaw drops as she gasps. "Don't look," she tells Janice. "Don't you move. There's a bug on the screen."

Janice resists the impulse to jump up and flee. "Where?"

"Behind you. I think it's a grasshopper."

"I'll get it." Neil steps behind Janice's chair and flicks the insect from the screen. He grinds it under his heel. He leans over her shoulder, his face almost touching hers. "I killed it," he says. She sags with the relief of his hand on her neck, its reassuring warm pressure.

Sadie's face tightens and her foot revolves around and around. "It's so silly," she says. "Afraid of insects. What can a little bug do to a person, anyway?"

"It's not an unusual fear. Most people find something or other frightening. I'm afraid of flying," Neil says.

"And I'm afraid of snakes," Sadie retorts. "But I learned to conquer my fear. I just talked myself out of it."

Neil whistles through his teeth, the Marianne Faithfull song about the woman never having been in Paris; Janice recognizes the tune. "Yes," he says, breaking off, "but this country isn't exactly overrun with snakes, is it? Especially not in this province."

Sadie pretends she hasn't heard. She becomes preoccupied with twisting the rings on her fingers, arranging their stones to the front.

"Grasshoppers aren't that easy to kill," she says, moments later. "How do you know you've really killed it? You can't always kill a grasshopper that easily."

❧

Janice and Neil are approaching the halfway point between Sparling and the city, a toy-like country church, a wrought-iron fence enclosing a graveyard. This was as far as Janice and her younger brother, Sonny, had been allowed to cycle along the shoulder of the highway. This thirty-minute drive was a day's expedition on bicycles, she tells Neil. It was where they ate their lunch of salty buns and green peppers. Sonny liked inventing tragic lives and deaths for the people buried in the cemetery. In that very spot, he had told her, flocks of passenger pigeons, millions of them, had blocked out the sun with their flight and turned day into night. The people buried there were likely the ones who had fished the birds from the sky with nets and clubbed them to death until the passenger pigeon disappeared for good.

She doesn't like to think about it, Janice says, or about the bison either. Their bones piled as high as the church steeple; and that was why Sonny had refused to eat meat. He was gone, now, she said. Neil nodded, listening intently as he always does, and, when he doesn't ask how, or why, but waits for her to give as much as she wants, she tells him.

Sonny was a curly-haired child who had once, on a dare, caught a girl in the schoolyard and kissed her. He drowned on a spring day just after his twelfth birthday. He'd been out on the swollen Sparling Creek on a raft, seduced by the lure of a free ride on spring currents. She imagines he stood tall on his raft, head held high as he glided past the cemetery where the tops of headstones stared out at him across a stone wall. Then the raft shot around a bend, and, balancing himself with his pole like a high-wire artist, on he flew to where the creek entered the Red River and the spot where once, as a young boy, he'd stepped into a nest of willet eggs. It was the only time she ever heard her father raise his voice, she tells Neil. He had been a quiet, steady man whose only real ambition was to be at peace with the people around him. But the sight of yellowish-green egg shells clinging to her brother's boots, the destruction of the birds, had angered him. Then the raft veered, snagging on a piece of timber jutting out from the shore and swung around and pitched her brother into the icy water.

What had Sadie done to bring this on? This is what Sadie's aunts and sisters wanted to know, Janice says. Sadie, what have you gone and done? What was it she'd done that had made God take the child from her? After the funeral they took Sadie into the church basement and sat her down, told her to look into her heart. Sadie should take the time, for once, they said, to think about what wrongs she may have committed. And Sadie excused herself, Janice tells Neil. She told them she had to go to the bathroom. Then she locked herself in it, climbed out the window, and went home.

"Your mother's got a lot of courage," Neil says.

"I didn't think so at the time."

I can't imagine such cruelty, Janice says. That was when my father put his foot down. He said my mother's family wasn't welcome in his home any longer, unless they spoke English so he could understand what was going on. I don't think she would ever have got over it if it hadn't been for him.

Janice thinks about what to tell her sisters. That Sadie put the shoes on a shelf in a closet. That she didn't promise to wear them. She thinks of her mother sitting on her chair, the book of photographs open on her lap. Of the faces of her childhood friends coming forward beneath the looking-glass Janice's father once kept in the medicine chest to better see the splinters or specks of glass embedded in a child's skin. Sadie saying to herself, "There's Alvira! And Frieda! Betty!" Sadie saying, "I never once had to clean out a barn or stook hay. I never worked my fingers to the bone washing dirty bed linens for the rich English, either. What did I do to deserve that, I wonder?" Janice imagines the black furry animal huddled against the foundation beneath the trough screwing up its impish face, holding its breath and listening.

The church steeple rises on the horizon, the halfway point between her mother's house and the city. "Look," Janice says, as she sees a spot of colour floating across the sky.

They exit off the highway, follow a path beaten into grass, drive across a field to a cluster of parked vehicles, and stop. It's a gathering of parachutists. An airplane lands and idles in the field. As she and Neil walk towards the scene, Janice becomes mesmerized by the staccato beat of rap music, how it clashes with the look of the high, clear sky, the smell of grass and musty earth of the field. The men who finished their jump gather together and talk quietly, passing a beer among them. Those about to go up pace among vivid parachutes spread across the grass. Several step from their jeans and pull on jump suits. They appear unconcerned when she stares. They're so damned alive, Janice thinks; and likely wouldn't last more than five minutes in bed. But it would be worth the shot, she thinks. She would like to experience their energy. She's stopped by her thoughts. God. Was that what her mother was thinking about when she looked at Neil?

As the airplane lumbers down the field, Neil brings a blanket and the spray bomb of insect repellent from the car. He spreads the blanket, anchoring its corners with their shoes. Janice watches with a rush of gratitude while he walks around its perimeter, carefully spraying the edges. She lies beside him, secure, her breath even, the sun beginning to warm her face; believing that she knows for certain that a man who makes his own soup stock is someone worth wanting.

"Those daring young men," Neil says. He reaches for her hand and curls it in his. "I don't think your mother would have been able to wear the shoes, anyway," he says. The muscles in her legs have probably shrunk, he tells her. Going to a flat shoe at this stage would probably give her muscle cramps.

"I think she was disappointed," Janice tells him. "She wanted that Mr. Bishop to be cheating on his wife."

"She wants to have something to think about," Neil says. "She's as bright as can be."

The pressure of his hand on hers becomes stronger and so does her awareness of him, his scent. It's been several years but the odour is a familiar one, she knows it from the days when she used to make love. Years and years ago, with her husband. She would joke afterwards that animals had come to nest in her armpits while she was away. It was an indicator of how lost she'd been, how given over to the act that allowed wild things to creep in. She exuded the odour of a burrowing animal, of damp earth, rusting metal, crustaceans.

"You want to know something?" Janice asks Neil. The impulse to say what she's thinking is a bubble rising to the top. If she tries, she can suppress it.

"What?"

The airplane begins its wide turn towards them and the landing strip, its body flashing. My mother has the hots for you. Janice almost says what should remain secret, whether the person about to be revealed is your mother or not.

"They're getting ready to jump."

"I've been thinking about those men," Neil says. "The ones who came to your mother's house? Do you think they were really after a jar of jam?"

Because Sadie left her first home so young, she has childlike perceptions of it, Janice tells him. "I have never trusted her memory."

"I don't know," Neil says. "It sounds like something an adult might tell a child. An explanation for an inquisitive child." He has read accounts, he says. Of rape. Sometimes entire villages of women.

Janice had often thought about that.

Had Sadie really crawled through the hole in the fence and run away? Don't cry, Sadie used to demand, and would turn away from them, angered by the sight of her children's tears, as though the sight of crying made her physically ill. Crying is for babies, Sadie would say.

Men begin spewing out of the belly of the airplane, guppies

spilling out of a mother's fish-body, specks ballooning suddenly into spots of colour that swim across the sky. They watch for minutes as the jumpers tack in a slow waltz from east to west.

⤙ ⤚

Even if it is family, Sadie finds entertaining tiring. Especially now when they demand she just sit in a chair while they take over in the kitchen. They expect other things from her now. Words. Exchanges of conversation that seem to lead nowhere. When once she was full to the point of bursting with things she wanted to tell them, there were never enough hours, nor was there interest. Now, instead of dishing up dinners, they expect her to come up with varied and arresting full-course meals of conversation that they take home, she knows, pull apart, misconstrue, or make sound ridiculous or amusing. They talk about her on the telephone, she knows. Nurse hurt feelings.

The clock ticks on the wall above her chair. She thinks about her children. She wishes they wouldn't come home so often. It worries her, how their lives are going. Not well, she can tell by the frequency of their visits.

She doesn't hear the back gate open, or Janice and Neil creeping through the garden hand in hand, the wine they'd drunk with their late-night meal at the Chinese cafe in town keeping them off the highway, and closing the gap between being just friends and becoming lovers. They giggle and shush one another to deny their fear, the slight terror they have of coming together. The act is more complicated than it might be if they were younger. They're too aware of what's really involved, this giving away, giving up of themselves at such a late stage. They have more to gain and to lose.

Neil's face is blotted out by shadows but Janice feels that he's smiling. Dampness permeates her shirt and jeans and she begins to feel clammy. I'm afraid, Janice thinks. At the age of forty-seven, she's never been to Paris, and what she wants to do now is to go to her mother's first home. Tramp around where she lived and try to uncover why Sadie turned out to be the kind of mother she was.

Neil draws her attention to a lit window in the house, Sadie passing back and forth in front of it.

"It's the bathroom," Janice tells him. She pulls him down onto her, traces his smile with her fingers.

"Bathsheba. In the bath." Neil laughs softly.


Sadie doesn't hear their cries, moans, as she goes out into the kitchen and turns the light on above the back door.

The house, the steps, and the garden leap forward, startling Janice. She clings to Neil, exposed, a pale-skinned animal brought to the light suddenly, eyes slitted against the shock of it.

Sadie leans into the stair railing as she comes down the steps hugging a cooking pot to her chest. Her terry robe, the bath towel wound about her head, make her look more substantial than she is. She steps down slowly, deliberately, as though studying each step beforehand. As though moving causes pain.

Like an old woman, Janice thinks.

Sadie stops at the water trough and pulls the towel from her hair. Water splashes as she dips the pot into it. She bends and streams rainwater over her head, rinsing her hair meticulously,

combing tangles free with her fingers. Then she winds the towel
back about her head, scoops a pot of water from the trough and
flings it at the false spirea.

The last of a dying breed, Janice thinks. The idea of it, a
whole generation of women vanishing, makes her want to weep.

Sadie pauses before going back inside the house. She looks
out across the garden for a moment, raises her hand as though
she wants to speak, but to whom?

She leaves the light above the door burning. A habit, Janice
knows, from the time when all of them, her sisters and brothers, came home after dark. She wanted to see them before they
could see her. "Who is it?" Sadie always demanded to know.
Knowing full well it was going to be one of her children. Janice
knows that she was preparing them. She wanted them to realize
that they shouldn't take her for granted. She aroused in them
the fear that one day they would return home and she wouldn't
be there.

"She didn't see us," Neil says.


Sadie goes to bed and falls completely asleep almost immediately; almost before she drew the blankets up beneath her chin
and tucked her hands between her knees the way she always
slept, had slept since childhood, for comfort.

She dreams that she's a young girl walking across a field. As
she walks, trees bend to the ground, dust particles split apart
and the air withdraws to allow her passing, and hooded fore-
fathers, their ancient hands hidden inside their cloaks, bow as
she arrives, deferring to her energy, the complexity of her sinew
and bones.

# The Man from Mars

❧

My mother must not have cut my father's hair at all during that long trip, because I remember curls at the back of his neck, straw-coloured and C-shaped. I was surprised. I didn't know his hair had a curl to it. But it seemed that the farther north we travelled the more enigmatic my father became. He no longer approached a store or filling station as though he were stalking it. He seemed to know, too, if a greeting was in order when he entered a place of business, a smile, or a "how do." Truncated greetings were the way of the English, he apparently thought, indifference, or a nonchalance he affected by pushing his straw stetson to the back of his head. It was as though a light had come on, he said. As though he'd never been away.

The temperature inside the car climbed to more than intolerable, and we had no choice but to be lulled into accepting it; heat thick and matted as uncarded wool. Wheat fields, a brassy gold, met the sky, and, on my side of the car, the Pembina Hills, blue mounds sprawled across a bank of clouds. We were approaching a junction, a place where a road going east-west met the one we were on. At the sight of a road sign, my father, Willie, seemed to come awake. He straightened behind the wheel and pointed to it, his jaw working as though what he wanted to say had stuck in the back of his mouth.

"Jordan," he said moments later, triumphantly. He leaned across my mother to look out her window. His eyes, red-rimmed from lack of sleep after countless days and nights on the road, filled with light, an eagerness. As we approached the crossroads and what looked to be a store, he pulled onto the roadside and stopped. The building had a boom-town front and faded lettering across it. "There was a cooler. Outside. For the cream cans." Willie craned his neck, as though he thought it would still be there. "The man always gave me a piece of ice to suck on." The store's windowpanes were broken and the yard was choked with goldenrod and thistles. My father remembered going to the store with his father to drop off milk and cream. His father had had an agreement with a cheese factory in Miami, he said. Others in their farm community hadn't approved of his father doing business with outsiders, just as in Campo 252 they hadn't approved of my father doing business with the ranchos of Mexicans or in any of their towns. Wild asters in the ditch in front of the abandoned store undulated as a wave of hot wind swept across the tops of them. "Elmer," Willie said to himself. The store-owner's name had been Elmer Scarfe. The farther north we travelled, the more it was coming back to him, he said, places, names, English.

As we turned east at the crossroads, the sun shifted from the map spread across my knees. There was a house behind the abandoned store that sagged at one corner. A dog tethered to a broken stair banister reared from tall grass as we passed by, bounding to the length of its chain, straining, barking at us fiercely. Dogs had barked at us during the night, too, when we had travelled, headlights darkened, across open country to the Canadian border. Again, the need for stealth, to fear strangers and barking dogs, I thought, as we travelled across open fields. The animals' strident alarm had driven us rigid with tension. Our own dog had once barked at strangers. At *campesinos* wandering the streets of our village in search of work, or at an Indian family that had come in begging for food. Now the dogs were barking at us. Later, when I learned to recite, "Hark, hark, the dogs do bark, the beggars are coming to town," I remembered that day, our turning east at the crossroads at Jordan, and the dog barking.

"Be still," my mother said, moments later. She meant she had heard something and wanted us to pay attention.

Willie pulled on to the gravel shoulder and turned off the ignition. Boiling water thrashed in the radiator. "Devil," he swore, and grabbed for his stetson lying on the seat beside him.

I knelt beside my sister, Helena, watching as my father rummaged through the car's trunk. There had been many breakdowns during our trip, but my father had always managed to fashion a part, mend a tire, or find work at a smithy while a part could be fashioned. Yet every time we stopped, I was afraid our forward movement had come to an end. Now, he threw an empty jerry-can onto the ground. He returned to us and slouched behind the steering wheel, fingers drumming against it, unaware that our hearts, Helena's and mine, drummed in our chests along with them. Eva, my mother, sighed and opened the car door. She sat sideways on the seat, feet dangling outside to cool them. "It still hurts when I make pee," she said to no one. She rolled down a sock and pressed a finger against an instep swollen with water. There is a candour about my mother, a lack of pretence that is often mistaken for simple-mindedness. She had been complaining more and more about her bladder, the pressure, and how she could pass only a tiny trickle of pee that scalded and didn't bring relief.

The car had broken down an hour and a half from the next dot on the map, the village of Lowe Farm. My father had once lived in Lowe Farm. In 1948, his family, along with fifty-three other families in Manitoba, had loaded their Holstein herds, Belgians, grain tanks, bundle wagons, implements, furniture, and chests filled with goose-down bedding onto a train that took them to Cuauhtemoc, Chihuahua. The chests, one of which I still have, had been fashioned in Prussia in the seventeenth century and carted off on an earlier *Auswanderung* to the steppes of Russia; later, Canada and, eventually, Mexico. As others before them, my father's family exchanged the black soil of the Red River valley for their new *Heimat*, a place of clay and gypsiferous loam on a semi-arid plateau peopled by squatters, *agaristas* who were taken by the newcomers' patois of *Plattdeutsch* and blue-eyed, blond children, by their relative wealth. Later, they referred to my father's people as being *muy astrasado*, by which they meant backwards, and, secretly, he must have agreed. He could remember living in Manitoba, the comfort and benefits of electricity and tractors whose rubber tires had not been taken off. Willie's people exchanged their wood-frame houses and white picket fences for adobe. Now my father was fleeing that Mexican Mennonite ghetto and a way of living that had remained unchanged since the time of Menno Simons. My father wanted to exchange a communal farm life for anonymity, a life in a city, Winnipeg, where he knew of a man, the elusive Johnny Peters, who had left Los Jagueyes before him and had been successful, he'd heard, in finding work in the railyards of that city.

My sister, Helena, my mother, and I sat in the car listening to the thumping of water in the radiator subside. We knew Willie would eventually stir and go looking for water to fill the jerry can. And we would stay with the car, and watch as he became a particle on the edge of the highway, and wait, sometimes the entire day, for him to return.

"Well, yes!" Willie exclaimed suddenly as, in the distance, a tractor emerged from a row of trees obscuring a lane. It turned and, like a huge grinding insect, came towards us. "We're in business," Willie said, dropping his Low German language for a heavily accented English.

The tractor slowed as it neared our car, and stopped. The driver, a man in oil-stained cap and coveralls, stared across the road at us. Willie was about to go and greet his rescuer with a handshake, but the man's intense scrutiny made him suddenly wary. The man climbed from the idling tractor and walked to the front of the car, hands on his hips, blatantly studying the storage box on the car's roof and our Arizona licence plate.

"A nose," my father muttered.

The farmer came over to the window and peered past Willie into the car, first at my mother and then at Helena and me in the back seat, nodding as though a question had just been answered.

"Returners," he said in Low German. "From Mexico." Were

we from the Sommerfelder, then? he wanted to know. Kleine Gemeinder? Russlander?

"Altkolonier," Willie said, his voice gone gravelly.

The man seemed surprised. Altkolonier were threatened with excommunication if they wanted to leave Mexico; my father left because he'd been banned. "High-minded" was a word attached to him. He had pushed against the limits; it had to do with business deals outside the community. But why we'd had to leave so suddenly, secretly, and at night, our dog, Oomtje, tied up in the summer kitchen so it wouldn't follow the wagon, lights left burning and supper dishes sitting on the table, was a mystery to me. I knew not to ask why.

"From which family?" the man wanted to know.

"Peters," my father said. His lie was like a slap across the face.

The man's eyebrows flared. "Oh, so?" he said. Peters from Steinbach or Gretna? he continued his questioning.

"Not," Willie said tersely and got out of the car. Did the man have water on the tractor? he wanted to know. My father had said the name of the man he knew in Winnipeg. Peters, not Hiebert. Willie Hiebert, well-driller from Campo 252 in the Los Jagueyes colony. Well, sure he had a barrel of water on the tractor, the man said, but it wouldn't be of much use. He pointed out a rust-coloured puddle under the car's bumper. Your rad's burst. He sounded strangely satisfied. It's kaput, he said, and kicked at a tire.

Eva got out of the car and stood beside the road, worrying, as the tractor moved across a field of sugar beets towards the horizon. The man had promised to return at the end of the day with a truck and take us into Lowe Farm. "What if Johnny Peters isn't in Winnipeg yet?" my mother said. She meant, what if he had left. The lie my father had told stayed with me. I had imagined people walking past our abandoned house and hearing the echo of our voices in its empty rooms, sound rippling out-wards. It was like that with the silence surrounding the mystery of why we'd had to run away. Willie's lie rippled, too, and didn't leave room for the sound of insects sawing in the grass, or a bird calling from a fencepost. To imagine our lives without the car.

Willie hitched the waist of his pants with the insides of his arms, a quick, jerky movement. Whenever my father returned from an auction, full of a good deal or a bargain he had made, he walked the easy loose-jointed lope of a desert coyote, a cig-arette dangling carelessly between his knuckles and a smile that seemed to have been airbrushed, soft and powdery. But what was more common than self-satisfaction was this nervous grab-bing at the waist of his trousers. His eyes drew inward to a thought just before he did it; a twitch of irritation as though he'd been bitten by a flea, and then he grabbed for his pants.

It felt good to hear Low German coming from another person, Eva told my father, her grey eyes blinking and turning away. She was taller than he and had the shape of a pear. It was as though her body wanted to be two people, almost gaunt to the waist, and then ballooning at the hips. The sway of her back accentuated the swell of pronounced buttocks that heaved beneath her skirts when she walked. A body less prone to heart attacks later in life but more than often, as in my mother's instance, the target of cruel jokes.

"Maybe that's the way it should be," Eva said. She meant that the radiator was supposed to burst, there, near one of the towns whose names sounded familiar. We were supposed to live in one of those villages, among the *Gemeinden*.

"It's not for you to say," Willie said. He spat. Spit bubbled on the gravel.

My mother left him then. She waded through clumps of fox-tails and the wild mustard growing along the edge of the sugar-beet field.

From a distance we must have looked like specks drifting in water. Tadpoles swimming in heat waves, advancing and retreating. One of those specks would suddenly stop moving and mushroom, Eva's dark skirt caught by a wind, its yellow and orange flowers billowing. Willie's white shirt flashing as he threw stones at a telephone pole. A mirage. And two smaller spots, Helena and me. Little women, miniatures of our mother in our apron-fronted, long, dark print dresses, hair looped in gentle blonde wings across our foreheads, heads covered in white flower-flocked scarves with fringes like white fingers splayed across our backs and shoulders. Ephemeral and so small we could have easily been mistaken as those things seen by strained eyes or the imagination.

Helena and I had been scouting the ditch while we waited for Willie to decide what to do next. We hoped to find drink bottles. This new-found endeavour had helped buy gasoline along the way. Helena called; she wanted me to hurry and come see what she had found. Just then a stone cracked against wood. The force of my father's anger shot from his arm as he pitched stones at the pole. The sound of stone hitting wood butted against my ribs. I was relieved when my father finally gave up on throwing stones and reached inside the car for his tobacco. He squatted, back to the door, and rolled a cigarette.

I could see my father's eyes follow my mother as she walked across the field, his fingers working, rolling, lifting the paper's edge to his tongue, tamping the cigarette against the back of his hand. "Go get a cover from the car," he told me, his eyes never leaving her. "Take your sister and find some shade. Take a sleep," he said, with the same guarded expression he had when, in the past, he'd tell my mother to keep us in the house, we were not to go near the barn, because, I knew, a mare had been brought to his stallion for servicing. If we had been his sons, our hands or bodies might have touched his during the course of work, or we could have felt his hand on our shoulder when we'd done well, a blow when we hadn't. He never touched us. He seldom looked directly at us, either, and if by chance our eyes met, his would look away, quickly, as though he knew things he didn't want us to know.

My father had been an *Anwohner* in Los Jagueyes, a man without farmland. He had built a well-drilling machine from scrap steel and machine parts and travelled to other colonies, Santa Clara, Swift Current, and Ojo de la Yegua, to drill wells. My mother fashioned black lace caps, *Haube*, women's Sunday church caps, and sent them along with Willie to sell in the villages of other Altkolonier. They had tried to put away money to buy a small unit of land. But it proved to be the will of God that a man without sons should remain landless. Eva had gone to the bone-setter often. There had to be a reason why her spine was so curved, why she'd had only two children while most had as many as ten and more. Willie used her often, she'd said, and so what could be the problem? It had been suggested that the reason why Willie had only two daughters and no sons had to do with his conceited ambition. God knew, he had likely drilled for more than water among the señoritas.

Grasshoppers sprang from the ditch as Helena and I crossed

it and made our way through a cornfield to a stand of poplar where we spread the blanket in the shade and lay, waiting for a signal to return to the car. I closed my eyes against the sun and a blood-red world opened behind my eyelids. Schuchull. Long Branch. Tyler, where we had harvested lettuce. Names, not places, to me, because we had always camped away from the other workers, away from the towns. Ajo, in Arizona, where Willie had worked in an open copper pit mine, sold our team of Belgians and wagon, and bought the car.

The car had become our home and what had been home had become alien. A place that had only been as large as its adobe-wall boundaries. The only powered vehicles allowed in the colony, tractors, had their pneumatic tires removed to discourage exploration beyond those borders. I had lived in a world defined as well by my school's only textbooks — the *Fibel*, a fourteen-page primer, Katechismus and hymns composed centuries ago in Danzig, scriptures in Gothic German. I advanced to the Luther *Testamentler* and into the *Bibler* class and would have completed school at the age of twelve had we not left halfway through my final year. Where they sat segregated, across the room, the boys were allowed elementary arithmetic, weights, measures, and volumes to ensure they would not be cheated in business transactions. But I had not gained a shred of information that was transportable beyond the hills that rimmed that horizon. I could see the hills from the school window. I thought they marked where the world ended. The car had taken us far beyond them, cupped us, given us weight; it contained us in the unfamiliar world that lay beyond its windows.

I lay beside Helena on the blanket, trying not to think about Willie and Eva, who were, I knew, inside the car. During the trip I would sometimes wake up thinking I had been dreaming about dogs fighting, and then hear a certain sound coming from among cedars in a wooded slope beside the road, or from among a jumble of sandstone boulders. I knew by my mother's absence that I hadn't been dreaming. The three of us slept on a sheet of plywood fitted in place once the car's back seat had been removed. Willie slept outside on the car seat, under a tree, or beside the car if my mother had heard something that frightened her. Sometimes I would wake up and Eva and Willie would be gone, and I'd hear a noise, a noise that sounded like quarrelling. I came to think that something wild had taken hold of my father, and connected it to the reason why we'd had to flee.

Willie's signal was a long, sharp whistle. I opened my eyes to what seemed to me a bleached sky, not a vivid Mexican blue. Here, I thought, the sky is paler. Nevertheless, there was a sky. We had passed through, and were on the other side of, the hills that had surrounded Campo 252 like smoky blue altars, and they were not God's footstool set at the edge of the world after all, but at the beginning of it.

᭞᭞

I followed the whine of the lawnmower across town and saw my father turn at the far end of a street, and as he crossed the gravel road, yellow dust billowed up, almost obscuring him. He emerged moments later on a grassy boulevard on the opposite side of the street, and came towards me, not seeing me.

I watched him leave for work that morning as I did every morning, and it was like watching a stranger. His shoulders had

a defeated slope beneath the criss-cross shape of his black sus-
penders. He would return to us late in the evening smelling of
gasoline, the rawness of freshly mowed grass. His head buzzed
with sound, he complained, his arms ached from the vibration
of the mower. In the evenings he sat at a workbench in the shed
behind the kitchen, rolling cigarettes or tinkering with a radio
he'd carted home from the nuisance grounds. Sometimes, in a
Mexican town, through an open window he'd caught a scrap of
music playing from a radio, but that was as close as he'd ever
come to one. Now he wanted to teach himself how to repair
them. It seemed that the pieces scattered across the table were
never moved, or had only been lifted and set back down again.

It turned out that it was my father who felt most lost without
the car. I had noticed it when we stepped down from the train
onto the platform, not at Winnipeg, but a small town called
Sparling, hours away from the city. We carried bundled in blankets what we had managed to bring from the car. People in the
street opposite the train station had gaped at us. Our profound
poverty of goods and knowledge must have made us appear
exotic. My family, with our strange other-world garb and talk,
resembled turn-of-the-century peasants, stoic and placid as
cows in the immigration sheds at Quebec. Willie cautioned us
to stay put while he went to buy tickets but didn't make a move
to leave us. Eva's eyes glittered with fever and her face had
turned the colour of pie pastry, slick with sweat. Eva had complained about a backache that made walking painful and
vomited beside the road. And so when a train stopped at a siding
to take on water, we boarded it as passengers.

The stationmaster had been watching for us, had grabbed his
jacket, and was still putting it on as he crossed the platform.

"He's the big boss," Willie said in a tone that implied our schooling had just begun. As Willie talked to the man, he fished for his wallet in his back pocket. On the train he'd attempted to purchase tickets to Winnipeg from the conductor but the man had waved his money aside as though offended, and Willie had sat glowering and silent. As the stationmaster spoke, my father turned away, his face becoming florid and confused. He didn't have enough money. As he turned back to us, his eyes held a nervous suspicion that he was flawed, an incomplete man.

"I hurt," Eva moaned, pleading with him. What happened next was how we came to stay in Sparling. Willie spoke to the man again, his voice low, confidential. He jerked his head in Eva's direction. Amusement jumped in the man's eyes while he fought to contain his laughter. We found out later that Willie had said, "My wife says it burns when she pees. Is there a place she can make her water?" and, with that, sealed the town's perception of us. Later, a visit to the doctor and sulpha drugs indebted us, and the ensuing outpouring of charity could not be refused.

Two months had passed since we'd arrived. Two months of humid heat in tight little rooms with windows that wouldn't open. Willie had paid a farmer to tow his car into town, had found a replacement radiator and was installing it. On several particularly hot nights he had slept in the car or outside on a tarp he'd found in the rafters of the tacked-on shed at the back of the kitchen.

The town had given us what was referred to as "the Edgar house" to live in. It stood next to the municipal yards, a typical early-period Sparling house. Built cheaply and quickly. Its roof sloped steeply from the front to the back, the sides forming almost triangular shapes. The house's siding had been covered with red insul brick that had chipped, and the unpainted wood showed through in patches. Left vacant after an old bachelor had died, and taken over by the town for back taxes, it was suited for those used to no better than a house made of mud.

A muscle in my father's face twitched as he came towards me now, guiding the lawnmower painstakingly, his movements mechanical-looking, a primitive robot. It was as though he thought the machine was alive and had to be watched.

Overnight, the landscape had withered. Vegetation had shrunk, leaves on the trees faded and clumps of them had turned the colour of dung. For several days the sky had been clouded with what looked like smudged bruises, clouds that Willie said held snow.

He said that to a man who had just waved at him to shut down the mower and come over.

"Not yet," the man said. "Soon enough, mind you. But not yet." They stood looking at the sky, Willie waiting, I knew, for the man to say why he'd called him over. There was music — a male singer accompanied by a guitar playing from a radio on the man's verandah. Curtains moved in the window of the house and I knew someone was watching. We were always being watched. I sensed it, and it made me clumsy and too aware of my feet. Walking had become a concentrated effort. My ankles were bruised from my heels nicking them.

"Why don't you tell your wife to come for a visit?" the man said to Willie. As their hands met, I thought my father had grown smaller. It was the way his shoulders came forward, arms gathered tightly into his sides. "Zeke," the man said. His name was Zeke Palmer. "Your wife and mine could be of the same persuasion," he told Willie.

Fear darted in my father's face and his expression went flat. A familiar expression since we'd come to live in Sparling. He plucked at a rag my mother had stuffed into his back pocket that morning and began mopping his brow. She had ripped it from the skirt of a dress she had pulled at random from one of the boxes of donated clothing stacked in a corner of an empty room. She didn't care who might see it. He could honk his nose on it, at least it would be good for something, she'd said.

"What I meant to say is, my wife speaks German," Zeke said, when Willie didn't respond. "She comes from a Mennonite background."

His wife had come out onto the verandah and stood at the screen door. The song on the radio became a plaintive refrain of loss and injury that I will always associate with Saturday mornings in the town of Sparling, people out on sloping verandahs, music, and the smell of bacon cooking. And my father, mowing the grass along the town's boulevards, playground, and golf course. The Municipal Hospital, where he'd once stopped to refill the mower's engine with its oil and gasoline mixture. He had seen movement in a basement window and been drawn to it, to a light hanging above a table and what looked like a fresh carcass of butchered meat on it. But when he'd seen the feet, he realized it was a man. A man whose ribs had been sawed through and his chest cavity wrenched open. He couldn't leave off, he'd said, even when the doctor had come back into the room, picked up a hacksaw, and begun sawing at the top of the man's head. It comes away like the lid of a jar, Willie had said to Eva with a mixture of fear and amazement. The doctor had noticed him then, had looked up at Willie staring through the basement window and smiled at him as he drew the blind. It must have frightened my father to see a man being taken apart, the doctor's hands probing what he believed held a person's innermost secrets.

"You have a radio," Willie said to Zeke, as his wife stepped outside. From where I stood across the street I felt the force of the woman's intense gaze. Sharp and bright eyes, vivid features in a heart-shaped face. She had a presence that would have stilled a classroom of students the moment she stepped into it.

"Well, of course I have a radio," Zeke said, as though he minded that Willie had brought it to his attention.

Just then, children swarmed from around the side of the man's house, shouting, and ramming into one another's bicycles as they shot past me, barely curious, while I can remember even now the colour of a plastic bow-shaped barrette behind an ear, a frayed shoelace knotted halfway up a running shoe. The last of them, a tall boy with hair so blond that it was almost silver, stopped at the gate, straddled his bike, and regarded me as though he thought I was interesting.

"Hi," he said.

I was the face in the moon of his pale blue eyes. He would blink and my reflection would disappear if I allowed my shame of black oxfords mottled with dust, the scarf knotted tightly under my chin, to keep me tongue-tied. I said hello, and felt my father's sharp glance, his surprise.

"Sun," the boy said, and pointed to it and then to himself. "Sonny," he said, and I understood.

"Sara."

"There, you see, quick as a fox," the man named Zeke said.

"Kids. It comes to them easily." It never ceased to amaze him.

Why weren't my sister and I attending school? he wanted to know. If it was a matter of not having money for supplies, my father could go to the drugstore and get what he needed and put it on the town's account. The list of supplies and books was posted on a corkboard in the store.

The man's wife leaned into the stair railing at the top of the steps, hands behind her back and one foot forward, toe pointed, as though she was posing for a camera.

"You're going to have to send your children to school," Zeke said. He was a school trustee, he explained, and responsible for seeing that my father did so.

Willie nodded and ducked to fiddle with the mower. There was something rigid about the way he had begun to part his hair in the centre, flipping it up on each side of its part in waves that looked as though they were varnished. He uses axle grease on his hair, I would later overhear. He goes door to door, begging like the Indians for sugar, coffee, tobacco. He went and threw out the jars of bacon grease we gave him. Perfectly good bacon grease. Could have been used for frying or baking.

"My wife needs soap," Willie said to Zeke, suddenly. "For washing. Would your woman let me have some?"


I held the jar of soap powder while my father went inside the drugstore. I saw him through the window, hands in his pockets, sauntering down an aisle. He stopped in front of a corkboard and studied it. A tall man in a white jacket came up to him, spoke, and Willie shook his head and fled. He strode past me on the sidewalk, forgetting I was there.

"There's a woman in town who speaks German," Willie told Eva, and it was as though he had brought her a gift. She followed him through the house, eager with questions, and then out to the yard when he went to split kindling, until he barked at her to let him be. He built a fire in the cookstove to eat up the dampness that had spawned a dark rash of mildew across the bottom of the walls in the kitchen. The walls began to absorb the fire's heat, releasing the smell of old cooking odours, pipe smoke, of winters when the rooms had gone unheated.

We ate our supper meal without speaking. The house snapped and creaked around us.

"Wait and see. When it snows, they're going to hand me a shovel," Willie blurted from nowhere, his words crisp as the sparks cracking in the stove, jolting us. But he was away, inside his head, and so we left him there.

"What choice did I have?" he said moments later, as though taking up an old argument. He seemed to come awake and notice us.

"What is it?" Eva asked.

"There I was," he said, "already knowing English. How can you stop knowing something?"

And the government, he said, had made it a law that they be taught school in English and his family had run from that law. To Mexico. "What choice did I have? I had to go along with them," he said. He'd only been ten years old.

"Well, maybe I can't read," Willie said, defensive. "But I can still talk it." He rose abruptly, toppling his chair backwards onto the floor.

"Willie, Willie." Eva sighed and reached, as though she wanted to touch his shoulder.

He turned on her, jaw muscles jumping. "You keep the pig's ass that you call your face shut," he said.

The heat of his anger radiated from his body as he passed by me and went out into the shed. He swept radio parts from the workbench onto the floor. Eva began clearing away the meal, her face working with words she couldn't speak. Willie reappeared in the doorway, holding the jar of laundry soap. He was going to finish fixing the car that night and drive to Winnipeg the next day and look for Johnny Peters, he told Eva. That was why he'd brought her the soap, he said softly, so she could wash his good shirt.

"All right," Eva said, taking it from him. "All right, Willie."

Perfectly good bacon grease that could have gone to make soap. His behind-the-ears need a good scrubbing.

I thought I heard the milk-hauler's whistle and Oomtje barking, as Willie's car left the yard early the following morning. I thought for a moment that a pump was thumping water onto a garden and that the street had grown noisy with children, each identical to the other so that they might all have come from the same parents. I saw the tops of straw hats, buff-coloured tortillas set against the red soil as they walked to school in bunches. But just as I thought I was hearing and seeing it, it vanished. It was as though Campo 252 was a spot cleared in frost on a window, the mist encroaching and the spot closed up before I could fully recall its shape.

When I came into the kitchen, I found Eva kneeling among boxes, clothing spilling from them onto the floor. "What am I supposed to do with these?" she asked, and held up a pair of black velvet mule slippers. She threw them aside and continued rummaging through a half-empty box. She smelled them, she said, their perfume, cigarettes, a fustiness that suggested sloth. They were like whores, she said, with their painted faces. Or else they wanted to be like men. "Bum cracks showing," she muttered, referring to the women who had come to the house with their offerings, the ones who had worn slacks. A baby blue sweater lay at my feet. What did she have in common with any of them? she asked me. Her eyes were deep in shadows from a night spent sitting on the back stoop watching Willie repair the car. Our eyes met as I picked up the light blue cardigan. It was cool in the house, I told her. The sweater had pearl buttons and tiny pearls stitched across the yoke in the shape of butterflies. Wearing it would spoil it, I thought, and my heart ached.

"Can you remember the way to the house of the woman who speaks German?" Eva asked.


It was as though Mrs. Palmer had been watching for us, the way she appeared at the screen door as my mother, Helena, and I entered the gate. She seemed prepared for company, too, in the pale green dress she wore, which looked as though it had just come off the ironing board. We were led to a room fronted by the verandah and filled with overstuffed chairs, a couch, and a piano. She drew aside drapery, letting in the sun.

"My, my," she said, taking us in with one sweeping glance. The woman was quick and her eyes moved constantly. They had lingered on Eva's buttocks as she'd turned to pull up a chair and then, sensing that I had noticed, she feigned an interest in the fabric of my mother's skirt. What was it? Eva plucked at creases in it, tried to iron them flat with the heat of her palm as the woman went into the kitchen to put the kettle to boil.

Eva's eyes scanned the room, a plaque hanging above a door, plaster-of-Paris geese flying across a wall above a couch, knick-knacks standing on tables and shelves, lining the window sill, fluted vases holding sweet pea blossoms, figurines of two Victorian women in ball gowns on top of the piano.

"Why do you have so many things?" Eva asked as Mrs. Palmer entered the room carrying a tray with tea and a plate of cookies.

She was about to answer, a quick retort, and then smiled patiently as though Eva were a child. She set the tray onto a tea wagon in front of the window. "When you have a large family, you get lots of things," she said. "Gifts. My children are always buying me things. And my husband, of course. Anything new in the store he buys for me."

A beautiful young woman with wavy auburn hair cascading down around her shoulders passed by the doorway. I saw how she screwed up her face and rolled her eyes as her mother spoke.

Eva pointed to the plaque above the door and its inscription in German Gothic script.

"It was my father's. He gave it to me when I married. He brought it with him when we came from Russia," the woman explained.

"What does it say?"

"'I came that they might have life and that they might have it more abundantly.'" As Helena read the words on the plaque, my mother blushed, a mixture of envy and pride.

"It was my father's," the woman repeated, when she had gotten over being surprised.

Helena still takes secret pleasure in disturbing people's perceptions of her.

"What does it mean?" my mother asked.

"It means . . . ," Mrs. Palmer began, and then faltered. "It's scripture."

As my mother reached for the cup of tea the woman offered she leaned towards her, a plea forming in her grey eyes. "I need underwear," she whispered.

"You need underwear," the woman repeated, as though she hadn't heard correctly.

"No one brought underwear." My mother glanced at Helena and me, not wanting to say more because we were there. Helena coloured, and I counted the number of sweet pea blossoms on a single stem.

"Didn't you bring any with you?" the woman said, not curious, but scornful.

Eva nodded, and ducked her head like a child about to admit to an error. "But I don't have any left and I don't have cloth to make them either." She fixed her gaze on her large hands spread across her knees. "He tears my underwear."

"Who tears your underwear?" The woman had felt for her chair and sat down.

"Willie," my mother whispered softly, shamed. "He can't wait." Then she smiled apologetically, as though begging the woman to excuse a child's temper tantrum.

"Well," the woman said, when she had started breathing again. She called for the young woman to come and take Helena and me away so she could have a good visit with my mother. She had been brought up speaking High German, not Low German, but they would manage. "If you girls need to make your water," she said, a slight smile pulling at a corner of her mouth, "Janice will show you how the toilet works."

Helena and I sat on the clothesline stoop and waited. We sipped at a sour iced drink that made our stomachs ache. I thought of the woman's intense eyes, the strange twist of a smile, my mother's hunger for someone to talk to. Her voice, too large and eager, could be heard outside. Happy at last, enjoying herself, oblivious that the woman's laughter was directed at her.

That night I woke to a presence in the doorway of the room. Willie stepped into the patch of light on the floor. His shirt-tail hung loose and the front of it was spattered with what looked like mud. Then he stepped back into shadows and disappeared. A sour odour lingered, hops, cigarette smoke, and fear, reminiscent of the night we had left Campo 252. A dog barked from somewhere in town. Everywhere we'd been, there were dogs. Packs of village strays, some with twisted hindquarters or permanently curled lips, survivors of distemper. All thin, their racks of ribs shivering with cold or panic. I moved past them, motions deliberate, picked up stones when they circled. I stayed awake beside the sleeping Helena listening to the dog barking, wondering what panic or fear caused my father to tear my mother's underwear.

"He wants to see you," Eva said, when Helena and I entered the kitchen in the morning. She was at the table kneading dough, her hair bound in a piece of blue cloth. "Go," she said, without looking up, indicating that Willie was in the shed behind the kitchen.

He squinted at us through smoke rising from a cigarette clenched between his teeth as he fiddled with a radio on the workbench. His hair hung loose across his brow, almost obscuring his eyes. He hadn't shaved, and I noticed a purple bruise and small cut beside the cleft in his chin. Static buzzed in the radio. He switched it off. "It needs an aerial," he said. He had borrowed a working radio so he could take it apart bit by bit, and discover the cause and effect of each part and connection. I saw a box sitting beside it jiggle with movement. Willie grinned. "A little Oomtje," he said, and brought out a squirming black-and-white pup. "It's a good little dog," he said, stroking its muzzle.

Did he get it in Winnipeg? Helena wanted to know. Was it from the city?

"Farm dog," he said and passed the animal to her. Just like the dog he'd once had. It had been a smart thing. Could coax it up a ladder onto the roof of the house. "And then I'd take the ladder away." He laughed. "He'd go crazy. Bark his head off. My dad would come and give the devil to me. With his belt. But you think that stopped me the next time?" He answered his own question with silence. His eyes pulled away as he looked out the window of the shed, across land. Not more than twenty miles from here, he said. The house was gone now. Gone to pig shit. Pig farming.

What, Helena asked, had he called his dog?

"Duke."

You can call the pup what you want, he said. Helena said, "Duke," without hesitating, knowing that was what he wanted. He laughed and reached for my sister. As he drew her between his knees, she grew rigid and her puzzled eyes asked me for direction. She pulled her head into her neck, a startled turtle, as he pressed his stubbled cheek against her hair.

Eva entered the porch carrying a broom. Her eyes grew wide when she saw him. "What is this?" she demanded and swung the broom as though she were going to hit him. "You leave her be," she said, her features swelling with anger. For a moment I thought he would grab the broom, curse, and send my mother into the house; but he didn't. He crooked his arm to fend off the blow. They stood eye to eye. "It's not right for a father to touch his daughter," Eva said, and it was Willie who turned away first, uncertain, and then deflated.

The town's constable came to the house later that day looking for the radio. It had been reported stolen, he said. Then he removed the licence plates from Willie's car. There had been a fight in another town, he explained to Eva. And in any event, Willie shouldn't be driving it. Not until he'd paid the town what he owed in assistance. Willie's name had been put on the Indian list and he wouldn't be allowed in any drinking establishments either.

Willie strode across the field beyond the house, becoming smaller and smaller, and I thought how everything moved away, here. Willie was being swung by some force and it was compacting him, flinging him outwards and away from us.

He returned later that day and we heard him get into the car and start it. We watched from the backyard as he drove off. When he was halfway across the field he got out, lifted the trunk's lid and took out a fuel can. He peeled his shirt off, threw it onto the ground and doused it with gasoline. He pushed an end of the shirt into the car's gas tank and lit it on fire. My mother ran towards him, calling. She was stopped by the explosion, an orange ball of roiling flames and a roaring rush of wind that vibrated in the window behind me. The air above the car shimmered, became glassy-looking and liquid. Willie's rage was eating the air. I saw it and felt the heat of it on my face.

୭ ୧

Snow on the window ledges had turned blue with shadows as Helena and I left the school. We had been kept late by her teacher, but I didn't mind because I was certain the other kids had already gone home. I wanted to go down into a gully that opened to a broad slough, which, except for a strip of ice the others had cleared on one side, was snow-covered with tufts of yellowed grass sticking through. On the far side of the slough, Sparling opened up to graceful tree-lined streets, stores and houses. The Lily house, where Eva was cleaning that day, was on 7th Street. It was an Italianate-style house with brick arches above its windows called hooded crowns, my teacher had pointed out on the walking tour of Sparling. Her grandfather had been the architect who had designed most of the more substantial houses in the town. Our house, she said, had been erected quickly, built for shelter and that was all. Willie had torn the shed off the back of it, sawed the boards into lengths that would fit in the cookstove when the town refused to provide fuel oil for the burner because Willie had refused their snow-clearing job. He filled his time walking, far outside of Sparling, hours trekking alongside the highway, Duke following at his heels, returning late, often after we had already gone to bed. Some days he scrounged at the nuisance grounds, brought home bits of wire and metal and a stringless acoustic guitar that he wanted to repair and teach himself to play. He had taught Duke tricks: dead-dog, to beg for a bit of cheese, and to roll

over. Come, my father said to Duke, and he came. Sit, and he
sat. It's time for bed, he said, and Duke crawled under the front
step. All his curt demands once directed towards others, the
Indians who had worked the well-digging rig with him, the
village herdsman returning late with the cows, my mother,
centred now on the dog. It hurt to watch. My sister and I went
to school and my mother cleaned houses.

I veered from the road to the side of the gully and Helena
called after me, her voice a reproach. Usually, after school, there
would be a swarm of kids down there where they had cleared
a strip of ice for jam-pail curling or sliding, and as Helena and
I passed by in the street, their noise and games stopped like a
tap shutting back water. Because it was late and almost dark
there were only two boys down there now. Their bulky winter
shapes almost lost in the light of the setting sun as they shot a
hockey puck between them.

What did you have for breakfast? Helena's teacher wanted
to know. Eggs, bacon, Red River Cereal, pancakes, toast. Oh,
and an orange. Helena, head down because otherwise she would
giggle and give the lie away. I want toast, she had demanded of
Eva, and so Eva had put slices of bread on the cookstove. The
toast looked as though it had been brushed with soot and
tasted bitter. "You ate all that for breakfast?" the teacher asked,
incredulous. She crossed her arms and aimed her nose at our
heads, a nose peppered with tiny black dots and red lines that
shone through her face powder. Show me your hands. How
many times did you brush your teeth? She stirred our hair with
the tip of her pencil and then gave us blue stars to paste onto
a square beside our names.

"Sara!" Helena called from the centre of the street, a

shapeless silhouette in a mouton coat. The coat, too large and heavy, hung down around her ankles and gave her sloped shoulders. She had pushed her arms up into the opposite sleeves and hugged herself.

"Come or stay," I said. I didn't care.

The short cut crossed the slough in a diagonal line that disappeared into shadows halfway across. And how did the ancient Greeks bathe, Sara? The teacher's voice changed when she spoke to me, as though it was an effort to be kind. Plants lined the window sills. Their leaves stuck to the frost on the windowpanes and tore loose when the teacher, singing *sun, sun, marvellous sun*, turned them. I felt cold radiating from the windowpanes and silence, as the class waited for my answer. The ancient Greeks bathed. In water? My answers always came out sounding like questions. Helena said she'd heard their laughter from across the hall.

"Sara!"

The slap of a hockey stick against the puck echoed.

Be quiet. You'll only draw their attention. Keep your head down. Never run. I turned, expecting to see Helena as she passed through a chunk of darkness between the streetlights. There was a blot of movement on the path behind me, shapes melded together. I heard the sound of panting and struggle. Helena yelped and I ran to the sound. She lay on her back, one boy held her legs while the other straddled her, grinding snow into her face.

Helena's voice was a whine, eyes pleading from the white snow mask.

I picked up a hockey stick dropped beside the path. I told them to let her loose and was surprised when they did. They were my age, but not in my classroom. I'd seen them at recess, throwing snowballs against the school, their voices dominating. As Helena got up, one of the boys kicked snow at her boots. "Your dad's a pyromaniac," he taunted as they backed away. "Your dad's a thief," he sang. "I bet your dad puts his thing in you."

Rage, and the desire to strike him across the face with the hockey stick swelled, but then died just as quickly. I heaved the stick at him and he avoided it easily; his laughter becoming a jeer. I hated Willie, then, for being the kind of person who inspired the telling of lies.


Eva was at the stove when we arrived at the Lily house, stirring a pot of tea towels with a wooden spoon. Her nose, she said, wrinkling it, was raw from the chlorine fumes. She bleached stains from towels that had been used too many times to clear spills from the floor, she complained. Mr. Lily had rubbed off scuff marks from the toe of his boot before heading out the door, imagine, she said. She had seen it with her own eyes, she said, as we walked home. Have you seen your father? she wondered. I didn't want to see him. Willie, just by being who he was, brought humiliation. My mother, on the other hand, had begun to wash and alter items of clothing we'd been given, to make them acceptable for us and her to wear. Like Helena and me, she'd begun to go out without putting on her head-scarf. "Look," she said, and pulled an apple from each of her coat pockets. It was our dessert, she said. Mrs. Lily had given them to her.

I knew I should be grateful. Mrs. Lily had given us apples. The town had given us a house. But I suspected we were the ones who were really doing the giving. We lived in a house that people could drive past and say "the Hiebert house," in a way that suggested nothing more need be said. A house viewed as though the occupants had designed it for squalor; perverse people obstinately pursuing poverty. We were examples of what not to be.

And then Willie did us a favour.

Willie tied Duke up one evening in spring, went walking, and didn't return. Days passed before we heard about him. Just outside of Minot, North Dakota, he had stepped into the path of an oncoming car and was killed instantly. I learned about my father's death at school through whispers around the sink in the washroom. "It's probably the best thing that could have happened to them," someone said. My ears began ringing and the cubicle walls receded. I had nothing to hang on to and would fall forward into blackness. I was dying, I thought. Like Willie, alone. I was dying while sitting on the toilet and they would find me, I worried, pitched against the door with my underpants down around my knees.

With Willie gone, the town's entertainment ended. Our starved minds craved learning and Helena and I gained reputations as being shy whiz kids, impossible to better at tests and examinations. Bookworms, but good at baseball and choir-singing. When Helena won a provincial essay-writing contest, the school congratulated itself for having turned out one of the best. People stopped my mother in the street to say how proud they were. It goes to show what can happen sometimes, when you give a person a bootstrap. Eva worked as a cook at the hotel, and when Helena and I went there after school, she'd be sitting at a table at the back of the restaurant, the one reserved for staff, on her break, always surrounded by people. She would be wearing blue plastic fan-shaped earrings that covered her entire ear, their iridescent stones refracting light when she lifted her chin. My mother's laughter always dominated the conversation at the table, as did her solid, sweaty presence and the aroma of her hearty cooking. Once, at the end of a day, I came into the house and found her standing at the kitchen window, singing, "*Sieg, Sieg, mein Kampf ist aus,*" a song sung at funerals. They put him in the ground the wrong way, she said, with bitterness. South and not east.

After that, she seldom mentioned Willie; not that she had put him aside, but rather she'd decided not to talk about him. For months she acted as though she carried a bowl brimming with water that she was being careful not to spill. I got the impression that by not speaking about him, she protected him. That she had swallowed all her memories of him whole, in a single gulp, and he walked around with her; inside, intact, safe.

Years later she married a customer, a retired Mennonite widower, a farmer who became a gardener and whose pumpkins won prizes for their great size. He had a teasing manner that she liked; his grown children seemed at ease in his presence and joked about being happy to be finally finished cooking for him. They married and moved, she said, to enjoy the more temperate winters in Abbotsford, British Columbia. But most winters they travelled to Arizona, towing their Streamline trailer. He took her to Mexico once, to visit her relatives. Her mother had died, she learned. And of the others, all she would say was that they walked funny. Hunched-looking, stiff limbs. It was as though they constantly braced themselves against the sun, the wind, or one another.

Helena went to university and edits books now, while I stayed behind and became the wife of a farmer whose family was among the first to settle in the area. I live in what was once an Anglican vicarage, and my husband and I fly, do crop-dusting as far south as Texas. It is at these times, when I see the workers, rows of men and women, their straw hats bobbing in a field of lettuce, the reddish soil, that I think of my father, Willie.

"Why do you think we had to leave Mexico?" I asked Helena. She had an hour's stopover at the airport in Winnipeg and called.

"Who knows," she said. "It could have been anything. But more than likely something quite small."

"Do you think it had to do with sex?" I asked. "A Mexican woman, maybe?"

She laughed. "God, then a lot of them would be in trouble." If anything, she said, Willie's leaving probably had to do with money.

Helena has been reading about Mennonites in Mexico. It's all right now to admit to having come from there. Books have been written, both scholarly and sentimental. Books of poetry, and fiction, too. The women continue to have as many as ten and fifteen children, Helena says, but radios and vehicles, including rubber tires, are commonplace now. They are beginning to teach some geography, she says, and health, in their schools. But nurses still tell stories of being chased from hospital rooms by husbands who want to have sex with wives who often have only just given birth. "It's like these guys are living on Mars," she said.

A man from Mars, I thought, would feel the pull of earth's gravity much more strongly. He would feel heavier, sluggish, and his blood might run slower in his veins. He would see things falling from the sky and know that his reflexes would never be fast enough to catch them. A man from Mars, I thought, is overcome by air too heavy to breathe or to speak the deserts and fires he carries inside.

# Phantom Limbs

❧

It was the time of day in December when the balloon of warmth in the house collapsed with the onset of darkness and falling temperatures, shadows darkened the floral wallpaper in Shirley's bedroom, and sighs, false endearments, were eroded by her lover's surreptitious glances at the clock on the bedside table. Shirley walked her fingers across what remained of Claude's index and middle fingers. The skin was purple and shiny and more susceptible to heat, cold, a touch. When she blew across the stumps, he said he felt her breath in the missing parts of his hand.

The telephone rang, and Shirley grabbed for it, cupping the receiver to block out any room sound. It was Marlene, reminding Shirley she was counting on her presence at their Christmas table, as per usual. The invitation was extended in the form of a lighthearted threat. Yes, Shirley said, with the usual ambivalence, of course, I'll pencil it in. However, she would prefer to work right through Christmas day, draw the blinds on her office windows and ignore it; though as the season approached, work slacked off at COS Research. Respondents were either too harried or depressed; more than somewhat uninterested in answering questions about sexual or chewing-gum preferences.

Just bring your appetite, Marlene said, a veiled hint of what should, by now, be understood. For Claude's sake, Shirley wasn't to bring wine as she and Stuart used to when the four of them, Stuart, Shirley, Claude, and Marlene, were friends twenty-five years ago. This was in another time and place, the north end of Winnipeg, where Neighbourhood Watch meant they reported who was on their knees praying because their period was late or the presence of a police car in front of a house. Things had changed since then. Claude and Marlene divorced and married one another a second time, and Stuart and Shirley, the couple from the old neighbourhood most likely to succeed, hadn't.

"So you're still game to give me a hand with the turkeys one night this week?" Marlene went on, reminding Shirley of their agreement, what had been the arrangement ever since they had renewed contact several years ago.

"Just say when." Shirley wanted to convey nothing more than a willingness to help, but as ludicrous as turkey night seemed, she had to admit she looked forward to it. She wondered how, in a world bent on self-destructing, when disenchanted citizens were rioting at the legislature, rogue elephants were tromping on children and splitting them open, God had the time or inclination to honour Marlene's pact. But Marlene was a woman who prayed for happiness and got it and insured it with turkeys. A husband and children who had been heading towards ruin; alcoholism, street violence, prostitution perhaps, had been diverted and set on the plane of productive, healthy lives because God had heard her request and agreed to it.

"Say what?" Claude asked, as Shirley hung up the telephone.

"Nothing much." Shirley had decided long ago not to tell him about his wife's turkey ritual. He had patted her buttock as she talked, let her know that he knew who was on the line. His hand rested there, a warm palm against chilled skin; a summary, Shirley thought, of what Claude meant to her. She rationalized in a strange way that, if it wasn't her, it would be someone else. Someone who would steal more than an afternoon once or twice a month.

They shared an orange between them before parting, Claude inevitably poking the orange seed into her navel. A sticky orange-juice kiss. The cake of soap in a drawer, wrapped in Saran, the same brand that congealed in a soap dish in Marlene's bathroom, ensuring Claude never returned to her with the scent of anything unfamiliar. The stream of water in the shower. Claude, barely concealing impatience to be away, blew a kiss off his leather glove, fingers made whole with cotton stuffing, and promised to return.

Whatever, Shirley said, as the door closed behind him. He was off, she knew, to celebrate the anniversary of the tenth year of his second marriage to Marlene, and his tenth year of sobriety.

As the door pinched out the cold air, the telephone rang, a shrill echo in the upstairs hall. Shirley thought she heard in its ring: Beware, disappointment. She had three children in various parts of the country. This time of year was for them loaded with the unspoken, with silences. She had begun to dream of being in India asleep on the floor when a rogue elephant entered the room, and of being unable to move or call out as it roamed among her sleeping children and very deliberately stomped them open.

"It's me again." Marlene's buoyant, it's-a-new-day tone had gone flat. "I need to talk."

Shirley feared discovery, recrimination. She couldn't imagine what Marlene would need to talk to her about, other than that. What problems Marlene had, she brought to a women's Bible-study group she met with weekly for guidance and prayer.

"I'm having second thoughts about the turkeys," Marlene said.

"We could do them next week, if you like. It's okay by me." Beyond Shirley's living-room window, rush-hour traffic streamed by.

"It's not that. It's just that they're so big. Twenty-pounders. I asked, but Safeway won't be getting in anything smaller."

I understand, Shirley told her. The cost.

"It's not the cost. It's eleven twenty-pound turkeys," Marlene said. "I'll soon need a truck."

"It's only one more than last year." Exhaust from idling vehicles crystallized instantly into white clouds billowing among tree branches as Shirley went on to tell Marlene about a farmer she'd heard about who had lifted a calf from the moment of its birth and continued to do so every day after. In the end, he was able to lift a fully grown, eight-hundred-pound animal, she said. She thought the story might be a myth, but it seemed fitting.

"I can believe that," Marlene said.

Shirley waited for her to say it was possible to move mountains, too. Oh, ye of little faith. You can't see air, but you breathe it. Nor faith, but the results of it: Claude, boundless energy, oozing good health, enthusiasm. Dispensing cheery encouragement. Hovering, touching, fussing, adoring. When Shirley had visited Claude and Marlene after years of being out of touch, her appetite became numbed. She went to the doctor complaining of chest pain. Their devotion to each other had made her sick. She'd gone home and looked in the medicine cabinet, but other than vitamin B and ENO, couldn't find anything for it.

"But the farmer didn't lift eleven cows," Marlene said, "he only lifted one."

Shirley stood at the window for a moment, looking out. The monotonous thrum of traffic vibrated in a loose windowpane. It vibrated, like Marlene's comment, in her breastbone. For some reason, Marlene was finding the ritual of the turkeys heavier than the birds.

∽ડ

Marlene hung up the telephone and left her onion- and clove-scented kitchen — a tourtière was cooling on a rack — and went to get the bags she'd packed that morning. She wanted to drop them off at the Union Gospel Mission before she met Claude. The bags contained the gifts she had made for the men who would come to the Mission for Christmas dinner. The derelicts and down-and-outers. A bar of soap, a pair of socks or mitts she had knitted, a bag of raisins, chocolate.

She had taken the crocheted cloth off the dining-room table and worked there, packaging and gift-wrapping. As she worked, she grew aware of the room: high-gloss walnut furniture, white doilies setting off the dark wood, the seat covers she had cross-stitched, violets and forget-me-nots on a beige background.

She noticed the crocheted scalloped edging on the window blinds. In the living room, the couch back and chairs, the end tables, the coffee table, every stick of furniture was sprinkled with what looked like large white snowflakes that she lifted to vacuum and dust. Hand-washed regularly, starched and ironed. The needlework had once brought contentment, pleasure in achievement, relief at having, at last, the leisure time to browse through pattern books, rummage about wool shops and craft stores. In their bedroom down the hall there was a crocheted wool bedspread that was too heavy. Every night when she folded it down and set it on a trunk at the end of their bed, she was reminded of its weight and her folly. How, the whole time she had worked on it, her arms had ached and she'd had a pain between her shoulder blades. The doilies, the hand-crafted cushion covers, doorstops, wall hangings, added warmth, she had thought at the time, and not, as she felt now, a look of desperation.

Comfort, Marlene thought as she showered and dressed, was like the deep plush carpet she walked on. It held you for a time, stroked your feet, cushioned you. But after a while, beneath the scent of carpet cleaner, your nose began to pick up the cloying odour of stale perspiration, dust, and whatever was brought in on the shoes from the outside.

The headlights punched holes in the winter blackness as Marlene edged her car into the thick of rush-hour traffic. In her mind, she had already arrived at the mall where Claude waited. She imagined the two of them seated in the Bombay Bicycle Club, where they had a reservation for their celebratory dinner. She imagined herself scattering the contents of a Ziploc bag across the table — a pearl blouse-button, a screw-on blue rhinestone earring, a lipstick-smeared tissue — and concealing what had gone from being anger to relief. When she confronted him she must either make herself large with indignation, she thought, or diminished by grief.

She turned on the radio, and the youthful, uneven voices of a school choir rose above the drone of the heater fan. She tried not to weep but, lately, news bulletins interrupting regular programming, any ceremony, marching bands, a figure skater coming out of a triple jump into a bad spill – these things made her want to weep. What did the singing children know about coming to Bethlehem, joyful and triumphant? she wondered. They were just a choir of parrots. She stifled her desire to cry. At a stoplight, she looked in the mirror. Objects, her eyes said, objects found in the car, Claude's overcoat, his sample case, added up to a single certain thing. She had the right to be indignant, but most of the time she felt almost giddy, as if with excitement, or as though she was on some sort of tranquillizer.

She watched pedestrians become clouded by churning exhaust as they hurried down sidewalks, soft-edged and fragmented: ghostly. If she told the women in her Bible-study group about the found objects, they would remind her of Job. They would press forbearance, prayerful waiting. Unconditional love. They would remind her of her first honeymoon, and she'd remember Claude, rowing the boat and, behind him, a shoreline receding. Claude's stringy biceps knotting as he rowed, a testicle leaking from his trunks. The boat rises on a crest of a wave and bangs down into a trough of lead-coloured water. His face looms towards her as the oars skip across a foaming crest. She must not forget how it felt, how her body went flying across the waves, or the roar of water in her ears when she went under.

God figures pretty much in my life now, Marlene remembered telling Shirley when, after coming across Stuart's obituary, she had called her and they had met. She had tried to explain what had happened to her in a way that wasn't a cliché, but she only wound up sounding too offhand, as though she wanted to minimize the truth of it. But Shirley's crossed arms, the way she'd held her head and stared unblinking into her face as she spoke, had stopped her from saying what she wanted to say. Jesus Christ saved me and my family. She resented how that immediately lumped you in with the likes of Tammy Faye and Jim Bakker. She would fare better, she thought, if she admitted to having committed a crime, or announced that she was a lesbian.

It was a blessing, she'd told Shirley, how bad times could be forgotten. The slate wiped clean. It was like forgetting the pain of childbirth. "I guess I'm in the final stages of labour then," Shirley had said, "because I feel like hell."

Love lifted me, Marlene wanted to convey. There were reasons for everything. Even Stuart's death. For the day on her honeymoon when she'd almost drowned. She'd called out to God and the boat was there when she'd surfaced; Claude too, clinging to it. Would she have been brought to an awareness of Him, if she hadn't almost drowned? She seldom read newspapers. There was a reason why she just happened to read one the day Stuart's obituary was printed. God's love can lift you as well, she wanted to say, but had been thrown off by Shirley's hard-rock bit of laughter.

— Tell me what I can do to help?

— I shit like a rabbit, Shirley said. Tiny pellets. Like wall-to-wall Glosettes every time I have to face a creditor.

— I'll pray for you, Marlene promised.
— Thanks, Shirley had said. But cash would be better.


Marlene and Claude strolled through Grant Park Plaza beneath hanging Styrofoam snowflakes, arm in arm. As they passed benches and shoppers resting knee-deep in parcels, Marlene felt eyes lift, felt a spirit of tenderness enfold her and Claude. He squeezed her arm and pulled her in the direction of a craft display in the centre of the mall.

"Oh, good, look. Handycraps," Claude said, using an expression coined by their only grandchild, Tara, who would be arriving with her parents within a week.

The usual stacks of knitted tea cosys, mittens and socks, the misshapen sweaters, made her feel lethargic. Then Marlene saw the egg tree. A tree branch spray-painted white, embedded in a pail of plaster of Paris. Hanging from its branches were what looked like sugar-encrusted eggs. As she drew nearer, she saw that the eggs had been sliced lengthwise and their insides decorated with bits of velvet and lace.

"I'd like to see the chicken who laid this baby," Claude said, cradling a large egg. Everything about him, except his laughter, had changed. There had always been something in it, a hint of the maniacal. It made Marlene go still inside; remembering the old Claude, his lurching and bumping into walls, her fear at the sound of his key scratching at the lock.

"It's goose," the salesclerk said.

Claude slid the egg from its branch and set it into Marlene's palm. A door had been cut into the sugary-looking shell, and in the door, a window the shape of a cross that split apart as she opened it.

"Some people buy them for tree ornaments," the clerk said. "There you go," Claude said, and took out his wallet. He thumbed through bills just as he did whenever Marlene showed an interest in anything. Think of what you would have missed if you hadn't married him the second time, Shirley was always reminding her. She meant Claude's magnanimous gift-buying, the trips, new furniture, new neighbourhood. She only needed to blink and he reached for his wallet, trying to make up, she always felt, for years frittered away in an alcoholic haze.

As Marlene accepted Claude's gift it felt as though her heart had just been shrink-wrapped. She knew she wasn't going to confront him with the found objects. She held the box with the egg as lightly as she could. It was almost weightless and more awkward to carry than a heavier one would have been. She grew anxious that it might collapse under the pressure of her arm, but the more lightly she tried to hold it, the tighter her grip became. What was the meaning of the found objects? she wondered. What was their purpose? What was she supposed to learn from this? As she passed by a shop she saw her reflection in a mirror, a flash of her cobalt blue coat, red highlights sparking in auburn hair. She didn't look like someone who wanted, at that moment, to bite the hand of God.

∽℃

"It's a goose egg," Marlene said to Shirley, as she lifted the ornament from its box.

The cross-shaped window in its door split apart as Shirley opened it. The walls inside the egg glowed a pearly green. In the centre of the egg, set on a golden pedestal, was a tiny vase holding a bouquet of Easter lilies.

"Strange theme for Christmas, if you ask me," Shirley said. As she closed the door the shape of the cross became complete, a cut-out that displayed the gilded pedestal inside the egg.

"To your tenth," Shirley said, and raised one of her best cut-glass crystal in a toast. A bottle of red wine sat on the coffee table between them along with Marlene's glass, which was full, untouched. There's no reason why you shouldn't have a drink now and then just because I can't, Claude said and, out of a sense of duty, Marlene tried, but wine only gave her a headache.

This was the night for the turkeys, clear, cold, but no wind, and if they bundled up they would be fine, Marlene said. She smiled, a meagre, preoccupied smile, and Shirley wondered, as she returned the smile, if she looked like a cat who had eaten a canary and concealed the bones under the couch cushion where Marlene sat.

Marlene reached for her handbag on the table, about to open it and take out the Ziploc bag. About to confide in Shirley, who would, she realized, only say that there were worse things that could happen in a marriage than the suspicion of infidelity. When she had once complained about clogged pipes, having to use a crochet hook to fish strands of Claude's hair from the bathtub drain, Shirley had said, You'd like him better if he didn't have any? And so she changed her mind. She'd been finding things all year. The button first. She'd kept it in her jewellery box, meaning to throw it out, but then she'd come across the second object and the third, the discoveries making her head rush. She began to notice things. A cluster of moles on Claude's forearm she hadn't noticed before. The squeak of his shoes. How his laughter hadn't really changed.

They drove through the centre of the city, its streets and avenues deserted; vacated, Shirley thought. The car stopped at a traffic light, and the turkeys slid forward in the trunk, a dull knocking together of their frozen carcasses. The reason Shirley had decided not to tell Claude about the turkeys was that there was no way she could say it that would not make it sound ridiculous. And, she thought, she didn't want to be responsible for breaking the spell. Marlene reminded her of someone. A girl from her past who had been adopted by an older couple in the town where she'd grown up. Shirley had been drawn to the girl by a rawness and susceptibility to acts of kindness. The child had invited Shirley home one day and took her into her room to show her a gift she'd got for Christmas. It was a chocolate box. But instead of chocolates, inside it were cartoon drawings. Drawings of rabbits in floppy hats and high-heeled shoes, flower lei wound about their chubby rabbit necks. The girl said her real father had given them to Santa to deliver, all the way from California where he worked as an artist for Walt Disney. Shirley remembered as though it were yesterday the girl's grief when she revealed the truth. Santa was not real. The result, after a storm of tears, was a strengthening of the child's resolve to believe a lie. After that, Shirley avoided the girl because she didn't know whether she envied or pitied her. Marlene had that same brand of hope, Shirley thought. A clean page, daring you to put a mark on it. Daring you to plant an earring in a sample case lying open, or to drop a button into the pocket of a coat draped over a bedroom chair.

They travelled down Arlington Street into the north end where the street widened and the houses became interspersed with pawnshops, corner stores, and gas stations. As they approached the Arlington Street bridge, it stretched up before them into a canopy of steel, its crest seeming to end in the black sky. Lights beamed from house windows, rectangles of warm yellow light that defied the cold and the ramshackle appearance of the houses' exteriors. This is Claude, Shirley remembered Marlene introducing him, drawing him over to the fence that separated their yards. Claude had looked gypsy then, his olive skin tanned deeply, his narrow face and cheekbones. He looked undernourished, uncertain over being introduced in a tone that suggested he was a trophy. The old neighbourhood: clotheslines, plastic curtains, and true confessions over coffee. Where Shirley and Stuart had moved from the country to jump-start their future at a time when all that was required for success was guts, cunning. Stuart, son of a farmer and full of the conceit of self-sufficiency. While Claude stumbled his drunken way from job to job, Stuart had got a loan, turned an airplane hangar into a factory. While Claude took a broom handle to Marlene, Stuart and Shirley spoke their schemes in the dark, fell asleep exhausted, warm and smug.

As they mounted the bridge that spanned the train yards, the turkeys slid back in the trunk, thudding loudly. When the car reached the crest, Marlene turned off the engine.

Below them, metal squealed, there was a clunk, and a reverberating shudder that shook the bridge as train cars were shunted off to another track. To Shirley the idea of Christmas was like the pinch of frostbitten toes, the pain of it flaring up on the first day of cold weather, which was why she anticipated turkey night; the pain abated for moments then. She felt called, as though she walked near a burning bush. Like Marlene, set apart for some reason. She felt watched and grew hopeful as they crept about the old neighbourhood they knew like the palms of their hands. The at-home business in garages, clandestine ventures carried out under the noses of the city fathers. Which corner stores sold liquor from the back doors; the yards that were safe to take a short cut through, those that weren't.

Each year Shirley went with Marlene through alleys and chose houses at random or on a whim, or because a child's sleigh leaned against the house, and they would leave behind a Butterball turkey on a step or just inside a gate, its enlarged breast gleaming like white marble in the moonlight. An unburnt offering. Eleven turkeys this year. Ten for ten years of Claude's sobriety and their wedded bliss, the eleventh to ensure the eleventh. Every year Shirley helped Marlene fulfil the promise she had made to God after her divorce. When, out of a wrenching emptiness, Marlene had telephoned the Oral Roberts Prayer Tower and asked the believers there to pray that Claude would come back to her, sober, for Christmas. She vowed she would show her thankfulness by giving a gift to a stranger each year. By helping Marlene with the turkeys, Shirley was assisting in the wreath-laying, saluting the memory of how, Marlene said, Claude appeared at the door only months later with a poinsettia and a white-gold wedding band. Shirley was participating in the celebration of how a door opened up for Marlene and her family, a door into a sunlit world of chirping birds and bubbling streams. A world Shirley thought she despised.

Marlene sat for moments, gloved hands turned up on her lap, staring through the windshield at the houses and warehouses, the places of business in the streets below, chunky blocks of light and dark.

Why have we stopped here on the bridge? Shirley wondered, but didn't ask.

"You know, when I lived here I knew what was coming," Marlene said, continuing aloud a conversation she'd been having with herself. "I knew what to expect." She got out of the car and went over to the railing. The bridge hummed. She could feel it vibrate beneath her feet, with the cold, she thought, or else it was the city breathing. Arlington Street dipped down into a tunnel of shadows on either end of the bridge and emerged dark, defined by the streetlights on either side of it.

"What we knew for sure was that we never knew where the next meal was coming from," Shirley said as she crossed the bridge and stood at the railing with Marlene.

Eleven turkeys, Marlene thought. Eleven ignorant and ugly birds.

A train whistle echoed across the city.

"A great place to troll for bluebirds," Marlene said, startling Shirley. It was what Stuart said whenever they crossed this very bridge. Shirley heard in the train's whistle an announcement, a call for help. She heard it in the sound of a telephone. How its ring bristled in the metal roof beyond the rafters in the airplane hangar. She imagined and imagined it, the telephone ringing that night, her angry calls gone unanswered. Thinking that the salesmen, business acquaintances, had dropped by at closing for a Christmas drink and he'd gone off with them. She imagined the chasm of silence on the work floor below while the ringing of the telephone echoed. Stuart was not large enough to accept the threat of foreclosure, or face the shame of bankruptcy, she thought. Then she heard the creak of the car's trunk and realized suddenly that Marlene was no longer standing beside her.

She turned and saw Marlene cross the bridge, cradling a turkey, her breath ice crystals, clouds escaping in billowy white puffs.

The frozen bird radiated cold through Marlene's coat to her breasts. Her fingertips burned with frost. It's not the object, she knew the women in the Bible-study group would remind her. It's the act. Vanity, Marlene thought. It's all vanity. Why else had she told them of her agreement with God in the first place? She wanted them to think that she had been singled out, favoured with wedded bliss. She had to admit, too, that every Christmas she dined on the glow of the good feeling it gave her to give these turkeys to needy people. She liked to imagine the recipients of her charity imbued with joy and gaining hope. She had not thought of them choking on a mouthful of dry turkey meat and wishing for ham instead.

Marlene uncurled her arms, extending the turkey, and for a moment, as she lifted the bird up, it looked to Shirley as though she was engaged in some kind of ceremony. Asking for a blessing or something, she thought, as Marlene stepped up onto a concrete ledge beside the railing and, with a little grunt and a hop, flung the turkey over it.

Shirley heard a sharp crack, frozen meat rupturing as the bird smacked onto the ground below and skittered away. Stunned, she leaned over the railing searching for a sight of it. "Jesus Christ. What gives?" she asked.

"Someone's bound to find it," Marlene said. A rail worker trudging home along the tracks, cheered by his good fortune, she thought, instead of burdened by charity.

"Look, I told you, I don't mind helping you with this. Honest," Shirley said, as Marlene returned to the car. Her eyes began tearing with cold, and the lights alongside Arlington

Street became glittery white auras. "You can't be serious," she said, when she saw Marlene go round to the trunk and take out another turkey.

"Yeah," Marlene said, "I'm serious. About as serious as I'll ever get," she said as she crossed the bridge, cradling another bird against her chest. "I've had it up to here with the turkey business."

"But you can't stop," Shirley said.

"Really, and why not?" Marlene said, her voice a challenge.

"Because," Shirley said, searching for an answer. "It's almost a tradition by now. After all these years. 'The turkey fairy strikes again!' " Shirley said, pretending to read a headline from an imaginary newspaper, attempting humour. "Or imagine this one: 'The turkey fairy has gone on strike!' " Her bit of laughter trailed off. "What about them?" she asked. "The recipients?" She nodded in the direction of the city, the houses stretching out beyond the bridge into the heart of the north end.

"This has never really been about them," Marlene said.

No, Shirley realized, it hasn't. It's been about having what you call faith. And now you want to give it up. And you can't, she thought. She needed to believe that, for some, trusting in what cannot be seen was possible, a talisman.

"It's like you're quitting or something," she said. She wanted to wrestle the bird from Marlene's arms.

"I don't know," Marlene said. She stopped short of the railing, clutched the turkey tighter, hugged it. She sighed. "I really don't know. I'd like to think I'm giving up, and not quitting. Giving up isn't always such a bad thing."

Shirley followed her gaze — Marlene's eyes moving out across the skyline, the city pulsating and glowing, the steady probing beams of lights from an approaching aircraft which, as it descended into its landing, looked as though its wings might slice off the top of the Twin Tower apartments. Marlene's mouth twisted into a wry grimace.

"Whatever happens, happens," Marlene said. "Uncertainty has its own kind of appeal, I guess."

"Even Claude hitting the bottle again?" Shirley said. "Then your marriage would be over. You know he loves you. It's so obvious." It was true, she had to admit, Claude's love for Marlene was always apparent in his lack of tenderness, his jocular casualness, the perfunctory terms of endearment. A stiff prick has no conscience. That's about all it had ever amounted to, an urge carried through. She didn't want to feel responsible for what might happen now, but she would, she knew she would. The lights along Arlington Street ran together in a single stream that wobbled and blurred. Claude loved you enough, Shirley thought. Enough to try. To throw in the towel and start over.

"You try eating chocolate cake for ten straight years," Marlene said, as she returned with another bird. She was being perverse, she knew, in light of Shirley and Stuart's tragic ending. But at least she was being truthful. Then she elbowed Shirley aside and threw the turkey over the railing.

"There goes ten years, come what may," Marlene said, as they watched the turkey plunge towards the steel bands of the rail tracks.


As they drove back across the city, Shirley's breath took shape in the car window. It became a swirling sky world, a ragged horizon of fir trees. All about the edges of the window, exotic plants and ferns grew, concealing floppy-eared rabbits. Hidden among the foliage as the adopted girl had been. When, later, the girl ran away with a sixteen-year-old boy, the police found them hiding like rabbits in a field beside a drive-in movie theatre. The shock waves rippled through the neighbourhood when it was learned the girl was pregnant and would marry. But the dismal forecasts for their future never materialized. He became a successful insurance broker and a member of the Knights of Columbus, and she a satisfied stay-at-home mother of four. When Shirley saw the girl last, it was at a school reunion. She told Shirley her husband had made good investments, they were financially sound, and she didn't need to work outside the home unless she chose to. And how was Shirley keeping herself together? she wanted to know. Shirley came back with, "Well, let's just say not on my husband's life-insurance policy, that's for sure."

"Look," Marlene said, and pointed to the Bay department store, where workers on ladders were putting the finishing touches on a life-size Nativity scene. "Yes, nice, nice," Marlene said.

All along Portage Avenue evergreen wreaths glowed with red lights, colouring the snow-caked median strip. "Nice," Shirley said and yawned. She had not told the girl that she was supervisor at COS Research, widow of a man who had taken his life on Christmas Eve. The season was loaded with silence that a crèche, festive lights, and carols could never fill. The season was like the elephant she had been dreaming about, coming to stomp her and her children open. The car's heater blew hot air, sucked moisture from Shirley's face and her cheeks stung. She felt drained, heavy. It was how she felt when the winter sun dropped behind peaks of houses and shadows coloured the elm trees along the boulevard navy blue. When, upstairs in the bedroom, the duvet on her bed was thrown aside, the evidence Claude had been there, inconclusive. It was the shape of his limbs, incomplete outlines in the folds of the bedding that made her long for him to return.

Marlene dropped Shirley off and drove through River Heights. She liked this neighbourhood for the sense that time had passed by with a certain grace. Once Shirley and Stuart left the old neighbourhood and moved here, it was as though they had left the province. A hurried message in a greeting card, that was all she'd ever got. It was as though they had never been friends. She'd never been invited to their house, an address on Cambridge; she'd driven past it often. Now she and Claude lived in River Heights. Snow-covered rooftops radiated moonlight and untrodden lawns, white aprons, met the edges of immaculately snow-cleared walks. Her living room was pastel. Soft blue and dusty-rose velvet furniture and window sheers that diffused the harsh sunlight. It was like her inner sanctum, she had thought, peaceful and pleasantly decorated; pleasant enough that God might feel the presence of goodness. Certainly an orderliness. She wondered now if God had found her decorating unimaginative or boring.

∽ℰ

"You're out late," Claude said as Marlene crawled into bed beside him. She wound her limbs through his to warm them.

"Shirl wanted to talk." She curled about his back and waited for him to sleep. "Claude?" Her mouth moved against his hot skin.

He drew her leg over his.

"It would be nice not to have to do Christmas this year."

"But Tara's coming. And Shirley. You know how she can use a boost this time of year," Claude said, surprised.

"But just the same." She wouldn't go to the Bible-study group tomorrow. She would telephone first thing and tell them not to expect her.

Marlene waited until Claude's breathing grew to a gentle snore and then she got out of bed with stealth, the way she had learned to do to escape a sleeping child during an afternoon nap. She crept across the room and picked up her handbag, which was hooked onto the doorknob. She took out the Ziploc bag and placed it on the bedside table where, tomorrow morning, on awakening, he would be sure to find it.

Then she drifted towards sleep. She saw her grandchild, Tara, standing in front of the Christmas tree unwrapping the goose egg from its tissue. She wanted to call out. To say, Watch! Claude, help her! Tara's going to break the egg. She saw the egg dangling from a branch. It was going to fall, she knew it. But when? Then her tongue became too thick for speech; and sleep, a heavy warm cat, sat on her chest and she was gone.

و‏ے

Shirley walked along the river to work the next morning. It would be a slow day on the telephones, she knew. Interviewers exchanging Christmas-cake baking tips with the respondents; skipping over questions; saying, Your guess is as good as mine. She unwound her scarf, exposing her face to the glare of sun on snow. Spots of shimmering colour hung on either side of the sun above the city skyline fogged with chimney gases and exhaust. What if it ended? she wondered. What if Claude and Marlene parted? Would he come round to see her more often?

Become a regular thing? She wouldn't want him then, she knew. Not even for half a day once a month or so.

Her footsteps sounded hollow, the snow crusted and porous with air pockets. It looks like skin, Shirley thought, the snow, opaque, pebbled, with its milky sheen. There was a line in it, as though someone had dragged a stick across it the length of the river-bank. Shirley followed the line in the snow where it had split wide open. She chipped at it with her heel and the snow's pebbly hardness gave way and a crevasse opened. She knelt. From up close, she saw polygon shapes in the snow skin. She pushed at the edge of the crevasse and it fell inward. Long silvery spikes of ice crystals gleamed along its edge. She plucked at one of the octagonal shapes, and it came loose. She drew out a thin spear of ice. Perfectly shaped, crystal clear. She stuck her hands inside the crack in the snow. Ice crystals clinked together as she riffled through them. The entire snow pack was made of shards of ice, crystal teeth that she plucked out, one after another, and sent skittering, brilliant against the frozen river.

All this time I have been walking back and forth to work, I have been walking on crystal, Shirley thought, the roof of a crystal palace, she imagined. The symmetry of frozen water, the randomness of beauty made her throat tight. It made her want to dig up the spikes of crystal, scatter them across the snow, roll in them. To fling them into the air and see the light rainbow in them. But there was no way, the immensity of the field of crystals was overwhelming; she could never take apart all of it. All she could do was stand back and admire it. In the distance, a black speck — a dog? she wondered — moved steadily away, down the centre of the river. Hoarfrost clung to underbrush and branches, drawing attention to the silence.

# The Two-Headed Calf

❧

Calypso music played from the speakers mounted on the roof of the Caribbean pavilion across the street from Sylvia's apartment, and the line-up of people, the patrons who had been waiting a good hour for the pavilion to open, filed towards its doors. Tourists. Culture vultures, Sylvia thought, as she watched the people bob and weave to the festive sound of steel drums. Anxious to experience the city's uniqueness during Folklorama, the annual festival of nations, during which its citizens oom-pa-pa with zest or perform the delicate gestures of kabuki, the mazurka, and jingle dance so harmoniously. For two weeks anyway, she thought. As she went to close the balcony doors the telephone began to ring in the room behind her.

Sylvia recognized Lucille Champagne's voice immediately but, still, she was caught by surprise, and the traffic in the street below the window, the music, receded. Even though she had called, Lucille said, she was not looking for visitors. This she wanted known right off the top. She didn't want anyone coming round to the Saint Boniface hospital where she'd been a patient for almost a month. It wouldn't do anyone any good to see how a body could be wrecked. It was as though she had memorized what she was going to say, Sylvia thought, but had not allowed for responses.

As Lucille talked, her voice, its accent strong, as strong as Sylvia remembered, conjured an image of russet-coloured curls, henna-rouged cheekbones. Lucille's accent and musical lilt had always brought to Sylvia's mind a scene from a movie, of *décolleté*. Lucille a charming flirt dancing in the court of the Sun King. Lucille with a tremulous Judy Garland mouth and manner, but finer-boned than the actress had been, darker-skinned, black eyes, her grin a high-powered beam of light when she raced her dogs on the river. She had once reminded Sylvia of an Oriental ivory carving. If Sylvia had inherited her mother's fair colouring, her voice and facial bone structure, she believed, came from Lucille Champagne.

"For some time there, you lived on Lipton Street," Lucille said. "And then it was Dominion. There was one year I couldn't find you. You weren't listed."

Sylvia imagined Lucille with the telephone directory in her lap, tracking her down throughout the years that had passed.

"I was away travelling," Sylvia said.

"That's something I was never interested in. Travelling," Lucille said.

The sound of Lucille's raspy breath filled the silence that followed. Her voice was heavy with fatigue and husky. From smoking? Sylvia wondered. Where the lilt in her voice had been there were gaps. Gaps filled with cautionary sips at air. The sound of a sick heart, Sylvia thought, with foreboding, the same sound she'd heard in her grandfather's voice during his final year.

"I heard you were married. Are you still?" Lucille said.

"Not for years," Sylvia said.

"It pays to ask, these days," Lucille said. "Hardly anyone I know is married to the person they started out with. But I've still got old Edgar."

Edgar the pimp was how Sylvia's mother, Betty, once referred to the apparent love of Lucille's life. Sylvia remembered him as being a wedge that had come between her mother and Lucille, what had been responsible in some way for ending their friendship.

"I need a priest," Lucille said, speaking finally, the reason for her call. "Your mother married a priest."

"An Anglican minister," Sylvia said.

"He's allowed to do Communion, isn't he?"

"Yes, of course," Sylvia said.

"I haven't had Communion for years," Lucille said. She explained that because of Edgar, the chaplain at St. B. had refused her request.

"What do they know, eh? The priests, the nuns," Lucille said, as though Sylvia was Betty and she was continuing a conversation held years ago when she asked Betty the question to convey that it was a waste of time to hope for reasoning or an accounting. Meaning, Sylvia guessed, Lucille's common-law relationship. Lucille's refusal to renounce Edgar Valcourt.

"It's so archaic," Sylvia said. "I can't believe they would deny you the right." She understood why someone would want Communion. Why, for some, the sacrament was still rife with significance. "I can't fathom people still being kept apart over religion," she said.

"Or love," Lucille said.

"Edgar."

"Well, yes, Booga-boo. Edgar, too. But what I meant was you. You and your mother. If you can imagine. Old Father Normandeau, he got it in his head our friendship, our three-some," she said, using their old phrase for it, "was dangerous."

Sylvia's throat constricted at the sound of her pet name. From having watched her own children, she had learned how children were. How, no matter what you did for them, unanswered questions could make rooms chock-full of furniture echo.

"Remember Thursdays? Good old treat day," Sylvia said. "Our light fantastic."

"I don't remember us calling it that," Lucille said.

Outside, the Calypso music grew louder and then changed suddenly, and a man, his voice amplified by the speakers, began singing "The Banana Boat Song." A good imitation of Harry Belafonte, Sylvia thought. But after the fifth straight night of it, the pleasure of listening was beginning to wear thin. The song signalled the beginning of the stage show, she knew. The doors would close and some of the people waiting outside would leave, hoping to gain entry at another of the thirty-five or so pavil-ions scattered throughout the city. People in jaunty tam-o'-shanters or chaplets, people clattering about in wooden clogs, anxious for the limbo dance to begin, people wanting the taste of samosa, tidbits of a culture from the Lesser Antilles. Some costumeless, pale-faced people who were shopping around for an ethnicity they could take home, polish up, and hang on a wall above a rec-room bar.

As if a knowing could be gained from sampling different cooking spices and modes of dress, quaint folk music. It was somewhat like claiming the hymn "Amazing Grace" as a favourite because of its unforgettable melody, its haunting essence, without wanting to know how grace could be amazing, or what it meant to be an unsaved wretch. It was wanting to be overcome by emotion and at the same time to remain aloof. Or to hunker down somewhere in between.

It happened that when Betty was seventeen she became pregnant with Sylvia but did not, as was the custom for unmarried mothers-to-be of that time, disappear and reappear months later, wan, pensive, looking back at the trip she had taken supposedly to care for an elderly relative in another province or some other such thing.

Instead, Betty had ballooned flamboyantly, gaining forty-five pounds, and with Sylvia floating inside had swayed and waddled about town, daring anyone to notice. It was after Sylvia was born that she had left the town where she had grown up, the east end of it, in an enclave of six houses owned and occupied by distant relatives and friends, those who had shunned city living and chosen not to farm. Those who had all arrived in the country years earlier at the same time and from the same place, and who had constructed a wood-frame church only large enough to hold fifty people. A place where they could practise their language and religion. They ventured out into the community at large to work only, or for charitable reasons, such as a basket of hot buns set on a back step for those known to be ill, or to present money the women's *nähverein* had earned for the hospital's maternity ward by selling items of needlework and preserves at country fairs.

When Betty went to the city, leaving her baby daughter in her mother's care, the old woman rolled up her sleeves and summoned the women to make a star quilt of yellow and blue patches. Whenever she put Sylvia to bed, the elderly woman hoped the child would fall asleep thinking of the sky and dreaming of heaven. She is not ours, her husband reminded her. Don't forget. We are her counsellors, her protectors, but we are not her parents. We *are* her parents, the grandmother had said when, one weekend, Betty came home from Winnipeg and brought a convict with her. They'd held hands as they walked down the street from the bus depot. This wasn't the first time Betty had brought someone home. She had brought home an Irishman, a lightweight boxer, and a Japanese who imported ivory carvings, elephants and the like. A Chinese junk with elaborate bluff lines and sails still sits on a shelf in Betty's curio cabinet. Betty had once brought home a man who painted sets for Pantages Theatre.

Well, the Bible says to love one another, Betty said, when her mother wept into her apron. It says love your neighbour, doesn't it? *Red and yellow, black and white, all are precious in his sight,* Betty sang, repeating a song she had learned as a child at a summer camp.

They were silver-haired people, her parents. Drawn in like shrunken sweaters and entrenched in the church pew when, years after Betty had completed her course of study at the Monarch School of Beauty in Winnipeg and had established a steady clientele at the hairdressing salon she'd opened across town, she came to claim her daughter. Betty had agreed to go to church for the exchange; she was large enough to allow her parents this ending.

The ceiling in the church cracked, as though there was someone in the attic creeping about. A male voice droned and, when it stopped, the sound of breathing surrounded the grand-parents, Betty, and Sylvia, many breaths becoming one. Hands on a clock clicked through numerals and then a quartet of scrubbed faces appeared, suspended around the pulpit. *When I survey the wondrous cross*, they sang and, as the grandfather joined in, his rich bass voice filled the sanctuary. *On which the Prince of Glory died.*

At the words "Prince of Glory," a window beside the clock seemed to grow larger and come off the wall, radiant with sun-light. Sylvia felt its heat, a pressure on her shoulders. *All my vain hope I count as loss*, a man with a lump on his bald head sang behind them. He had always sat behind Sylvia when they were at church. But the woman whose lap she sat in, whose visits to the house usually came every other weekend, had not been to church with them before.

The page of Betty's hymnal quivered: sugar-induced tremors. A symptom she had eaten the wrong thing before setting out to church. She would have to make some adjustments now. There was the child to consider. Reading over coffee at break-fast would have to go, the gin-and-tonic evenings be scrapped. At least until Sylvia grew up and Betty could once again let go. What Betty wanted was to burn out. She wanted a blazing, roaring, burning glory of fire. Like Joan of Arc. The fact that the Anabaptists, so-called extremists and enemies of the Reformation, had gone singing to their fiery or watery deaths had never entered Betty's mind; that the inclination to want to throw herself on a burning pyre just might be racial memory. As the congregation sang the Communion hymn, a plate holding cracker chips and a rack of glass tubes jiggling with grape juice was being passed from hand to hand towards them.

Betty drew her chin into her neck and her peachy mouth wrinkled. This church thing, Betty reasoned, she would leave to her parents to carry on without the benefit of her presence. Her hymnal closed with a dull thud.

Sylvia looked at the woman whose lap she sat in. Betty's strawberry-blonde hair caught up into a ponytail, jade-green eyes outlined in black. Mama, Sylvia thought. The word the grandmother had taught her to call the woman — "Mama" — came to mind as an illumination, a blast of sunlight in a window, a knowing. This woman is my mother, Sylvia thought.

"I'm out of here," Betty said.

There was a sucking intake of breath around them. Someone had disturbed the sanctity of the act, someone whose eyes glittered with a raging impatience.

The grandfather raised his head; it turned slowly, shining silver in the light streaming through the windows, wrinkles in his neck unfolding, new ones forming, a clot of disappointment working up and down his throat.


Lucille Champagne waited for them outside the church, a trim figure in a dark coat, its hem flipping in the wind. She swung her arms across her chest to keep warm. Sylvia rode Betty's hip and, as they crossed the road, sunlight made her eyes tear. Lucille seemed to jump towards them and split in two, her head a crystal refracting light. There was another person beyond Lucille, standing beside a car. A man with a corona of fire leaping out of his cap. Ice covering potholes in the road reflected the sun and became beams of light shining from the black earth.

"What's he doing here?" Betty asked.

"He gave me a ride into town. He says he'll drive you home, if you want," Lucille said.

*On which the Prince of Glory*, the saints in the church sang, their voices melodious, bass and treble; young and old.

Lucille swayed, as though waltzing. It sounds nice, she said, their singing. "There's no music worth singing at our church." She was petite but, at fifteen, she could carry a sack of flour from the mill in town, three miles along the river, fifty pounds, all the way home. She raced dogs on the river in winter and outran Father Normandeau's horse, not just a pokey farm horse, she liked to clarify, but a pacer he'd brought with him from Trois-Rivières.

"Sure. Why not a ride home?" Betty said. "It's bloody cold."

Frost nipped at Sylvia's fingers, her mitten dangled, her hand clenched about the stem of an artificial Easter lily.

"Bloody, bloody cold, isn't it, Booga-boo?" Betty nudged Sylvia's cheek with her icy nose.

"*Il fait froid*," Lucille said, putting her face close to Sylvia's. She exaggerated her tongue movements, wanting Sylvia to see how the words were shaped.

"*Ich bin kalt. Sehr, sehr kalt*," Sylvia said.

"The little Kraut." Lucille laughed. When she laughed it looked as though a finger poked her in the cheek, denting it deeply; her dimples were like that.

"I'd settle for her speaking English, never mind French," Betty said.

There came a fluttering of black at the top of the street, what looked like a huge bird about to swoop down on them all.

"It's the old crow," Betty muttered. She meant Malvina

Champagne, Lucille's mother. She'd borrowed the saying from
Lucille. It was what Lucille called the nuns at the convent school
in Saint Jean Baptiste.

Lucille darted off to meet the swooping bird, past the man
who stood beside a car. Her feet fractured the ice in the potholes as she ran, and left a trail of puddles brimming with what
looked like splintered glass. The fiery corona shooting from the
man's cap vanished. The Prince of Glory became Lucille's
brother, Arthur, a man with dark curls falling across his forehead. A wiry, small person who had once tramped three miles
on the Red River on a single snowshoe to invite Betty for
supper. He had lost the other snowshoe, but that didn't stop
him. Betty had gone over there for a meal of beans, which had
been heated in the can and plunked onto the table, bannock,
and tea so strong you could strip paint with it, she told her
mother afterwards.

"They have the bush in their hair," her father had said. He
meant that the Ojibwa in their blood made them half wild,
uncivilized.

Malvina Champagne, still wearing black after twelve years,
Betty had reported, gave her dirty looks the whole time she was
there. Betty guessed the old crow thought she was trying to get
her claws into her precious Prince Arthur.

And are you? Betty's mother had once asked, her crocheting
needle missing a loop.

That's not the point. The point was the looks Malvina always
threw at her. They were the same kind of looks Father
Normandeau threw at her when she'd gone to mass that one
time with Lucille. Swinging his damned incense burner in her
face, trying to smoke her out, as if she didn't know.

They keep a squirrel in the house, Betty told her mother. It lives in the couch and the smell of pee is the first thing that hits you stepping inside. Lucille and Arthur's younger brother had brought a saw to the supper table and sawed away at a corner of the table throughout the entire meal of beans, and no one blinked.

Her mother's crocheting needle was stilled by her astonishment. Above her, a cuckoo bird shot out of its house, cuckooing the hour. Betty hated that damned clock. It reminded her of a place she didn't know. Her parents had dragged all their outdated influences with them to this country, including that damned clock with its blunt, one-dimensional sound. They had bundled themselves, fled the Arctic, arrived in a tropical country wearing their fervent beliefs like layers of clothing they sweated in but refused to shed.

*When I survey the wondrous cross, on which the Prince of Glory died, all my vain hopes I count as loss*, they sang inside the church.

Marriage to someone not of our way is just asking for heartache, Betty's father had once said. One pulls one direction; the other, the other.

Malvina Champagne ignored Lucille's entreaties to leave well enough alone and strode, arms swinging, through the water-filled potholes towards them.

She sews for people, Betty said to her mother.

What does she sew? she wanted to know, crocheting needle once again flashing.

She works with fur. Mitts and muffs, hats. Mends coats. Makes braided mats.

At the mention of braided rag mats, the mother's face closed. They had come knocking on her door, hoping to sell their rugs, the tiny birchbark canoes, teepees, deerskin slippers. Broad-hipped women from the reserve who smelled as though they lived outdoors. Children with inquisitive or knowing eyes that she took to be cunning clung to the women's skirts. If she had clothing out on the line, she made sure she brought it in. She had them sit out on the back step and fed them. Stale buns and jam. She never gave them money.

Malvina thrust her long, narrow face into Sylvia's. A face with a strong nose, black hook-shaped eyebrows. Her breath smelled of tea. She reached for the ribbons on Sylvia's bonnet, untied them, and drew the bonnet away. The woman's gaze, the vicious intensity of it, seemed to want to pull Sylvia inside. She touched Sylvia's hair, twirled a white-blonde curl between her fingers. Her grimace cracked open to brown teeth, a triumphant smile.

"You ask me to believe it?" she said to Betty. "You think I'm a fool? It's clear as the day, this girl is no relation of mine."

"I couldn't care less what you believe," Betty said.

Beyond them, the church doors swung open and the worshippers stepped outside, a tight group, fingers on hands moving down a sidewalk towards a string of cars parked alongside the road. Betty's parents were the last to come out. They stood on the stairs for a moment, looking down the road at Betty and Sylvia, hesitant, as though lost and not knowing which way to turn.

A door slammed, a car's engine started. Malvina Champagne disappeared inside it. The Prince of Glory drove off.

"*Ich moechte Hoause gehen,*" Sylvia said. She wanted to go home to the sound of the cuckoo clock, the clock Betty despised, a tiny kitchen pantry where she played with the pots and pans and watched red ants marching across its cracked floor carrying away crumbs of sugar cookies.

"We are going home," Betty said, her voice brittle and broken, face running, wet, peachy mouth turned down in misery.

That night Sylvia went to bed in a salmon-coloured room above Betty's hairdressing salon. A room that smelled of fresh paint. Through the cream-white rods of the iron bedstead, she saw crescent moons, stars, and flaming suns bursting from a royal blue closet door. A light hanging in the hall beyond the bedroom door, its shade draped with a fringed scarf, swayed whenever Betty and Lucille passed through the hall and came to the doorway to check on her. Had Sylvia vanished? Was she still breathing? Too hot, or too cold? Was Booga-boo waiting for a visit from the sandman? When Sylvia slept, finally, it was to the sound of their voices, laughter coming from the television, strange music, and even though her yellow and blue quilt smelled of the grandparents' house, it was as though she had fallen asleep in another country.

Throughout the summer months and later, during school vacations, Sylvia's second-floor view of the world from the apartment above the salon was exchanged for the smell and feel of the earth in the grandfather's garden, as his cottage, the place she loved most, became home again.

Although the walk from Main Street to the east end of town took her only ten minutes, it seemed she had travelled a great distance. As always, as she arrived, she noticed that the air in the garden was different. It felt moister and silky with heat. She greeted her grandfather and the dusty odour of his dark twill jacket made her think of enclosed varnished rooms the colour of walnuts. He'd been married in the double-breasted jacket, he once told Sylvia. He wore it to church twice weekly, when they collected the mail at the post office and when he worked in his garden. Sylvia went into the garden with him, squatted in the dirt to listen to his stories. She preferred his stories to the ones she heard in the salon.

Sylvia's city and country cousins visited regularly and they would be arriving later in the day. She and her grandfather were harvesting the garden so that when the uncles and aunts came with their monthly offerings, books and magazines, envelopes crackling with dollar bills slipped into his palm during the farewell handshake, he, in turn, would present his. Bushel baskets of potatoes rested against the house, washed clean, still wet. He would fill gunny sacks with carrots, beets, and turnips. What about melons? she wanted to know.

He smiled. It was time now. He hadn't forgotten his promise. She could come with him and choose a watermelon. As he pushed a wheelbarrow through the garden she followed, setting her feet into his boot prints. Her eyes moved up to the small of his back and a feather of dust on his dark jacket. The jacket, she knew, was a gift from a Count Nicholai Petrovich Urusov, chief of the Red Cross in Russia, for whom he had served as Secretary for the Department of Nurses as a young man. When he said the word "Odessa" he lifted his head and gazed out over the garden, at the tops of plum and apple trees at the back of it.

The grandmother was at the kitchen window cleaning an already spotless windowpane in preparation for the visitors. While the grandfather was the keeper of the garden, the grandmother was the keeper of the house and of the ghost in its pantry. She had seen the ghost of a young girl, a girl with yellow hair who smiled at her while reaching for the flour tin on the middle shelf. She had first seen it when she had the flu. A high fever had induced an hallucination, Betty had explained. And what she continued to see was the creation of her imagination. The grandmother longed to see Neta, a daughter she had left behind in the old country, and so she imagined a ghost. An extraordinary child, Neta, an angel in human disguise with saintly and perfect features, they always said.

Sylvia watched the grandfather tap his knuckle against the side of her watermelon, his ear pressed against it, listening intently. He listened, he said, for the heartbeats of musicians. An orchestra of seeds inside the melon.

"Playing a serenade in B flat," Sylvia told him, remembering the music from "Let Us Listen," a school radio broadcast.

He shook his head. "Don't forget about the trumpets," he said. He meant there were also fluted orange-coloured blossoms in the seeds, trumpets toasting the future births of other melons.

He rapped the melon on all sides and listened intently. "I'm not sure if it's ripe," he said. "Maybe not."

Then he did something Sylvia had never seen him do before. He took a jackknife from his pocket and opened it. She was amazed he would cut into a melon still attached to the vine. He made three small incisions then pulled out the triangle and peered into the wound.

"It's not," he said. "Take a look."

She set her eye against the hole. She thought she saw pale seeds floating in a stringy forest.

"Did you know that seeds have memories?" he asked, as though it had only occurred to him. "They can remember every garden they came from. Even the garden of Eden," he said, with reverence. "Seeds are the Alpha and Omega," he went on to say. "The beginning and end of every garden."

The cousins arrived in the early afternoon. Sylvia heard a car enter the lane and went into the front yard to watch. Moments later, another car turned in from the road. The cars travelled along a narrow tree-lined path that opened suddenly to the yard where she waited. The path opened to an arbour of vines, a water pump almost hidden among the spikes of delphinium, phlox, and sweet William gone wild in random spurts of colour.

Immediately the yard filled with people, their greetings, the women reaching for one another, the men comparing gas mileage, the amount of time the trip had taken, trying to cover their self-consciousness over wearing shined shoes and Sunday attire on a Saturday afternoon. Then Betty appeared at the top of the lane carrying her hairdressing kit, her slender waist and firm round breasts accentuated by the pink nylon work smock she wore, its belt knotted tightly.

As Betty stepped into the clearing, the men fell silent. She was always alone and she wasn't just any single woman they could tease good-naturedly or avoid; she wasn't a widow to be pitied. They had no term of reference for Betty they could speak aloud, and they resented that. They resented not knowing how to look at her, where to put their eyes and still remain inno-cent. They imagined frenzied couplings in stubble fields, of coming upon her in the barn and cornering her in a stall, mounting her like a stallion would a mare; their teeth at her neck, her cries.

"So, you came." The elderly woman spoke as if against her will this pleased her.

"Why not?" Betty said. "I have the right, don't I? And I brought my tools, that's what everyone wants, isn't it? A free haircut?"

We're glad to see you, the women said quickly, wanting to overwhelm Betty with their embraces and assurances of love, to heap burning coals of fire on her frizzy strawberry-blonde head.

They moved at once to the side of the house and the shade of its extended roof where spindle chairs had been set out, boards covered a water trough, becoming a table covered with a starched cloth. The grandfather followed but stood away from them as they gathered in the shade. His hands dangled at his sides like spotted potatoes. Someone opened the hood of a car and the men, grateful for the diversion, leaned over its engine, their oblique and truncated discussions beginning.

Her cousin, David, had grown taller, Sylvia noticed, as they walked to the front yard and entered the diffused light of the arbour. His father had taken a longer route, he said. They had driven miles out of their way across secondary roads in order to cross the Red River on a ferry at Saint Adolphe, because David had asked them to. He had had rheumatic fever and was not allowed a normal child's play; his parents compensated any way they could. He couldn't wait, David said, for the trip home and the danger of the car inching down a steep slope onto the ferry.

The women began calling them. It was time to come for lunch, they said, for singing, for saying grace.

"Your mother is so pretty," David said, as they saw Betty emerge from the house carrying a tray of water glasses. "It's no wonder they don't like her."

That Betty was not liked didn't surprise Sylvia but, rather, the thought that she might be beautiful. It was true, Betty's complexion was not marked, or mottled by the sun, but a seamless beige mask. Her expression held an enigmatic pout that made her appear exotic.

"But pretty is not going to get her into heaven," David said, his voice parroting an adult voice.

Sylvia ran through the garden because she knew he would not follow. She leapt over hedges of potato plants and felt the breeze, cool in her skirts, on her thighs, against her stomach. She felt the bite of corn leaves as she plunged through the stalks and out the other side to a row of fruit trees edging the garden and the tall grass between them, where she could hide. *A foolish man built his house upon the sand*, the words to the children's song came to Sylvia. The grandmother had taught her the song, singing in a voice her chest condition of late rendered wobbly and plaintive-sounding, and, whenever Sylvia sang it, it was with the same vibrato. *And the rains came down and the floods came up.* Sylvia leaned into her haunches, listening to their high and low voices, the clink of dishes being set out on the makeshift picnic table. She pictured it: the last people alive in the world huddling on a mountaintop, about to be engulfed by a wave. Betty about to be swept away, her orange mouth gasping for air, fingers like claws scratching at the sky for mercy and finding none. Sylvia had swung between Betty and Lucille, weightless, suspended in the air by their hands as they walked down the street singing Paul Anka's "Diana" song. She had marched with them across a clipped lawn to admire a KEEP OFF THE GRASS sign. She had gone through doors at the DO NOT ENTER entrance. Set her palms beside theirs in the wet cement of someone's new sidewalk. Snuck into sideshows on Fair Day from the back of the tent. Everywhere she went with Betty and Lucille they managed to stick out. There was always that danger. It had followed her to the grandfather's garden, it would follow her to heaven.

"Sylvia!" the women called, their voices high with a faked cheeriness, but Sylvia heard the panic in it.

"Booga-boo!" Betty called, when they couldn't find her in the house, or in the front or back yards.

From where she hid, Sylvia then saw her grandfather, his face taut as he walked faster than she had ever seen before, down the road to the river.

"Sylvia!" Betty shouted. She yanked the belt of her smock loose and shed the garment. It dropped to the ground, revealing the white halter top and shorts she had put on beneath it hoping to catch the last bit of sunshine later, when she would suntan on the apartment roof. She kicked her sandals free and sprinted after her father.

Then all at once Sylvia was there behind them, the aunts, uncles, cousins waiting in silence, watching the trees along the river for the grandfather and Betty to emerge. The grandmother saw Sylvia first and pulled her into her stomach in an embrace and cry of relief.

"We found her," the women called, hailing the grandfather and Betty.

Moments later Sylvia felt Betty's hands on her shoulders trying to turn her away from her grandmother. Wanting to draw Sylvia into herself.

"Be ashamed," the grandmother said, meaning Betty's cleavage slick with perspiration, her bared stomach heaving. "Is this what you do? Go about half-naked in front of the girl?"

"Give her to me. She's mine. She's my kid."

"No one is denying that," the grandmother said. "But that doesn't mean you can do what you want. Where were you last night?"

"Where do you think?" Betty said, stepping away, releasing her hold on Sylvia. The women sighed and drifted out of hearing. The men jingled change in their pockets and studied the treeline beyond the river.

"I don't think so," the grandmother said. "Already past midnight, and there were no lights on at your place."

The grandfather arrived mopping his brow, his breathing shallow and laboured.

"You were spying on me," Betty said to her father.

"We're concerned about your reputation. For the sake of the child," the grandfather said.

"Look," Betty said. "I'm sorry. I'm sorry I'm not Neta. I beg your pardon, everyone. I beg your pardon, world. I beg your pardon, God, but I'll never be dear Neta!" Betty shouted. "I have no desire to be six feet under."

They turned from the sight of her buttocks jumping beneath the white shorts as she bunched her pink cotton smock against her stomach and strode from the yard.

The grandmother was in the house at the kitchen table, a lamp set down onto it and shedding its light across the pages of an open book. "Spiders talk to each other," the grandfather said to Sylvia. It was late in the evening and the company had left. They sat in the semidarkness on a bench beside the kitchen door, their backs to the house, looking across the garden. Fruit

trees sprawled against the purple sky, their crooked limbs glinting with light as spider silk billowed in a cool breeze. Spiders
talked about what they were afraid of. Sylvia had read "The
Wizardry of Webs" in *Reader's Digest*, too. Spiders talked about
hunger and desire, the article said.

"They speak to one another through their threads," the
grandfather said.

Spiderlings fly away from their mothers on strings of silk,
over fields. Over mountains. Over oceans? Sylvia wondered.

"There was ice in the garden the year Neta left us for heaven,"
he said, as though taking up a story he had begun earlier. "There
was so much rain that year the creek flooded into our yard and
froze. The children were sliding on it. Back and forth, wearing
their felt slippers. Our little Neta, too. One would try and outdo
the other. See who could go the furthest." He gazed at the fruit
trees as though he might find the children among them.

"But then a man came. One of the bandits. There were
always plenty of those. We never knew when they would come
or go. He had a gun and was prodding a young man with it,
making him go to the back of our yard. Out towards the barn.
Who knows why? Maybe the young man had committed the
crime of butchering a chicken without a permit. Or he had hid
a bit of silver somewhere." Behind them at the window, moths
battered at the kitchen window, trying to get at the light.

"The children knew something bad was going to happen.
They'd already seen so much by then. And they began to run
for home, all at once. The man was far enough away, and because
he was occupied with this other man and had his own intention, I didn't fear for the children. I turned from the window. I
didn't want to witness another killing. And so I didn't know that

Neta had slipped on the ice and couldn't get up. I didn't realize this until I went to the back door to meet her. It was then I knew that the man had let the young man go and, instead, had taken little Neta off to the barn. He was going to do to her what other girls, women, had too often endured. Much later, he came to me. Said he couldn't sleep over it. He begged my forgiveness. He told me Neta had said she would pray to God for him. It was then that he became angry and killed her."

The kitchen window shivered with the grandmother's rapping. "Papa!" she called loudly, angrily. "It's too late for stories."

He sighed. His hands became large white fans unfolding across his thighs. "And now it's time for tomorrow," he said and, with a groan, rose from the bench and walked stiffly off into the garden.

"He's tired," the grandmother said, and set a shopping bag with Sylvia's belongings onto the bench. "Please tell your mama. We're growing too old for summer vacations." She had twisted sugar cubes into a handkerchief and pressed them into Sylvia's palm.

"We will still be here, everything will be here, just as it is. You can come on Saturdays. And Sundays, after church," she added. "But not for nights any more. I am too old for babysitting all night while she goes out and makes a name for herself," the grandmother said, more to herself.

Sylvia looked at the water trough where she bathed to cool off, the greenhouse set to one side of the yard incandescent with the light of a single bulb left burning day and night, at the garden where the grandfather walked, stooped and slow. She went into the garden to inspect her melon before she left, already longing for her grandparents' house, its clocks ticking in every room, the enfolding stillness of it; for the gaunt lament of the clock cuckooing the hour during the night and their step on the floor as they moved from room to room. She felt a melancholy that reminded her of the sound of moths' wings beating against a windowpane. Red ants swarmed around the plug in the watermelon, looking for a way inside it. She pressed the triangular piece firmly into the melon to secure it; so that the melon inside the melon, inside the melon, would not be lost. She heard the grandfather's step on the path behind her and then smelled his dry papery odour as he dropped to his knees beside her.

"Do you know who my father is?" Sylvia asked suddenly. She imagined rescue. That, some day, he might be a place to go to.

The grandfather jabbed the earth with a finger and then drew a vertical line through it. "This is the beginning," he said. Then he drew another vertical line, a wide space between it and the first one. "And that is the end. Watch," he said, as he drew a horizontal line between the two lines, his finger stopping midway between them. "See? That's you." Finally, he drew an ellipse the shape of a melon seed, and enclosed all the lines. "And that's the almighty God, your father. He already knows your beginning and your end. Do you think when he sees you, he sees your mother and your father, too? No, He sees only you. So just be who you are. Be you."


"Well, that's a nice thought," Betty said to Sylvia, months later. "But we are living in this world, aren't we? And if, years ago, your great-great-grandfather was a horse thief, you can be sure people would want to check your pockets before you left the grocery store."

The topic had arisen when Sylvia asked Betty to give her a boy's haircut. She wanted to find out, she said, if people would treat her differently. If they would want to know who she was and not just notice her hair. Stop calling her Goldilocks.

"They'll only notice it more, you cut it short like a boy's," Betty said. "Unfortunately, this world is not filled with people who will just let you be you."

"I wish," Lucille said.

"Never you mind," Betty said to Lucille consolingly. "You've got the best of two worlds."

*Mitchif*, Sylvia thought. Half-breed. The word sounded like "mischief," a word she thought described Lucille and her brothers perfectly.

This was on a Thursday, the day they "tripped the light fantastic," as Betty called it. She closed the shop and, during school months, Betty let Sylvia miss a day. Today the bathing suits were packed in Betty's tote bag. They were going swimming at the Sherbrook pool. Betty made deep-fried plum fritters for breakfast, rolled them in sugar. She cooked herself a pan of scrambled eggs cut with cheddar cheese; protein to keep her hands steady all day. Lucille timed her three-mile walk from the farm to arrive just as they sat down to eat. Pork selly, Lucille called the plum fritters; *portzelky*, Betty corrected. From time to time, Betty prepared one of her mother's recipes, for Lucille's sake. Lucille had grown up on beans heated in a can. Sylvia had noted the feigned nonchalance in Betty's voice as she dropped the sizzling fritters into a paper bag and shook the fat from them. Glue, Betty said, it's just flour, milk, and a few acidic plums. Imagine what it's going to do to your guts. As though she had not sweated over asking the grandmother for a jar of wild plums; sweated over the hot fat in the deep fryer, heard the old songs being sung.

There was an edge to Betty and Lucille's chatter that grated on Sylvia as she waited for them to be ready. When they made up their faces in front of the salon mirror, it was with intense concentration, as though there was so much at risk, a blotch of mascara smearing, a crooked line that might give the eye an odd shape. When they were done, tubes of colours, wands of colours, eyelash curlers, hairpins, brushes, and damp sponges lay scattered across the counter in front of the mirror. They lifted hand mirrors, scrutinized their profiles in silence. Finishing powder sifted down through the light, settled on the counter, a fine beige dust that smelled faintly of chalk.

"I hate swimming," Sylvia said.

"We'll eat Chinese first," Betty promised.

"Where do you tell your mother you go on Thursdays?" Betty once asked.

"I lie," Lucille said.

"You need to lie?"

"It's less trouble that way. Once in a while I go to confession and I'm in the clear."

"Sounds too good to be true," Betty said.

Often they went to a movie at the Capital. Bowling, to the zoo, or idled the day shopping. On one of their shopping trips Betty found a piece of red taffeta. Lucille designed and Betty sewed a dress for Sylvia on the event of the town's first, and only, amateur talent contest. Lucille accompanied Sylvia on the piano as Sylvia sang "On the Sidewalks of New York" in a voice unsteady and full of breath. She swayed and shuffled her feet the way Lucille had rehearsed her, and the audience laughed and then sighed when she was done.

When Sylvia received second prize, Betty and Lucille congratulated one another as much as they did her. The grandmother had been sitting beside the radio all evening, waiting to hear, thinking that the event was of such importance that the results would be broadcast.

"What did you sing?" the grandmother asked. "Did you sing a Christian song?"

Sylvia didn't know what tripping the light fantastic meant, or where New York was. It was as though she'd been singing in another language.

"She sang, 'Gladly, the Cross-Eyed Bear,'" Betty said.

"Make fun," the grandmother said. "See where it gets you."

"Laugh," Betty said. "I dare you. Your face won't crack. Honest."

As Sylvia feared, at the end of the day they wound up at the Sherbrook. The pool filled her lungs with heat and body with a wariness. There were always men pacing around the pool's perimeter and, as Sylvia emerged from the change room, they were there, as usual. Pacing as though impatient for something to happen.

The pacing stopped abruptly when Lucille and Betty appeared from the change room and set the towels draping their shoulders onto a bench. Sylvia noted the men's muscles bunching, chests rising. Ooo-la-la. Lips kissed the air as the women chose their spot and sat dangling their legs in the water, waiting for sufficient time to pass after having filled up on Chinese in Chinatown.

Sylvia dog-paddled across the pool, propelling herself along with the tip of a toe against the bottom. Lucille spoke and Betty laughed. Their sudden laughter caught their bodies unprepared and their nipples jumped under their bathing suits.

"Watch! Watch me!" Sylvia's shrill demand for their attention bounced off the glass doors at the pool's entrance. She could see the shapes of people behind the steamed glass; a hand clearing moisture, and then eyes set against the spot and turned onto the two women. A wall of marine-blue tiles became a backdrop for Betty's pink and Lucille's orange floral bodies while they sat as though joined at the thighs and shoulders, still hoarding whatever had made them laugh. They appeared not to notice or care about the eyes turned on them.

"I've got to stop working here," a man said.

Another laughed, ruefully, knowingly. "It's the only age a woman looks good. Enough to eat."

"I'll have the dark meat," the other said. "A bit of wild game is always good for a change."

Sylvia floated to shut them out, face down, arms trailing and her body bobbing with the motion of water. Her ears boomed with the muted sounds of laughter, voices, a whistle blowing. She floated, wanting to stay under for as long as she could. Wanting, as her chest tightened from lack of air, to know how it would feel to need air and not be able to breathe. To understand the terror of realizing you are about to be engulfed and swept away. Suddenly she felt hands on her body, flipping her over, yanking her to the surface.

"Brat!" Betty said, and struck Sylvia on the cheek. The sound of the slap echoed. "Don't you do that. Don't you ever, ever do that!"

"You hit me!" Sylvia shouted, stung more by astonishment than injury.

"Yes, and I will again. If you ever do that again."

"What was I doing? Tell me!"

"Just don't do it." Betty said.

Ceramic tiles ran with moisture in the change room and the air turned to steam. Bathing caps popped free as streams of water hit the floor in the shower stalls. From where Sylvia sat, she saw Betty and Lucille's suits drop and become puddles of crumpled flowers about their ankles. If the shower ran too cold they'd scream, or sing with pleasure if it was hot. That day they sang and raised their arms and smiles up to the strings of water, oblivious, it seemed, to the glances of women around them who showered with their bathing suits on. A pinched disapproval hung in the air as Betty and Lucille vigorously sudsed their armpits, the furry change purses between their legs, fingers fishing about their folds as if searching for coins. As they curled to their task, their breasts swung. Their bodies were translucent, beaded with moisture, taut-skinned like grapes and about to split open. They seemed not to notice, or chose not to, how spaces opened up around them, that the benches they'd sat on were wiped down with a towel or avoided if at all possible.

Sylvia cowered in a changing cubicle, her back against the door in the event someone came barging in. She dressed hurriedly, furtively, resenting the sound of Betty and Lucille's heightened voices as they towelled dry, powdered their bodies, and then rolled their wet suits up into their towels. Plastic bags crackled. The scent of shampoo and rose talc hung in the moist room. They prolonged their nakedness, Sylvia knew, relished it, flaunted it.

During the return trip home, Lucille slept, her dark head swaying with the motion of the bus. Betty sat beside Sylvia, chatting across the aisle with a woman, their voices underscored by the drone of wheels against pavement. Two nuns sat in front of Lucille, and when she'd got on the bus she'd greeted them by name and with a shy reverence. They spoke to Lucille for a time, in French, questions, Sylvia guessed, questions Lucille seemed reluctant, or unable, to answer.

Outside, a harvest moon hung above the fields. It seemed a rotund furnace containing a glowing still fire. Except for the bonfires lit on the fields to burn off stubble, there were no reference points. A spot between Sylvia's legs buzzed with the vibration of the bus. She pressed against it to make it be still, but it erupted suddenly, the sensation radiating outwards, making her shake and wanting to curl into it. Then, suddenly, pillows, shopping bags, cigarette ashes, and a silk scarf floated in the air. The bus flew up and off the highway. It rolled. Glass shattered. Metal sheared open.

Later, Lucille and Betty's voices came through to Sylvia on either side, muted, as though underwater. Her heels met on the table and her feet splayed outwards forming a V through which she viewed a window in the operating-room door. Something was expected of her. That she remain still. She concentrated on the effort not to give in to the pressure on her full bladder while the doctor stitched the wound on her knee. She pictured the harvest moon above the fields, that still fire, round fire. She would make herself into that. Grow round, large enough to keep everything in.

Then the bearded face of Father Normandeau appeared in the window. The door opened, destroying Sylvia's concentration.

"The sisters said I would find you here," the priest said to Lucille. "I've come to take you home."

"I gotta go, Booga-boo," Lucille said, her cheek flushed as it descended for a kiss.

"You don't have to go with him," Betty said. "You're old enough to decide where you want to be."

"Yes, she does," the priest said. "Her mother wants her at home. I want her at home."

"So, what's his problem?" Betty asked Lucille.

"It's not that difficult," the priest said. "She doesn't belong here."

"And just where *does* she belong?" Betty said. "Somewhere down around your knees, I suppose."

"Spoken like the devil's daughter," the priest said.

"What fucking nonsense," Betty said, as Lucille left the room, the priest behind her.

"Oh," the doctor exclaimed at the sound of urine meeting the toe of his shoe, the sight of it trickling off the table.

It was loneliness Betty thought she heard in Sylvia's howl, and not indignation. It brought to mind the time she'd left Sylvia alone for most of a night. She had gone to a house party and worried the whole time that Sylvia might be snatched from bed by a stranger passing through town. Or that her father had gone for a late-night walk and carried her daughter off. She had chanced staying at the party in spite of her worries. She had walked home barefoot, a bit drunk, the sky already lightening, risked losing her child over a silly party, over a hurried, unsatisfying tumble among coats on a bed. She had risked Sylvia's life in the swimming pool and could have lost her on the highway.

"*Our father who art,*" Betty breathed. As she smoothed the hair from Sylvia's forehead, she thought, Thank you.


Shortly afterwards Sylvia learned that Lucille Champagne and her family had moved away. She learned about it in the post office, from the man behind the wicket. The Champagne family had given up their post-office box. They had gone to live in Saint Boniface after the old lady, apparently, had discovered she qualified for a widow's pension from the railway.

"I knew they were going, but I didn't think it would be so soon. Gone to become French," Betty told Sylvia.

Malvina had decided, Betty said, if anyone should ask, that they were French Canadian. That they were descendants of the first paddlers and carriers who came from Quebec. There had been no marriage in the custom of the land in the Champagne family. Lucille, with her convent schooling, had picked up a few things along the way and had a better chance of pulling it off, Betty said. The brothers, however, were another thing.

Sylvia had heard about the brothers' escapades. They worked in a meat-packing house and hated it. They disliked the tedium, the stink of blood, the fat rendering. They spent most of their pay at the Belgium Club and racetrack to compensate. They'd become known for their incongruous enterprises. Jumping off rooftops just for the sake of it. Surprising women who were leaving the cathedral on a Sunday morning by lassoing them with their lariats. Throwing hunting knives at one another. They were clowns without horses, dreaming of becoming rodeo

riders or stuntmen they had seen in the movies, and were prac-
tising the various ways of dying in preparation for the big
break.

"Never fear, we still have the Mexicans," Betty said one
Saturday morning to Tillie Olsen, an elderly woman who came
twice weekly to clean her salon in exchange for shampoos and
hair permanents. Betty meant that there was someone else in
town to talk about now. An indigent family from Mexico who
had appeared so mysteriously.

And then after not hearing from her for nearly half a year
the door opened that day and Lucille Champagne walked into
the salon with a beau, Edgar Valcourt.

It seemed to Sylvia that Lucille introduced Edgar to them
with an intense shyness, that she was begging for approval
while at the same time bracing herself against certain rejection.
The man was much older than Lucille, a man in a white fedora.
After he left, Lucille told them how her brothers, Noel and
Arthur, had shot their guns off at Edgar when he'd come to
pick her up that morning at the house the Champagne family
had rented on Des Meurons Street. Lucille had watched for
Edgar at the window and, at the blast of gunfire, he had shifted
his cigar from one corner of his mouth to the other, but kept
on coming down the walk as though being shot at was something he was accustomed to.

Edgar had business down the highway in Saint Jean Baptiste
and had offered to drop Lucille off at Betty's hairdressing salon
along the way. It was Fair Day in town and the three of them,
Lucille, Betty, and Sylvia, could make an evening of it, he said.
A poster in the salon window promised new attractions, an
Indian elephant and a two-headed calf. He could come by the

next morning and take Lucille back to the city and save her the price of a bus ticket. If she wanted.

"How magnanimous of you," Betty said.

"It'll be just like old times," Lucille said. The three of them would paint the town.

When Lucille had introduced Edgar Valcourt, he tipped his fedora and stuck it on the back of his head. He peered down at Sylvia through a puff of cigar smoke and chuckled in a scratchy voice; a good-natured enough sound, but it was unsettling because it seemed to imply that he knew something about Sylvia that she didn't. He had a solidness, Betty said later, that on some men she found inviting. His seemed to be all muscle, a self-protectiveness disguised as self-assurance.

"Turn," Edgar said, and Lucille turned, twirling slowly in the centre of the room to show off her new look, the batwing-sleeved blouse knotted at her midriff, a full blue chambray skirt that swirled from her hips.

Then he circled her waist with his hands. "Nineteen inches," he said.

"I wouldn't know," Betty said. "I've only sewn for her for umpteen years."

He said he thought Lucille could do better with her hair. Better than the upsweep, the jumble of curls gathered on top of her head. His eyes roamed the gallery of faded life-sized posters hanging on the walls. A collection Sylvia had dubbed "One of These Days Coiffures," because Betty's clients would often study them wistfully, and threaten to change their hairstyles at some vague time in the future. Edgar pointed to a model with a short bob. He liked that. It was kind of cute. The haircut was on him. When he went for his wallet, Betty told him to keep his money, with a snarkiness Sylvia noted.

"He thinks he's king of the road," Betty said, as he drove off in a new Impala. She didn't like the way he carried his head, square jaw lifted like that. "How does he make the bucks?" she wanted to know.

"Horses," Lucille said, defensively.

"Raises horses?"

"No, he bets on them," she said, as though Betty was at fault for not knowing.

"He's a gambler?"

"Why not?" Lucille said, and shrugged. "He makes a good living at it."

Then she showed Betty the bracelet at her wrist, American ten-cent pieces welded between silver chains.

"He bought it for me in Minneapolis," she said.

"Why did your brothers shoot at him?" Sylvia asked. It was, she knew, impolite to listen in, but in a hairdressing salon it was impossible not to overhear other people's confidences or confessions. The head she worked on, belonging to the elderly Tillie Olsen, had given up trying to think of small talk to cover Lucille and Betty's conversation.

"Because they still have the bush in their hair," Betty said. She seemed to relish the word "bush," as though she had coined it. She gave it a *whoosh* sound the way Lucille or her brothers might have said it. Never tango with bush, Betty once said. You got a taste for it and everything else would seem boring.

Lucille laughed, and ground the cigarette she'd been smoking into a beanbag ashtray cradled in her lap.

Sylvia worked at a sink across the room, shampooing Tillie Olsen while Betty snipped away Lucille's henna curls.

How was school? Tillie enquired. Her voice was a mourning dove, a hollow *hoo-hoo*ing sound in the bottom of the sink. People thought the woman eccentric ever since her husband died, because she'd begun to ride a bicycle. What was thought of Betty's salon, its new pink and purple interior, a steel girder in the centre of the room decked year-round with Christmas lights, Sylvia didn't need to know. Consider where the gossip comes from, Betty said. Some people have permanent-pressed minds. No matter how you try to set them straight, once there's a wrinkle in their thoughts about a person, it stays put forever.

"So just why did they take their guns to Edgar?" Betty asked.

"Talk," Lucille said.

"Such as?"

"Cheap talk."

"Where there's smoke," Betty said.

"He's going to buy Ma'mere a pair of budgie birds. The lady next door has budgies. When Ma'mere saw them she went crazy. Dragged Edgar over there just to see them. He's going to take her to the track, too, next time we go."

"Yes," Betty said. "I guess she would approve. He fits the bill, eh? He's French and he's cat'lick."

"And I'll wager he's married," Tillie Olsen said to Sylvia in a whisper. Sylvia suppressed a giggle. She enjoyed Tillie. She liked the woman's pink coconut skull covered with wiry white hair. Tillie had lost weight since she'd begun to ride a bicycle and the skin on her underarms hung like crepe. Tillie had once let Sylvia pinch it to see how it held its pucker.

"Ma'mere approves because I like Edgar," Lucille said. "Stantons," she said suddenly, extending a petite foot so Betty might admire the shoes she wore, open-toed, with a thin strap about her ankle. "I got them at Clarks. They said it's a new line."

"The new car isn't hard to take either," Betty said.

"And you'd like him better if he didn't have one?"

"I'm just concerned, that's all."

"He treats me well. Give him a chance, eh? I like him. More than like, I think."

"Really?" Betty said, her eyebrows flying upwards.

"He touches me. Anywhere. The shoulder, my arm. Just touches, and I almost come."

"Well, count your lucky stars, girl," Tillie Olsen said. "I used to crawl all over my Jimmy. Frontwards, backwards, sideways, and I never got a darn thing out of it."

Their laughter, Sylvia thought, was a relief, a cloud bursting open, finally, after threatening to all morning.


The midway was off limits to Sylvia until Lucille and Betty arrived. The fairground had changed, Betty said, when Sylvia objected. It crawled with what Betty had come to believe were bums, lowlifes, creeps. Fuck that nonsense, Sylvia had said, and got a cool reprimand. Only people with a very limited vocabulary use foul language, Betty said.

Sylvia was impressed by the size of the Indian elephant. But when its keeper, an undernourished-looking gum-chewing girl, explained how the mammal could be tethered by a single spike and length of flimsy rope, she felt let down. She watched the animal plod and sway mindlessly around a makeshift ring of snow fencing, wearing a muddy trail in the flattened grass. The animal could not be tempted from its fixed course by hands cupping peanuts or offerings of grass.

The tent exterior of the two-headed calf looked even less promising, its garish sign faded and cracked, the paint having peeled loose from the canvas so that the image of the calf looked as though it was a jigsaw puzzle and pieces of it were missing. But as Sylvia entered, the canvas flap dropped into place behind her and became a rich blue tapestry that shut out the odours of trampled grass and the honky-tonk looseness of the midway scams and spinning rides.

She was stopped by the sight of a glowing white cube set on a raised dais at the far end of the tent, dazzling and impermeable-looking as a diamond. The cube was lit by spotlights below and from above. As she drew nearer to it, the two-headed calf emerged in what seemed to be a solid, sculpted cube of ice. Its fuzzy caramel-coloured heads turned away from one another slightly, as though avoiding eye contact. The identical heads erupted from a single shortened neck. The Jersey calf's delicate noses and languid eyes seemed to follow Sylvia when she moved.

Which head, Sylvia wondered, had determined when the calf slept, woke up, ate, what direction to go? She imagined the striving of its limbs when one had the need to lie down, the other to gambol about the farmyard. The calf had two brains driving one body. It made her wince to imagine the heads straining on the single neck, the yanking and tugging against its own flesh and muscle. Or had it, she wondered, even before emerging from its mother's body, become an adroit acrobat, a contortionist, the heads working in tandem, anticipating each other's impulses and desires before they were thought, or felt? The calf's eyes looked to the left and, at the same time, to the right. Its heart would react according to what its eyes saw, the message the two brains sent to it: prepare to do two things at once, flee and stay. Sleep and eat. Laugh and cry.

Perhaps, Sylvia thought, as she hurried to the fortune teller's tent where she was to meet Betty and Lucille, one message cancelled the other and the calf's heart had stopped beating.

The Ferris wheel turned, carrying Sylvia to the top and then it stopped to take on several riders. Her seat rocked gently as she was held, suspended in midair. The landscape she had only come to know in bits and pieces became complete. Main Street was partly obscured by elm and cottonwood. The suite above the salon faced a perpendicular street that ended in the row of six houses, the grandparents' cottage enclosed in a square of greenery at the end of it.

She saw the bend in the river and a whiff of smoke rise near the place where the Champagne family had lived. Arthur Champagne had shot his gun off that morning at Lucille's first beau. Betty was pouting over it. Betty and Arthur were jealous for some reason, Sylvia thought suddenly. Then it came to her, like an illumination of truth, like the one that came to her that day in church when she realized Betty was her mother. Arthur Champagne was her father.

As the Ferris wheel began moving, Betty and Lucille's upturned faces came into view. Lucille had changed her clothes and wore a perky white straw hat with a single red stand-up feather. An apple-green scarf knotted in a floppy bow set off the coppery glow of Betty's hair. They were both wearing white. Betty, a crisp cotton shirt-waist dress that was meant to be a subtle reminder that she was now the responsible citizen, a school trustee, petitioner for the construction of a swimming pool in the playground. Organizer of community Halloween dances where energy in hormone-driven bodies could be expended in a better way than in random vandalism. Lucille wore a stylish suit nipped at the waist, its double revers draped gently across her small breasts. Sylvia thought, I have inherited my mother's colouring. But she could see now her own features in Lucille's face.

The women's faces disappeared, then reappeared and receded as Sylvia swept past and up again. Betty grew small and her red shoes looked like gobs of jelly stuck onto the end of her legs. She was slightly pigeon-toed and her head was obscured by the floppy apple-green bow. Red shoes, green scarf don't match, Sylvia thought. It was obvious who was high fashion now.

Once again Sylvia saw the rooftop of the grandparents' cottage. Neither my parents nor his wanted us to marry, Betty had once told her. But she would never say who Sylvia's father was. My mother rolled up a newspaper and beat me about the head and shoulders as though I was a dog, Betty said. And when I did tell her, she beat me with the fly swatter. My father stopped the beating. It doesn't matter who the father is, he said. The child is a blessing. Everything seemed clear to Sylvia now. Arthur Champagne, who had once kept a squirrel in the house. Whose brother sawed off a corner of the dining-room table. A meal of beans heated in the can. Arthur and Betty. The grandparents' home was a place, Sylvia realized, where God loved not only the pure in heart, but the faint of heart as well; cowards and traitors, murderers and thieves, but there wasn't enough room, apparently, to allow for two different worlds.

From the top of the Ferris wheel Betty looked like a kid who's been sent to a corner for punishment. Sylvia knew what this felt like. How it wasn't really punishment for wrongdoing but rejection, a shunning. She guessed this was what Betty had been experiencing all these years. She set the tip of a finger on top of her mother's apple-green head and rubbed it. I understand, she said, and felt herself grow older; vowed to, in the future, overlook her mother's glaring shortcomings.

The Ferris wheel rocked to a gentle stop and a wood ramp slid in place. As Sylvia stepped down, she was surprised by the sight of Edgar Valcourt's white fedora. He beckoned and called out in his scratchy voice for Lucille to come over to the Crown and Anchor Wheel. As Sylvia joined the women, she heard Lucille, apologetic, saying, "I told him he could. I didn't think you would mind."

Edgar set his hand on the small of Lucille's back and drew her to his side. He needed some cash, he said.

Betty looked on, disbelievingly, as Lucille took her wallet from her handbag and handed him several bills.

It grew dark and the Ferris wheel became a pinwheel of lights, and in the midway the hawkers' frenetic barking for attention softened to flirty comments when women strolled by, or a bantering passed between the barkers and the men at the women's sides. Sylvia could see the two-headed calf from the bingo tent where she waited for Betty, who had spent most of the evening playing bingo with an intense energy. The calf was a block of light glowing eerily inside its inner canvas courtyard. Spectators, shadows, loomed against tent walls as they followed the rope aisle leading to and from the glass cube. I am not remotely interested in freaky things, Betty had said, and refused to go and see it.

Edgar was still going strong, Tillie Olsen, who had joined

them at bingo, reported. She'd put on a mauve petal bonnet for Fair Day that resembled a blooming African violet. Lucille's beau had lost and won back over two hundred dollars so far, she said. There was quite a crowd watching.

Betty shot her a sideways glance that said she didn't want to know.

As Sylvia helped Tillie keep track of her bingo cards, they talked and Sylvia heard something new in her own voice. She thought she heard a sprightliness, an attractive energy.

Then, a woman's voice rose above the sounds of the midway. It held a kind of hysteria that made Sylvia follow Betty and Tillie to the Crown and Anchor Wheel. There a woman danced a strange jig in front of Edgar, beating the air with her fists. Her words were swollen and unintelligible. Two children at her side looked on with a serene solemnity that was unsettling to watch.

"It's his woman," Tillie said. "I should have put a wager on it." She could, she said, smell a married man up to no good, miles away.

Lucille stood at the Crown and Anchor Wheel table, her face expressionless, watching carefully as the screaming woman danced and punched the air. It was as though she wanted to memorize the woman's rage, her contorted features, the clown's mouth turned upside-down. When Betty touched Lucille, she started.

"He's married," Betty said.

The feather on Lucille's hat had bent and bisected her face in a red slash. She took off her hat, wet her fingers, and preened its feather straight.

"I know," Lucille said, finally. "He never tried to hide it."

"Look. He's got kids."

"And so?"

"Even if he wanted to, you know your church would never let him marry you. Ever."

Lucille smiled, a tiny smile of regret that didn't reach her dimples. She shrugged and made a move as though she might give the hat to Betty.

"Is that so bad?" she said.

"People will never let you forget it," Betty said. "Don't get hooked up with him. Stay here. Stay with us."

"No, but thanks," Lucille said. "In the city, what people don't know can't hurt anyone."

"Fine," Betty said. "But don't come crying to me. You've made your bed and you'll wind up having to pay for it."

Sylvia was stunned by Betty's rebuke, angered that she had repeated the somewhat fractured cliché that in the past she herself had railed against.

⸙

*Once I was a child who had a child*, my mother would often say. *The time just came for me to grow up and so I did.*

The bus accident that occurred years ago had been written up in the newspaper, and in a startling way, of course. It was not difficult for me to find it on microfilm at the library. A crash, the newspaper article said, and not what it was: a lazy flying upwards and rolling. A flying bus, an impossibility, yes, but for moments it did fly and we flew with it, waltzing among a storm of dust particles and tumbling objects: a silk scarf, a banner the colour of daylight unfurling from a bag and winding itself around me. I stared through the glare of the microfilm reader screen.

"Oh, that," Lucille said. "I'd forgotten about the accident."

"I still have the scar on my knee to prove it. I remember, there was a priest," I said.

"Nuns," Lucille said. "There were a couple of old crows on the bus. I've been searching my mind," she said, "and I've been thinking. It's funny how you never realize it at the time, but those were about my best years. Look at me, eh? Looking back. I hope you're not doing that. Not at your age."

I said she couldn't stop me. I wanted to come and see her.

"No way."

"What if I just popped in?"

"Oh, no, you don't, kid," Lucille said. "Look. It's not that I don't want to see you, okay? It's just that I'm not proud of myself, eh? I wish I was, but I'm not. Don't ask why."

My mother had received a letter from Lucille when Malvina died and she sent condolences composed in the carefully worded manner of those whose profession is to bring solace. Other than notes exchanged through Christmas cards, I don't believe they kept in touch. The last time my mother saw Lucille — it could have been twenty years ago — I was there. On a city street, walking past a downtown hotel in the early evening. A car had pulled up to the curb in front of us, and Lucille stepped out. I recall the flash, a California kind of glitz. Purple Spandex tights, gold lamé stretched to the limits across her swollen stomach and breasts. White rabbit fur slung across a tanned shoulder; an exaggerated smile pulling her face to one side as she teetered on pathetically thin legs and high heels into the hotel.

Drunk, my mother said, and flung an arm across my chest as though it was a spectacle I needed shielding from. She warned me not to speak as a man got out of the car and followed Lucille into the hotel. We saw Edgar, then, behind the wheel, drive off. "I knew it," my mother said. "He's nothing but a pimp." I wished for regret in her voice, or sorrow, and not what sounded like satisfaction at being proven right.

Lucille's white rabbit shoulder disappeared into the glimmer of the darkened hotel foyer and then the plate-glass door closed and reflected our images, my mother's greying hair, clipped short and hugging her round face. The woman who once wanted fire had settled for being the wife of an Anglican minister. A middle-aged woman, such as I am now, wearing socks with her Birkenstocks, a dirndl skirt and long T-shirt to accommodate a rather comfortable girth, and the platitudes, homilies that substitute for caring now that her life seems predictable and safe. I looked too anxious, my marriage was failing, I blamed myself. I was torn between going after Lucille to prove my mother wrong, but feared that she was right. She entertains with pot-luck suppers in her rec room and at backyard barbecues. People of all shapes, sizes, and ages attend, often people whose lives are flying apart. Why not Lucille then? I wanted to know.

She's always known where I am. If she needs me, all she has to do is ask, Betty had said.

I remembered waking some mornings as a child and finding my mother and Lucille on either side of me, wiry strawberry-blonde hair tickling my face, a dark head set against my shoulder blades; a brown hand on the pillow beside me, its slim fingers splayed against the white sheet as though clutching at air. But what I recalled most vividly was how their bodies smelled like wild roses and felt like a flannel cocoon.

"So why did the priest think that your friendship with my mother was dangerous?" I had asked Lucille on the telephone.

I imagined he feared Lucille straying, losing her faith and language, as if she wouldn't, by becoming French, lose the largest part of herself.

"I guess he thought that it might be unnatural," she said. "You know what I mean. Funny."

"And was it?" I asked, immediately hating how that sounded. My mind raced to make room for images coloured by memory. I recalled the dismal sound of snow pellets, like sand, flung against a window, a saxophone playing, a woman's voice – Billie Holiday, I imagined. I remembered their shadows rising and receding on a wall as they danced, swaying to the music. Their alarmed whispers at the sound of footsteps on the stairs. Heavy footsteps mounting the outside steps at the back of our apartment, as though each movement was an effort. I was never allowed to take the back stairs for fear of rotting boards, an open stair railing where a small body might slip through and tumble down into a yard stacked with egg and milk crates, soft drink bottles, the barrel for burning garbage, cardboard cartons, the things the backsides of shops are composed of. I heard a knock on the door, a glove pulled off, and the sound of the bared knuckles was succinct and sharp as though the person was not asking for admittance but demanding it as a right. The priest's voice calling for Lucille. Their inheld breaths became my inheld breath, my chest paining with their silence while they waited for him to go away.

"Are you asking was our relationship queer?" Lucille asked. "Gay."

"Your mother was just being good to me, that's all."

There was a muffled sound as though Lucille had dropped the receiver and fumbled for it among the blankets.

"I guess he wondered just what she'd be wanting from the likes of me," she said. "It was confession, I suppose. I was pretty naive then. I said what he wanted to hear. But the short of it is that I loved you and your mother very much."

Days after Lucille died of breast cancer, I drove to Lake Winnipeg. I wanted to think of the young Lucille eking out a meagre love from us. I imagined the emaciated, yellow-skinned Lucille — the vivid scarves binding her head, turban style. A different colour every day and earrings to match, my mother said. She had gone to the hospital with her husband, Joe, and the Anglican Book of Common Prayer. The brothers, she said with a scathing tone, had refused to visit Lucille to the very end. Arthur, she said, had six children and a baby-making machine for a wife who had the face of a Pekingese. Though she knew she would be denied burial beside her mother, Lucille had died at peace. And Edgar, a day later in the bachelor apartment where they had lived, was found with seven .22 bullets in his body, the final one entering behind his ear. The police put it down as suicide, my mother said. Seven shots, beats me. Cigar still burning in the ashtray beside the telephone when the police broke down the door. He must have been determined.

She made her bed, I said.

That's not a very charitable thing to say, my mother said, as if she'd never said it.

The sky above the lake was clear and the water calm, only a gentle wash that pulled at the shore. Windsurf boards lay beached on the white sand. From time to time, voices rose from among the dunes behind me. Voices of the nude bathers, I knew, from having stumbled across them in the past, embarrassed more at being clothed than by their nakedness. There was one particular bather I saw often, and he was there, that day, too, wearing nothing more than a deep tan and a Tilley hat. His place to sunbathe was a cleft in a sand dune where a fallen tree allowed him to hang a string hammock. Because of the solitude that the space separating the conventional bathers from the nude ones afforded, I was willing to chance these encounters.

For a year Lucille couldn't find me listed in the telephone book because, rather than paint the walls of my house, I had sold it. With married life over and two children gone to opposite ends of the country, I dug out what perennials I had, planted them in my mother's back garden, and although my grandparents had died long ago, I went looking for them.

Red brick walls tumbling down were all that remained of their house in Ukraine, broken fruit trees, a supposed paradise reduced to chunks of plaster, a tangle of barbed wire; a garden strewn with garbage and pools of glass, thousands of tiny pear-shaped bottles. The map had been drawn from failing memories – a road, and tiny squares on either side of it with family names printed on them, the names of the people who had lived on the same street as my grandparents in the town where I grew up. I was to look for a particular grove of trees, a large oak tree. You will find your grandfather's barn in the north corner of the yard, behind it is the creek, I was told. But of course, the barn was rubble, too, the creek had dried up and was choked with weeds. Somewhere in the garden lay Neta, my grandmother's example of perfection, a whetstone for my mother, an improbable paragon. What sounded like wind in poplar trees filled the air above their yard, the sound of electricity in power lines strung across the valley. Above the village where my grandparents had lived, a colony of summer houses spread up and across gentle hills. Dachas. Small wooden dwellings with not an inch of space more than necessary. Identical to the house my grandfather had built in his new country. He'd built a temporary summer dwelling, a brief respite from the extraneous world and, for a time, he'd let me inside it.

*Just be you,* I remembered, lying on the warm sand of the beach. *Just be you,* my grandfather often said that. But how was it possible not to be imprinted by other people's histories, their secret fears and desires? Whether we accommodated this inheritance or pushed against it as my mother had, the result was the same. I was my mother's daughter. To just be would require a miracle. Circumstance. The right moment, merely a certain kind of pause.

A hot breeze wafted over me and up, swept across the ridges of dunes at my back, drawing cool air from a distant horizon. The nude bather rose from his hammock, strolled to the water and stared across it, scratching a buttock. A gull rose, its flight a phantom moving across the stilled surface of the lake. I closed my eyes to allow the man his privacy. I would have liked to be able to do that, to shed my suit, risk possibilities. Then I felt, rather than heard, his footsteps on the sand. I opened an eye and saw his Tilley hat, the jiggle of his penis as he walked towards me. As his shadow passed across my body, I wished I could let go, let all matters of the mind vanish. The breeze began to blow in from that distant horizon, the water rippling a darker blue, marking the air's advance and crossing, then wisps of white sand began drifting along the beach. The pause was over now as the air reached me, cool against my limbs.

I squinted against the sun and watched how it seemed to break apart and flit off to the right and to the left, how it became globes of yellow light hovering, distorted, then, and blurred by the heat waves.

# Disappearances

ॼ

With the way things were going with his head, Donald thinks this could well end up being their last motoring trip. And so, when they stopped at Virden for gas earlier, he decided to take a southerly route along the U.S. border. Best, he told Frances, to avoid the heavier traffic on the Canada number 1. Donald's intention is to enjoy a more leisurely pace and to delay their arrival in Saskatoon.

There are fewer settlements straddling this highway, and fewer gas stations, and the road looks used up and abandoned. Lambs-quarters clump along the fencelines which form a straggled delineation of the groomed fields beyond and the wilderness that bursts up from the ditches, encroaching on the road with weedy patches of purslane and wild aster. Here, the highway seems a grey corridor, cracked, but inexorably straight and bound for the horizon and the clouds hanging above it. While the landscape makes Frances feel untethered and weightless, Donald feels gathered in, enclosed in a circumference of light. His head will not act up on him here, Donald thinks.

"You'd think there was a bug going around," Frances says. She puts aside a newspaper she's been reading since their stop at Virden for gasoline and to let Buster, their schnauzer, out for a widdle.

"How's that?" Donald inclines a grey shoulder speckled with dandruff, and invites Frances to elaborate. Donald is a grey man in a grey suit. People tell him he resembles Alfred Hitchcock.

"There's another person gone missing," Frances says. "A woman, this time round. Went for a walk three miles down a road to visit her mother and never got there. Had a tiff with the hubby, apparently. She was forty-two. Same age as Marjorie," she adds.

At the mention of their daughter's name Donald blinks rapidly, as though to clear a speck of dust. Rolling hills appear suddenly, greening dromedaries loping towards the horizon. Flat one moment, hilly the next, Donald thinks. The sight of them catches in his throat, and he feels the knot of words stuck there, stories, poems perhaps.

"You recall in winter," Frances says, "there was that man and his son?" So they will not be overtaken by thoughts of Marjorie and the girl, Frances wants to build on the virus theory, a virus that makes people disappear. "The house burned down and no remains were ever found. And then there was that case last autumn. The man who went off to a meeting of some sort. I don't think they've found him, yet."

"A church meeting," Donald says, "if I remember correctly. I think he was a deacon." As Buster, their dog, rearranges himself on the back seat, Donald hears the clink of his chain collar and feels a pang of guilt. He should, for the sake of the dog, turn on the air conditioner. He can take off his suit jacket if it gets too close in the car, but the wee fella, he thinks, can't do anything but bear it.

They approach what was once a homestead, a square of overgrown vegetation with a house in its centre, its windows framing an interior that looks gutted, blackened by age and the elements. Its door, askew on its hinges, gives the appearance of a toothless mouth, wry with objection as they pass by.

"Looks to me like caragana gone wild," Frances says. "It's all they seem to know on the prairie. That, or honeysuckle."

"Likely," Donald says.

From the strict look of the house, its front door gaping in midair, Frances supposes its inhabitants were from among the Galatian or Ukrainian. More than likely. More than likely people who hadn't thought twice about eating gophers during the Depression. Loud-spoken and hot-blooded people who might well have a tiff with the hubby, go for a walk and not return.

Last spring, Frances remembers, according to a newspaper account, a woman in Alberta had gone rolling in mud. She'd returned home after being missing for several days covered in clay and bits of twigs and dried weeds stuck to her hair and clothing. She needed a breather, a family spokesperson had said, and didn't invite further questions. Frances would have loved to be a fly on that wall. Then, there was that winter thing near Saskatoon. The parks person grooming ski trails and hearing a snorting in the underbrush. Thinking it was a deer or something, until he saw the woman's naked body thrashing about in the snow. When Frances read about it, her heart had

been in her mouth, fearing, what with all of Marjorie's problems with the girl, it might be Marjorie who had gone rolling
in snow.

"Frostbite to her extremities," Frances says, and giggles. The
hospital spokesperson had not elaborated. She is caught by her
reflection in the side mirror, a younger face flitting away as soon
as her eyes meet it. She approves of the soft arrangement of
silver curls across her forehead and the cluster of coral at her
ears. The peach top, which she plans on wearing to the pre-
liminary hearing. She simply cannot imagine being inside a
courtroom.

"What was that?"

"Don't forget about those two women, disappeared," Frances
says.

"Which ones would that be?"

"The landscape artists," Frances says, as she has come to refer
to the women. Making mud and snow angels in the wilderness
for others to come upon and wonder what kind of animal had
been there.

"I don't believe," Donald says and stops. They have had this
conversation before, he thinks, or is it *déjà vu*? Or is it one of
those things with his head, beginning to happen?

"Mind you, I could be wrong," Donald says carefully, listening for what he's supposed to say next. "But the landscape
women didn't disappear. They came back, didn't they? You
oughtn't trust my memory, though," he says with a rueful smile,
before she can say it.

"Of course they came back," Frances says. "How else would
the newspaper know they'd been out making their mark?
But it's as though they disappeared because they couldn't

remember a thing about it. Not how they'd got there, or where they'd been. Or why they'd been rolling." Frances has made this point before. She suspects Donald's forgetfulness. She suspects that Donald's fulfilment of the pattern of what happens when a man retires is her punishment for wanting to sell the house and move into the Oaks and Pond enriched housing.

"Yes, I suppose you're right," Donald says. "If they couldn't remember where they'd been, it would seem as though they had disappeared, at least to them, it would."

But Donald can always remember where he's been. He remembers being in the Centennial library paging through back copies of the *National Geographic* and attending a wine and cheese party at the same time. He'd seen himself put in the request for the magazines, heard himself speak to the library clerk while engaging in conversation with someone at a wine and cheese reception. A short woman, a round face turned up to his, framed by a slash of blonde bangs. During the bus ride home from the library, he emerged from both worlds uncertain whether he would find scraps of notes or a cocktail napkin in his pockets. It's as though he sometimes finds himself on both sides of a window, looking out, looking in. What happens is not memory lapse or Alzheimer's, the doctor said, so you can put that worry out of your head. We could do tests, the doctor said, but I'm almost certain we wouldn't find anything. The doctor told Donald about other cases that had come to him recently. A young woman, a professor, he said, whose children noticed she wasn't there and brought her in to see him. She was away for over two hours, the doctor said. It was something he was seeing more and more frequently. Donald wonders if the times are grinding down and glitches are occurring in the system; the creator blinks and laws are suspended and, for moments, some of us are left dangling, he thinks.

"They'll likely be coming down for tea now," Frances says. "It's that time, isn't it?" Sunlight glides across the dashboard; he feels its heat on his hands. They are managing nicely, so far, Donald thinks. There's a bit of a headwind, but still getting around 150 clicks per quarter-tank with the air conditioner shut down. Donald grows anxious whenever the needle on the gauge drops to the halfway point. It comes from being raised on the prairies, Frances used to say, gaily. Years later, Donald hears the apology in her voice when she says it, the regret, an indication that allowances must be made. Perhaps it explains his lumpiness and lack of colour.

"Time for your snooze, you mean," Frances says.

"I just can't get used to tea and visiting in the middle of the afternoon," Donald says, as though it puzzles him why he can't.

Gone only half a day and already Frances misses the apricot brocade armchairs, the mint-green walls, and the satiny sheen of light on water in the pond beyond the lounge windows. A bit of a problem, our Marjorie needs us, Frances had told the doctor. He was a retired general practitioner, another happy inmate of the Oaks and Pond was how he'd introduced himself, as though the doctor knew Marjorie and had been there as she stumbled her way through childhood. Beyond the car window, the humpbacked hills vanish suddenly to a flatness, and oil pumps, prehistoric cranes, poke their beaks into the earth. Frances fears the distance between where they have come from and where they are going to; the trip, the car's wheels thumping against the cracked pavement, white sound covering the rift widening at their backs. If she turns and looks, she'll see tyndal stone cliffs, the Oaks and Pond tumbling into the abyss. The images blur as Frances's eyes fill.

"Donald, for pity's sake, will you just look at yourself, you're dripping," Frances says. "Turn on the danged air conditioner."

"I hadn't thought of that," Donald says. A metaphysical or mystical disappearance, if not an actual one, he thinks.

"May I ask, just what was the point in buying a car with air-conditioning if we never use it?"

As Donald plucks a tissue from a packet clipped to the visor, Frances smells him; body talc, aftershave lotion, a yeasty odour that drycleaning fails to remove from his favourite suit. What was the point in buying the new jackets and slacks at Tip Top? Jackets and ties, suitable attire for the dining room, the director informed them when they'd come for their orientation tour of the Oaks and Pond towers. Dressy pantsuits for the ladies were, of course, acceptable. You folks going on a cruise? the salesman wanted to know, and Donald had said, it's kind of like a cruise, isn't it? Except that you can never get off the ship. Donald's new wardrobe remained in garment bags in his closet.

"I, for one, intend to enjoy what I paid for," Frances says. "Right, Buster?" The dog raises his head, his eyes swivelling across her face.

"Why not crank down the window a bit?" Donald says.

"It'll hit me square in the neck. I'll wind up stiffer than a board."

The air conditioner drones to life and an air-freshener clamped to a vent exudes the spicy scent of lavender.

A ridge of budding trees appears and, above it, mallard ducks. Six drakes, Donald counts, pursuing a female. Must be water beyond the trees.

"How long do you think it'll go on?" Frances asks, as the ducks pass overhead and disappear from view.

"How's that?" Assiniboia, Donald thinks, if he remembers correctly, is the next major town along the way; he'll be able to gas up there, if it gets too low.

"The court hearing."

Donald bunches his hands around the wheel, his grip tightening as the car meets a pothole. He braces himself against the possibility of a deer bounding up from a ditch and into their path, their forward movement stopped abruptly by the solidness of an animal's body.

"I don't rightly know," Donald says.

"I'd like to put that girl over my knee," Frances says. She sees the fiery cloud of the girl's hair, the chin clamped to her chest, an emaciated shoulder jerking away from a touch. Frances recalls the feeling of impotence, of being unable to satisfy, no matter what. It was as though the girl was born not knowing the word *contentment* and was always looking off to the side of every moment, pining for what she imagined she was missing elsewhere.

୬୧

"Just look at all the American clunkers," Frances says as they walk along Main Street in the town, past cars parked diagonally into the curb. As Buster stops to urinate against a building, Donald shoves his hands deep into his jacket pockets and glances up and down the street. A car passes by, and heads turn in their direction.

"Why not let him off the leash?" Donald says. "I don't think anyone would pay any mind." Dogs in prairie towns often run loose behind packs of children, Donald remembers, or imperiously stare down pedestrians from the backs of pickup trucks.

"I haven't got a plastic bag," Frances says, slapping her coat pockets.

"Yes, you're right. Better not. We can stop on the way out of town," Donald says.

"I can't for the life of me imagine anyone wanting to call a place like this home," Frances says, as they continue their stroll. When Donald had left engineering at Dorval airport to teach electronics in various community colleges, he'd had the luxury of uniformity, a community of fellow workers, a common language, while Frances had had to battle it out with Marjorie and Aaron in strange prairie cities. It took some getting used to, after being raised in a city like Montreal. But it's given her a broader view, she thinks, a tolerance for the inconsistencies in people, an ability to live and let live. When she takes inventory, the nights when she lies awake in her new, wide room at the Oaks and Pond, listening to the thrum of traffic on the city bypass, she counts her blessings. She names them out loud. Donald, first of all. She knows she has wound up among the fortunate in life.

As they pass by a store, the door opens and two people emerge. A man, tanned face shiny with perspiration, scowls as he steps into the sunlight. He adjusts his distended paunch as he walks towards them, legs bowed as though by the weight of his blue chequered stomach. A spindly woman skips up from behind him and latches onto his arm. Green plastic earrings the size of bread-and-butter plates, Frances notes, as well as the slash of grey at the woman's part, carrot-coloured hair sticking out from the sides of her head in springy curls. As they meet on the sidewalk in front of a cafe window, the man lurches to a stop and Frances is forced to avoid coming up against his belly. She is aware of people in the cafe, sitting at the window, watching.

"I've got one of those," the man says. He squints at their dog through a spiral of cigarette smoke. "Identical. Same markings and everything."

"Oh, do you?" Frances exclaims and Donald notes the forced brightness. Since their move she dresses beautifully, he knows, as well if not better than most. But she looks and sounds tense, he thinks, like someone uncertain whether or not they have over-dressed for a party.

"It's not the same," the woman says. Her caved-in mouth is an orange smear drawing down at the corners. She tugs at the man's arm to draw him away.

"Identical." But the man's dark eyes waver and slide away from the dog as though he's beginning to have doubts.

"His name is Buster," Frances says. "Schnauzers are such wonderful dogs, aren't they?"

The man clicks his tongue and pats his knee for Buster to come over. His brown and slender fingers rove through the animal's coat and stop to scratch its ears. When he straightens, his breathing is a whistling sound, as though he has a hole in his throat and the air is escaping.

"Yours is not one of them schnauzers. It's a good old Heinz 57," the woman says. The comment is a rebuff intended for Frances. The woman holds a smugness, and her unwillingness to look Frances in the eye is a kind of belligerence. Frances knows she has, for some reason, offended her.

"Did you get yours from a breeder?" Frances asks.

The man struggles to reply and gives up with a look of

impatience. He slaps the air and turns away. "You should bathe it," he mumbles. "I'm going home to do mine, now."

"Yes, it's that time of year, isn't it? Time for the spring grooming," Frances says.

"Lyme disease," the man calls as he crosses the street. "Wood ticks are the dickens. You bathe that mutt if you don't want it getting the Lyme disease."

"Emphysema," Donald says. "He meant well."

Donald notices the women sitting at the table in front of the cafe window, one of them licking an ice cream. He rubs his palms. "This looks like the place to be on a Saturday afternoon," he says. "What do you say we go in and have a bite to eat?"

"It'll be dark before we hit Saskatoon," Frances says. "You know how you are for night driving." A television screen inside the cafe blinks with the light of a baseball game, and when Frances sees it, it occurs to her how a picture would connect them with the girl. A television news report. A picture of Marjorie. Donald and herself, at Marjorie's side, leaving or entering a courtroom.

"All right," Frances says. They could stop at a motel somewhere along the road and stay overnight. A breathing spell, Frances thinks, a bit more time to consider how to prepare Donald.

"Now that's what I call a good dog," one of the women sitting at the table in front of the cafe window calls as they enter. She nods her approval at Buster, who is beside a bicycle rack, his leash lying loose on the pavement beside him.

"Oh, he's good when he wants to be," Frances says. "But if he takes a notion not to, let me tell you," she says, and rolls her eyes, grateful for the woman's generosity.

The three women nod and smile knowingly, and for a

moment, Frances fears they may invite them to share their table. She notices their similar hairstyles, permed and clipped to sharp points at the ear, teased high on the forehead, their oversize T-shirts drawing attention to their trouble spots. A man and a boy sit at one of several tables along a wall. Across from it is a counter, a high glass case, which, except for a plate of bran muffins, appears empty.

Frances chooses a table beside the door so she can watch Buster. Wall panelling near the ceiling has swelled and sprung loose at the seams, and the floor tiles, maroon and grey, are rippled and chipped. The cafe feels temporary, Frances thinks, a summer place given over to the frost in winter. Vegetarian burrito, the lunch special of the day, is posted on a chalkboard and, as Frances sees it, she suddenly feels hungry.

"You folks are from Manitoba," the ice-cream-eating woman says. She nods in the direction of their Accord parked across the street.

"From Winnipeg," Frances says.

"Winnipeg," another of the trio says, "I've never been there. Not yet, anyways."

"We're heading up to Saskatoon," Donald says, and Frances sends him a darting, cautionary look.

"Saskatoon," the women repeat, as though they find it surprising anyone would want to go there.

"It's a beautiful city," Donald says. He likes walking early in the morning with Marjorie along the river. He likes the way the river bisects the city, its connecting bridges. He thinks of silt drifting, a mirror reflecting the glass towers and church spires.

"I've got a sister lives in Winnipeg," the woman who eats the ice-cream says. "In West Kildonan."

"West Kildonan can be very nice," Frances says. "Lots of trees there."

"Water beds in every room," the woman continues, as though Frances hasn't spoken. "I couldn't get a proper night's sleep because of it. That and the noise of traffic."

The man sitting at the table with the boy snorts at this. "I wouldn't give you a dime for one of those things. Harder on the back than anything. You can't beat a futon for the back."

The three women nod. "Or a piece of plywood under the mattress."

"Pretty far south for Saskatoon, aren't you?" the man asks Donald. A hard-looking small man with a day's growth of beard so dark it looks blue. The boy with him turns sideways in his seat and stares at Frances.

The boy has the same skin as the girl had when she was his age, Frances notices, the colour of skim milk; she can see the veins in his neck shining through it. It was as though the girl was determined to be undernourished, different, just for the sake of it. The air moved when she entered rooms, a blur of motion. Flying up the stairs to change her clothes, pester Marjorie for money, and be off again. Hi, Gran Whitmore. A cool, meagre little mouth set against Frances's chin, a smile that opened up only wide enough to display her front teeth. A mouth shaped like her own.

"You doing home schooling again this year, Fred?" a clear, young voice calls out from behind the counter, startling Frances.

"You can bet on it," the man called Fred answers, "Plan on keeping Joey with me for as long as I can. Right, buddy?"

The child, still turned in his chair, nods, dark eyes steady on Frances's face. There is something not quite right, Frances thinks. His eyes. The way his heavy eyebrows flare up like wings.

"I sure admire you for that," the voice behind the counter calls out.

"Oh, this place must be self-serve," Frances says, apologetic, as though they've been in error for assuming to be waited on.

"Shelley, you've got customers," one of the women says, and a young face peers across the glass counter, bushy hair caught up in a ponytail at the back of her head.

"Tell me what you'd like, old girl, and I'll go on over and order it," Donald says, rising, clamping a hand around Frances's shoulder, giving it a light squeeze.

Frances senses the women's attentiveness, a stillness. She leans on her arms, fingers clasped and at rest against the table. The fullness of her brushed silk skirt drapes from her hips in gentle folds. Frances knows she was never beautiful, her face is far too long and bony, her eyes set too deeply for that. Handsome at times, graceful, she hopes, brave enough to have attempted elegance, even when in her early twenties and lugging groceries, a squirming Marjorie under the arm, Aaron hanging on to her coattail, three floors to their walk-up in Montreal.

Donald returns to the table, dabbing at his forehead with a handkerchief. Too pale, Frances thinks. It's as though his features are layered with white dust and blunted. Donald is shedding, dissolving at the edges, becoming translucent.

"They're out of the special," Donald says.

"It's all right, dear," Frances says, because he looks worried. "Why don't we share a burger?" It's her fault, she thinks, for being too optimistic, hoping she'd get anything else in a place like this.

"With or without onions," Donald wants to know.

"Without." As he returns to the counter, Frances notes how his suit jacket has creased from the trip and rides up his back.

She packed his blazer with the Legion crest on its breast pocket. She had decided to wear a mother-of-pearl pendant with the peach top. She thought it couldn't do any harm; that it might make an impression, for Marjorie's sake. The closer they get to Saskatoon, the more she recognizes the weakness of her thinking, the frivolity of it, as if their presence in the courtroom counted a hoot in the scheme of things. Except for Marjorie, of course. Since this latest episode, Frances can't bring herself to say the girl's name. Can't imagine them ever having been related.

"Would you be wanting mustard and relish?" Donald asks, startling Frances.

"Oh, Don, for goodness' sake," Frances says. "You should know by now." She attempts a bit of laughter for the sake of the women who, she knows, are listening. Men do that, she wants to confide in them, as he returns to the counter. They conveniently escape into clogged arteries and foggy memories, leaving us to take care of the details.

Donald returns once again. "The grill's turned off," he says.

Frances raises her chin, and her eyes become the colour of pewter. "That's strange," she says. "I seem to remember this place had a sign on it outside that said, SNACK BAR."

"Shelley's Lunch Bar," the young woman behind the counter says, and Frances recognizes the eyes have gone wide with a feigned innocence, a mocking smile lingering beneath the surface.

"May I enquire if you have tomatoes?"

"I think so." The girl nods and flounces her ponytail for emphasis.

"And do you have bread?"

"Yah. Likely."

"We could go somewhere else," Donald says.

"Well, if it's not too inconvenient, we'll have a tomato sandwich," Frances says.

"The Duchess of Windsor with a shovel up her bum," the ice-cream-eating woman says *sotto voce* as she lights a cigarette. The women's breasts jiggle as they chuckle silently and become preoccupied with the appearance of someone passing in the street.

Though her neck stings with heat, Frances tells herself she does not need their approval. It has become unnecessary at this point. There is no virtue in playing down to win the approval of anyone, she thinks. This is what the Oaks and Pond has given her. A community of the fortunate who are not inclined to apologize for it. And why should they? she thinks.

"Would that be with, or without, mayo," the young woman says.

"And I'll have an ice cream cone," the boy chirps at Donald.

"Hey, button 'er up there," the man called Fred says to the boy. His gruffness is filled with pride.

"I'd like to do that," Donald says. "Let me treat the lad."

The child slides from his chair and goes over to the glass case next to Donald. He peers down into the glass counter at the tubs of ice cream. Donald feels the heat of the child radiate against his leg.

"What'll it be, big fella?" Donald says. A ceiling fan turns, and he hears the soft whirring sound of it, the sound of the television, the roar of the crowd. *I'll have vanilla*, Donald hears himself say, years ago. He's in another room, similar, but the light has changed as though a blind has been drawn on the window. He sees a grainy silhouette of a man wearing a billed cap, standing in front of it.

"I want lime and I want chocolate chip," the boy says.

"Here now, one scoop, you little beggar," the father calls from the table.

Donald hears denim whisper, sees a hand spotted with cinnamon-coloured freckles emerge from a pocket, a coin rests in callused folds; he inhales and smells the familiar dusty odour of alfalfa, the sweat of horse in the denim coveralls of the man standing beside him. Donald wants strawberry, he wants lemon, so why does the word "vanilla" always come out?

"Why not have both?" Donald says to the boy.

A hand comes towards Donald, bearing ice cream, and Donald reaches up, as tall as he can make himself, to receive it.

"Do you folks have relatives in Saskatoon?" the young woman asks, as she hands a double-decker cone to the boy.

The grainy silhouette of the man in front of the window fades.

"Yes," Donald says. He blinks at the sight of a shelf lined with food containers, a clock above it emerging where the other world vanished. It leaves me bewildered, he told the doctor. But it's not the right word to describe what he feels when this happens. Discombobulated, he'd said, to make light of it. It's as though he has been held between sleep and waking, or being and not being.

"So, do you go up to visit them often?"

Donald sees the girl's red mouth moving.

"Who?"

"Your relatives in Saskatoon."

"Yes," Donald says. "My daughter and granddaughter." He

is relieved, as the room jumps forward with clarity, brightness of light and sharp edges. Sunlight glances off arborite, cigarette smoke trails across the windowpane.

"My daughter, Marjorie, and Samantha. Prokipchuk," Donald says, forgetting what he is not to say.

"Samantha Prokipchuk?" the child's father asks. The question holds the room still. Donald feels their faces turn away, hears the clink of the chain on the ceiling fan against the metal blades.

"Yes," Donald says.

"That's not the same girl who beat that old couple to death up in Saskatoon?" the man says.

She was not alone, Donald wants to say. There were two others, boys. She happened to be at the wrong place at the wrong time with the wrong kind of people. He sees Frances rise and flee, the dog scrambling after her, its leash trailing. Donald sees the flap of Frances's blue skirt, her flat heels kicking pale blue waves as she runs across the street.

୭ ୧

"I wish I could die," Frances cries. Her voice is ripe with phlegm. She wishes for the oblivion of unconsciousness, and yet she clings to her skirt, its blue silk bunched in her fists and twisted into knots. Frances hangs on for dear life, or risks flying from the face of the earth.

Donald watches a row of sparrows lift from a telephone wire; the birds' wings, jittery dark commas, hook for a piece of the sky. Bewildered, Donald thinks, lost; he has seen the worry in the girl's eyes on family get-togethers, as though she knew she should be able to make sense out of a room full of people, but failed to. He sees the scuffed underside of her shoes as she climbs the steps of a slide in a playground. He remembers her fierce concentration on the ride down it, her noisy objection to being caught in his arms. There are many things Donald does not understand because he has not been made privy to them. He has been spared, he knows, the details of Marjorie's unlucky choice in husbands. Samantha's growing truancy and shoplift-ing. The drugs. Day-care, Donald thinks, a poor substitute. Television. Food allergies; he has often wondered. He keeps remembering her as a lurching, determined child and can't believe she is guilty.

"Turn this car around," Frances says. "We're not going to Saskatoon."

"It doesn't matter what those people think, Fran. They're strangers. We'll never see them again."

"As if it was only that," Frances says. "Oh, god. Think of it, Donald. Manslaughter," she says, her voice breaking. Man slaughter, Frances thinks, and feels her body go rigid. The word, split open like that, brings the taste of blood to her mouth. A man bludgeoned with a tire iron, a baseball bat, his attackers' boots. The woman's windpipe broken by a telephone receiver.

Frances and Donald had watched the newscast, had seen the police rolling out the stretchers, the mounds in body bags, a man with a large stomach, the woman stricken with arthritis. Chosen because they were defenceless, Frances had said, and thank god for the security system, the video cameras and guards at the Oaks and Pond. Frances and Donald had clamped their jaws shut at the sight, not knowing there would be any connection to them.

"If you don't turn around, I'll jump out of this car," Frances says. She draws away as Donald tries to touch her.

"Marjorie needs us."

"You know what Marjorie needs," Frances says, bitterly, "What Marjorie needs is our chequebook." Once a parent, always a parent, the retired general practitioner had said; even on the deathbed, the kids are either demanding you live or die, for their sake. But there are limits, Frances believes. It begins with a man and a woman and it should end that way.

"We will do what we have to do," Donald says.

"We are not going to throw good money after bad."

"She's one of ours, Fran."

"Jesus bloody Murphy," Frances says, her voice rising. "She helped kill two people, Donald."

"We don't know that," Donald says, so softly Frances can barely take it in. "That's what this hearing is about."

"We know," Frances says. "I know. Marjorie knows."

Donald is drawn by the clouds hanging above the watery horizon; the slice of moon, its faint horns defining the space between them. Don't, Donald thinks. Please don't.

He will soon find out anyway, she thinks. There is no way around it. "They found hair. Blood and tissue. On the girl's boots."

The drone of the engine fills Donald's head, circles around and around his brain, echoes in his ears; telephone poles spring up from the earth and fling themselves at him. Trees topple backwards into the horizon.

"Of course. She was there, but that doesn't mean . . . ," he says. "Does it?" It sounds like a plea and not a question.

"And fingerprints. Hers. On the receiver of the telephone.

Look, whether or not we believe it won't change a thing," Frances says. "Facts are facts and we have to face up to them."

Donald pinches his eyelids, rubs them to ease the strain. Jack Sprat could eat no fat, Donald thinks, his wife could eat no lean. The words of the rhyme come to him, unbidden.

"Why do you think Marjorie needs the best money can buy? They'll plead not guilty, but she *is* guilty."

Something moves beyond, on the shoulder of the highway, as Frances speaks. A brown spot, Donald thinks, and watches to see if the light will dim or rise, for the colours of whatever place will emerge from the highway in front of the car. The spot jiggles, grows elongated, becomes a strange-looking creature.

"Look," Frances says, as she sees the creature, too. What appear to be coattails flap as it lopes down the shoulder towards them. Then the animal begins to run, an awkward but resolute sideways gallop, as though having confirmed its recognition of them it hurries now to greet them. What looked like coattails become gangly limbs and a tasselled tail, flying in all directions.

"It's a calf," Donald says, and his shoulders drop with relief. He steers the car onto the shoulder and stops.

Frances sees its pricked ears come forward, a startled look, and then the animal lowers its head, as though disappointed. The calf backs into a ditch and stands halfway down among the reeds, studying them. Buster leaps up and sniffs at the window.

"It must have got out through a hole in a fence," Donald says, as he notices a herd of cattle in a pasture beyond. He gets out of the car.

Was that it? Frances wonders. A matter of a hole in a fence, inattentiveness?

The calf stands shoulder-deep among the reeds, and as Donald comes round to the front of the car, the animal sees him and begins to swing its head, backing away, deeper into the rushes.

"It'll wind up hit by a car," Donald says to Frances, who has rolled down the window. He looks for a stone, finds one, and pockets it.

"There's not been a whole lot of traffic, so far," Frances says.

"A man loses a calf, it could mean his profit for the entire year," Donald says. He begins wading, thigh-deep, through the weeds along the edge of the ditch. He means to give the animal lots of room, skirt around it and get it in the rump. The animal stands motionless, peering out at Donald, as though calculating what he will do next.

"For pity's sake, Donald, there's likely water down there," Frances calls. "You'll ruin your shoes."

The whine in Frances's voice sets Donald's teeth on edge. He would like to smash something. Slam his fist down hard, punch a hole in a window.

"They're my shoes, Frances, and if you don't mind, I'll take the risk of ruining them."

His anger sets Frances's heart racing. It's unfair, she thinks, to take it out on her. Put it where it belongs, squarely on the girl's shoulders.

As Donald steps lower down into the rushes he doesn't feel the chilly water filling his shoes and rising to his shins. He sees patches of the animal, a flank, its taffy ribs heaving. A cow moos, a baleful groan from among the herd on the other side of the highway. Over there, you little bugger, Donald thinks. He heaves the stone and it flies too far, splashing down beyond the animal. The calf swings away from the sound and crashes through the reeds towards him. Grab an ear, Donald thinks. Both ears, turn it by the head, and send it up past the car and onto the other side. He smells the animal's heat, sees in its limpid eyes a blindness brought on by fear.

"Here, boss!" Donald calls and waves his arms. "Go! Over there! Here, boss! Go, boss!" The calf stumbles and lunges towards him, the reeds flattening as the animal's legs fold up beneath it and it goes down. "Go!" Donald shouts, as the rank water swirls around its silky brown neck. The animal snorts, and frothy bubbles clump its nostrils and mouth. "Get! You get!" Donald says, not realizing he is weeping as he grabs hold and feels its ears, warm flaps of skin and gristle in his hand. The animal scrambles up, its flanks dripping algae and mud. It shakes his hands off and backs away and, for a moment, Donald fears it means to charge him, but it veers around him, up and out of the ditch. Donald stands for moments, watching, aware now of the chill and wetness creeping in, and he shivers. The calf lopes across an open field, growing smaller. Then a silence moves in, a stillness he has heard only on the prairies. A quiet so intense and full that he used to think he could scoop it out of the air and cup it in his hands. A red-winged blackbird flits down onto a fencepost. The calf stops, turns to look at Donald, raises its head in a plaintive bellow. Go on, you little bugger, Donald thinks. Make a noise, it's not going to get you where you want to go.

His chest tightens from exertion as he climbs out of the ditch. He notices a house down the highway, a bungalow half-concealed by trees. The least he can do is let someone know they have a calf on the loose. His shoes squelch with water and sour-smelling muck smears the car seat as he slides across it.

"The silly thing would sooner go up a chimney," he says. "I tried, but it wasn't having anything to do with it."

Frances sees the soft pleat of skin beside his mouth, the nest of grey hair inside his ear, his chest rising and falling as he waits to catch his breath. She sees him as he must have been as a boy in a country school, dozy from being up early with morning chores, chewing on a ragged sweater cuff. Solid, profoundly loyal.

"We've got to get you out of those wet trousers," she says.

"Yes," Donald says. "Yes."

The farmyard they drive onto is weedy, spotted with patches of mallow, the grey earth trampled by feet and worn to a shine. The bungalow sits on a slight rise, straw bales banked up its sides. It exudes stillness; the windows reflect the clouded sky. Children's toys, bright pieces of plastic, lie scattered beyond the back step as though the children were called suddenly from their play. Frances notices a brackish dug-out pond off to the side of the car, set down against a backdrop of white birch. Its surface, black and oily-looking, suggests a great depth. And no fence, Frances thinks, noting the children's toys lying about the yard. Is it any wonder, she thinks, the frequency of the accounts of farm accidents? Words, warnings, were not enough to keep a curious or determined child away. Or a fence, either, for that matter; an attraction to some.

She watches Donald standing on the back steps, hands on his hips, gazing across the yard as though he expects an answer to his knock may emerge from the shed in a field beyond the garden. Alfred Hitchcock, Frances thinks. A rumpled man in a grey suit. Ashes holding the shape of what was once a solid chunk of wood. Daydreaming, or forgetting more than likely, why he'd gone to the door in the first place.

And I am not the Duchess of Windsor, Frances thinks. But

no matter how she tries, the rigid stance is there, she knows. She knows too well how she appears to others. She has never been able to do much about their misconceptions but accept them.

"Don!" Frances calls. It's somewhat like learning of an unexpected pregnancy, she thinks. The dread, fear, anger perhaps, but then you get on with it. What choice do you have? And it's inevitable, they *will* get on with the trip to Saskatoon. It pains her to think what it may cost in the end. But they will do it. He's right, she thinks, Samantha is ours, like it or not. She can only hope for explanations for the evidence, reasons she can grow into and come to believe. She must remember the child, how she enjoyed holding her. As much as one of her own. She recalls the girl's energy, her spirit beating against its cage of bones. She could feel it in her own hands. Frances used to think she understood the perplexed look in Samantha's green eyes, a pleading for acceptance and understanding.

As he comes down the stairs and begins to walk across the yard, Donald waves, wearing a smile that is wide and sunny and crinkles his eyes. Frances thinks he may have read her mind, and is pleased that she has decided they will do what Marjorie expects of them. His step becomes energetic, jaunty even, as his arms swing and the sodden, stained trousers flap about his muddied shoes. He waves again, and calls hello. Frances returns his wave, but he seems to be looking beyond her and so she turns, expecting to see someone, the owner perhaps, coming through the white birch beyond the pond.

Donald feels a chilly autumn wind off the lake. Grey pebbles roll underfoot as he carries a jacket for Aaron, a sweater for

Marjorie, both of whom are hunched like spotted toads at the end of the pier, absorbed in counting their toes, Donald supposes, or perhaps a fish has just glided into the shadows near the dock.

Frances rolls down the window and searches the stand of birch where its leaves, dots of light, begin to flutter as a breeze moves in from the fields. Leaves flipping white and then silver and white again, stippling the surface of the black water with light as Donald marches towards the dug-out pond, his grey shoulders squared. She thinks she hears Donald whistling, but it's not that, it can't be. Donald has never whistled.

"Don!" Frances calls, unable to take in what she sees, Donald's forward motion, his lack of hesitancy as his feet rise and fall. She sees how they lift, how they come down. She sees the outline of his thin legs in the wet trousers, his hips, his waist, shoulders. She sees Donald, disappearing.

# Rooms for Rent

❧

When the doorbell rang at seven o'clock in the morning, Lila Sanders was about to submerge herself in a bath. She stood for a moment percolating with indecision, one foot plunged into a froth of warm bubbles, the other planted firmly on the floor. She urged herself to ignore it, not to risk a pounding heart from rushing down the stairs to reach the front door before the caller walked away. But as the doorbell rang once again, she reached for her nightshirt lying in a silk puddle on the bathroom floor. She was of that generation who are compelled to answer a knock, a ringing doorbell or telephone.

As Lila crossed the hallway to go into the spare bedroom and to the window, whoever was at her front door began jabbing at the bell button. The sound of it bristled sharply above the door leading to the third floor and the two large rooms that Jim had converted into a television room and a hobby room. Jim had put the bell's ringer on the second floor so that the sound of it would echo in the upper hall where his rooms were and down in the hallway on the first floor. Wherever they were in the house they were able to hear it. But the bell echoed too brightly in the rooms on the third floor; they were empty now except for a fold-down couch she'd hung on to because she liked the smell of it. The ringing finally stopped, and as she hurried towards the window she heard the murmur of voices below and then, "Shit!" and a thump against the door as someone kicked it.

Half a dozen people were on the boulevard staring at her house. Several men, unshaven and sour-faced, looking like they'd just tumbled from bed, and women with uncombed hair, one pushing a baby in a stroller back and forth to soothe its cries, waited on the sidewalk. An accident, Lila thought. Perhaps they wanted her to call for an ambulance or the police. The window, swollen from recent rainfall, shivered in its frame as she lifted it. "What is it?" she called, and looked down into the upturned face of a man with a long white ponytail and bright yellow T-shirt.

"The ad says seven a.m.," he said, and held up a newspaper and shook it at her. A woman moved out from the overhang of the verandah roof and Lila wondered if she'd been the one who had kicked the door. The woman's cloud of maroon hair had a metallic sheen to it in the early-morning sun, and when she looked up, Lila saw that the woman's mouth was purple like her hair, her eyes heavily rimmed with turquoise, and she'd painted an orange and yellow butterfly on her cheek. "We've been here since six o'clock," the woman said.

"This is seven seventy-five Westminster?" the man said, and once again rattled the newspaper. "It says seven seventy-five."

Probably an advertisement for a garage sale, Lila thought. "It must be a mistake," she said. "I'll be right down."

As she pulled her rain-and-shine coat from the wardrobe in the downstairs hall, she thought about garage sales and how they used to be an adventure, would mean a leisurely bicycle ride through the neighbourhood beneath an arch of elm trees on a Saturday morning, stopping here and there to sort through other people's white elephants and belongings that had become outdated or redundant; stopping to admire a garden, a new fence or add-on. Now, the people who came to garage sales bickered rather than bargained over prices, cursed and stalked from the yard if they'd been unsuccessful. There were garage sales in the middle of the week, and on Sherbrook and Broadway streets several people had begun to hold them as often as five times a week. Lila would look the other way as she walked past these depressing displays of used clothing strung along fences and the litter of broken toys and grease-encrusted cookware scattered about on car blankets. Although she didn't believe kicking away at doors was warranted, she knew the people waiting outside were desperate. Desperate for a bargain, she thought, and, as she slipped the coat over the nightshirt, tying it firmly at the waist, she decided she would speak softly and kindly. She went out into the verandah.

"It says here under 'Rooms for Rent, Furnished,'" the man with the long white ponytail said once again, his voice like a dog snapping at her face. "'TV, Carpet, clean. Welfare recipients, pets, children welcome. Rent Negotiable.' See?" he said, and jabbed his finger at a column in the want ads.

Several others had joined what was a crowd now, standing on Lila's front lawn, their impatient murmuring punctuated by the sound of a grocery cart, its bent wheels clacking against the sidewalk as the young woman pushing it hurried towards Lila's house, the cart stacked with cardboard cartons and a cat's scratching post lying on top. She dragged along a cat crate on a rope and it scraped harshly against the cement, making Lila's throat suddenly feel raw.

"There's been a mistake," Lila said. She opened the verandah's screen door intending to stand on the top step and tell them all loudly and clearly that there were no rooms for rent. It was all a mistake. I'm very sorry, but there are no rooms for rent, she was going to say when the woman with the maroon hair lunged for the door.

"*We* have references," the woman said as she wedged a bulging handbag in the door. "I'm sure they don't," she said, indicating the people on the boulevard. Then she squeezed through the opening and into the verandah, pulling the man with the pony-tail in behind her. The people outside moved forward, protesting angrily.

The woman stood for a moment, flushed and panting, and Lila noticed that the butterfly on her cheek glistened with moisture and a wet circle of perspiration ringed the underarm of her cobalt blue tunic. "Look. Someone has made an error," Lila said, "I do not have any rooms for rent."

"Come on, lady, we've got a right to see the rooms, too," a man called to Lila through the screen door. He glared at her, hands on his hips; a weightlifter, she thought, from the size of his chest and narrow waist. He wore a black tank top lettered in white across his chest, Z.T.O.H. She had seen him before, walking past the house as she'd sat out one morning in the verandah eating her bowl of Shredded Wheat and doing the crossword. She'd noticed him in particular because of the way he had studied her house as he passed by. Others looked at it too, admired it, she knew, especially now when the front gardens looked so much like brides, the way the white peonies and Queen Anne's lace, the ferns billowed from them. But when this man had passed by she'd noticed that he studied the house with a shrewdness, eyed the alarm horn jutting out from under the eaves, and she had said to herself, "Never you mind. You just keep going right on by, mister."

"It's all a mistake," Lila said, her voice barely a whisper as he stepped inside the verandah. This is a bad dream, she thought, I'll wake from it and find myself in bed. The man's skin was silvery-looking, his whole body, she was sure, silver with faded tattoos, his movements jerky, apelike. From behind her came the sound of the front door closing, and a *thud!* as the deadbolt shot into place. She realized with a start that this wasn't a dream. She was locked out of her house and the man with the ponytail and the woman with the butterfly painted on her cheek were inside it.

"It's no mistake," the burly man said. "There are empty rooms in this house. Rooms you can't possibly use." Then he thrust his face in hers and she could smell something sweet come off his body. The smell of baby talcum powder. "You think you have the right to live alone in a house this big when there are home-less people?" he asked. Then he strode to the locked door and began pounding on it. "Open up. Let us in. These people outside have the right to see those rooms, too," he shouted.

His comment was a slap across Lila's face and heat rose in her cheeks. "I beg your pardon," she said, "but I have every right to live alone in this house. I own it." Her retort was lost as several

other people began to push and shove their way into the verandah, yelling, complaining, and shaking their fists at one another.

"There are no rooms for rent, no rooms," Lila shouted. She
could smell their bodies as they crowded around her, bodies
acrid with perspiration, cigarette smoke, the metallic odour of
the dye in their cheap clothing and cologne, onions, the sour
odour of an empty stomach, the smell of road dust.

"Mrs. Flipjack!" Lila cried as she fled across the street. "Mrs.
Flipjack! Mrs. Flipjack!"

The door was already opening as Lila ran up the sidewalk to
Rosa Filipczak's house. Rosa stood waiting for her on the top
step, her flowered head-scarf knotted under her chin, holding
in place, it seemed, Rosa's perpetual childlike smile. Beside her,
propped in the front window, was the hated sign; a black sign
with red and gold lettering: SATURN ALTERATIONS. MEN
AND WOMEN'S APPAREL. It was the first thing Lila saw
every morning when she opened the venetian blinds on the
living-room window to let in the morning sun. Rosa let the back
rooms of her house to a tailor and received an extra ten dollars
a month for displaying the sign. Lila knew she would be within
her rights to object – the street was not zoned for commercial
use – but she had kept silent. Industrious, hard workers, clean,
Jim had said when the Filipczaks had moved in across the street,
we could do worse for neighbours.

"Call the police," Lila said.

Rosa's smile dissolved into worried reluctance. Her eyes
shifted from Lila's face and she began to twist at a button on
her sweater.

"*I'll* call the police," Lila said, remembering the older woman's
inherited mistrust of any official, any person wearing a uniform.

Lila had never been inside Rosa Filipczak's house before. They had been across-the-street neighbours since 1960 but the broad street between them might as well have been several miles wide. They had only viewed with mild curiosity across that distance the rituals of their lives. Children growing to adulthood, their graduations and weddings. But loneliness was a word they both understood, and it was the death of their husbands, Rosa's a year earlier than Lila's, that had finally brought them face to face one day in Vimy Ridge Park at a picnic table, conversing, Rosa in broken English, half Polish, Lila surprised at how much she could understand, filling in the gaps of Rosa's understanding of her English with hand gestures and pantomime.

But all Lila knew of the place where Rosa lived was the plants lining the front window in the winter and the row of ceramic cats that replaced them in spring. More recently, and all year round, there was the tailor's hated sign. She knew Rosa's backyard from riding past it on her bicycle, its clothesline crackling with plastic bags Rosa had rinsed clean and hung out to dry, her immaculately turned-out vegetable garden. Rosa had also begun to blue-box, which Lila had found surprising because recycling was not mandatory and only a few in the neighbourhood, mostly people with young families, seemed to bother. And so when Lila stepped inside Rosa's house she wasn't prepared, and for a moment her urgent intention to call the police vanished. There were flowers, everywhere. Absolutely everywhere. From floor to ceiling, all four walls of Rosa's large front room were painted with daisies, nasturtiums, tulips, hyacinths, hollyhocks, daffodils, morning glory vines twisting through them; flowers Lila didn't recognize, vibrating with colour.

"Over there," Rosa said, indicating a small table covered in painted poppies. The telephone sat in the centre on a round doily.

"Yes, I see," Lila said, not wanting to stare, trying to take in the whole room at once, the light of a candle flickering at the base of a framed picture of the Black Madonna, and for several moments she couldn't turn away from the serious look of the Virgin. Then Lila recognized a photograph of a younger Władek, Rosa's husband, set on one side of the Virgin, with a picture of the Pope on the other. She became aware, too, of a cloth hanging on the wall above the picture. Pinned to it were shiny votive metals, twinkling in the light of the candle; an altar of some kind, Lila thought, too depressing. As she crossed the room to the telephone, the walls became a kaleidoscope turning with vivid flowers, the patterns changing.

"Please, you must sit," Rosa pleaded, bringing a chair on whose seat bloomed a vivid needlepoint sunflower.

"Is this an emergency?" Lila wondered aloud. She had never called 911.

"No one's dying," Rosa said.

"Illegal entry into my house," Lila said and picked up the receiver.


"That's all I can tell you," the policeman said to Lila. "We'll send a car as soon as possible. We respond according to the emergency of the situation and right now there are other calls that must be given priority. You must understand, we'll do the best we can."

"You understand," Lila said, aware that Rosa was standing

behind her, listening. "I'm locked out of my house and there are these two people, total strangers, inside it. Do you hear me?" Outside, a man's voice rose above the voice of the crowd that had now gathered, and then Lila heard the sound of glass shattering. "They're breaking my windows," Lila shouted.

"We'll try and get there as soon as possible," the policeman said, and the line went dead.

Rosa was already standing at the front door looking out through the lace curtains on the window when Lila, shivering and panting, got there. The woman with the stroller had spread a blanket and had laid her crying child down on the grass. She and another woman were wading through the front flower beds, yanking the heads off the peonies and throwing them out at the crowd, who egged the women on. The ponytail man in the yellow T-shirt stood at the railing on the second-floor deck over the verandah, raising a finger to the people below. Behind him, bedroom sheers billowed through a shattered pane of glass.

"Stop it! Stop it!" Lila cried from the door, moving quickly down the steps. Her terry mule slippers slapped against her feet as she strode across Rosa's lawn shouting.

"Can it!" the silvery-skinned man shouted at the crowd. He stood on the top step, hands cupped to his mouth. "Listen to me! Everybody shut the fuck up and listen. We want rooms, not a jail cell! Next person throws a rock, they get a rock in the head."

"Who says?" someone yelled.

"Me," the man said, shaking his fist, "and the Zero Tolerance of Homelessness Committee. I said, can it!" he screamed at the two women dancing in the flower bed and they froze, peonies dropping from their hands. "Sorry, ma'am," he called, and bowed in Lila's direction. "But there's a point to be made here today."

The crowd turned and stared at Lila, who was stricken by the sight of shredded peony blossoms like white confetti across the lawn. The belt of her rain-and-shine coat trailed across the grass and the coat gaped open, revealing the peacock-blue shirt, the swell of Lila's large breasts and stomach against the soft silk, her chubby white knees.

The patio doors on the second-floor deck slid open again and now the woman with the maroon hair stepped out onto it. "Hello!" she called across the street when she saw Lila. "Can you tell me where you keep the bed linens? There aren't any on this bed in here."

"That's my pinwheel crystal!" Lila cried. "What are you doing with my pinwheel crystal?"

The woman looked down at the bowl in her hands and then, as though remembering why she had come out, offered it to the man. "Popcorn," she yelled, "I microwaved some popcorn."

Hungarian, Lila thought suddenly. The woman's maroon hair and mouth reminded her of the Hungarian refugees who arrived by the thousands during the mid-1950s. Desolate and outraged people with sad or angry faces, and full-lipped women with hair the burgundy colour of wine. Just then, a battered red van, spray-painted with peace signs and the letters Z.T.O.H., veered sharply into the curb and braked to a stop. Two sinewy-looking men wearing khaki shorts and T-shirts jumped from it, opened the back doors, and began heaving nylon bundles onto the boulevard.

"Go home!" Lila shouted. "All of you, please leave and go home!"

The crowd fell silent. "You think we'd be here if we had someplace else to go?" someone muttered.

"Get off my property," Lila said, loudly and firmly. "I have called the police."

The young woman with the grocery cart filled with cardboard cartons had let the cat out of its crate and the orange tabby nibbled at food set down in a dish. She scooped the animal up quickly as though frightened that Lila might harm it. "You think because you bought and paid for this place that you own it? You think that you can actually own a piece of the earth?" she said. "That's so . . . so — WASPy, if you ask me. So typically Eurocentric. You're nothing but a has-been android!" she spat.

"Hoo-hoo," Rosa called to Lila. "Mrs. Sanders, please, please, you should come inside. Come, I'll find something for you to wear, make it some coffee. Please, it's no good to stand on the damp ground in your slippers."

"I would have had my face slapped twice if I'd talked to an adult like that. By the person I'd spoken to, and then by my parents when they found out," Lila said to Rosa, who stood in the bedroom doorway, back turned, waiting. As Lila stepped into a pair of the elderly woman's acetate bloomer-style underpants, she avoided looking at the crotch dangling at her knees, not wanting to see a speck of anything that might be there.

"I agree," Rosa said. "Canadian children are spoiled. They need it good spanking."

Lila looked at her sharply, hearing in the words what she'd always suspected and resented about the Filipczaks. How they viewed themselves as being Polish first, Canadian second. Even though Rosa's children had been born in this country, they had spoken their parents' language in the home. Most of their friends had been either relatives or people from other Polish families; and ever since it had become possible to travel freely to Poland they'd begun to send Rosa photographs taken during their frequent pilgrimages to her birthplace.

"I have every right to live in my house alone," Lila said as she stepped out of the nightshirt and reached for the dress Rosa had draped across one of the beds. "It's my house. Jim and I worked hard for it. We saved and paid out the mortgage sooner than we needed to so we could afford to live on Jim's pension," she said and felt her heart squeeze with worry the way it had begun to every time she talked about managing on her finances. "I could leave that house empty if I wanted to," she said, "and it would be nobody's business but mine."

Rosa's solution to inflation had been to turn her upstairs rooms into a suite that she rented to university students and let out the back rooms on the main floor to a tailor from Central America. That left Rosa with two rooms and the kitchen. "Ahhh, what do I need all that room for," Rosa had explained to Lila in Vimy Ridge Park. "In Poland we lived in one room. Some families still live in one room," she'd said with a sigh. "Yes, but that's why you came here, isn't it?" Lila had protested. "You came to have a better life, didn't you?" "I no need it more room," Rosa had said, brushing her comment aside, and Lila had thought how sad it must be for her, and how brave Rosa was being.

"*Bardzo ładnie,*" Rosa said as Lila turned to face the mirror. "*Bardzo, bardzo ładnie.*"

A real frump number, Lila thought as she looked at herself through the strings of rosary beads hanging on Rosa's bureau

mirror. Thirty-five years as neighbours and not much more than
a wave across the street if it couldn't be avoided, and here she was,
standing in Rosa Filipczak's bedroom, the woman's underpants
rubbing against her skin, wearing a dress that smelled like old
roses. The dress was like all Rosa's dresses, a dark acrylic knit with
elastic at the waist, shapeless, unimaginative, and didn't explain
at all the exuberance of colour on the floral walls. Rosa's bedroom
had been a surprise, too. Two armless couches covered with russet
handwoven spreads formed a right angle in one corner of the
room. When Rosa and her husband slept, their heads must have
touched, Lila thought. Again, it had been the walls in the room
that had overwhelmed her. They were hung with dark weavings,
and threaded among the fibres were bits of amber, single earrings,
lockets, strings of beads, silver spoons, cards with pictures on
them of the Virgin, saints, and, Lila realized with a start, hanging
above one of the couches was a leg brace. Its leather strap vibrated
slightly with the *whirrt!* noise of the tailor's sewing machine in the
adjoining room. What in God's name is a leg brace doing hanging
on the wall? Lila wanted to ask, when she heard a loud clatter, a
sharp metallic sound, and shouting in the street.

They had pitched tents on Lila's lawn, three of them, yellow
tents whose sides bobbed with the movement of the people
inside them. The woman with the grocery cart squatted, unpack-
ing one of her cardboard cartons, setting cooking pots down on
the bottom step. The noise Lila had heard had been the sound
of an aluminum ladder falling to the ground, she realized, as she
stood out in Rosa's yard now waiting for her to bring the lawn
chairs from the garage so they could sit and watch and wait for
the police to arrive. The burly man from Z.T.O.H. had picked
up the ladder and swung it against the side of the verandah, but

the man in the yellow T-shirt kept kicking at it through the deck railing. "Look here, man," the Z.T.O.H. man shouted. "Don't you get it? How many times do I have to explain it to you? The point of this whole exercise is to make a point."

"Yah, and then what?" the ponytailed man shouted. "I was there making a point about Vietnam and then what?"

What exercise, Lila thought, what point? The ad had not been a mistake, after all, she thought. It was him, the weightlifter look-alike, who had put it in the newspaper. One of the sinewy, dark men who had unloaded the van stood halfway up another ladder, holding the end of a banner while another man unfolded it and laid it down across the lawn. FIVE YEARS FIVE EMPTY ROOMS, the bright red letters proclaimed. More like four, Lila thought, because one was too small for anything but a baby's crib and a chest of drawers. She'd finished it in a creamy wallpaper with tiny blue cornflowers and blue carpet, and dubbed it the Blue Room. A room to be alone in, to read in or listen to music. It was where she went to write letters now, cheerful and sometimes humorous letters to her sisters and children who worried, she knew, about the old neighbourhood changing and had begun to suggest that she should "think seriously" about getting a dog.

The young woman with the cooking pots gathered her long, dark hair up and twisted it into a knot, pinning it to the top of her head. Then she bent over the bottom step, flicked a lighter and a flame uncoiled from a propane stove. She ripped open a bag of linguine pasta and dumped it into a pot. From the side of Lila's house the stove vent fan churned out the sweet smoky smell of bacon cooking.

"I have been patient," Lila said to the policeman on the telephone. "I've been patient all day. And, no, I don't think they're about to give up and go home. They claim they don't have anywhere to go to!" The two men had driven off in the van, and standing in its place beside the curb was a blue comfort station. "Next thing you know they'll be setting my house on fire," she said, "just to make some silly point."

"Well, in that case, you would have to call the fire department, and they would issue a full report to us. If there were any charges to be laid, we'd investigate," the policeman said. "In the meantime, I assure you that we're doing the best we can." And now, for the fourth time that day, the line went dead.

Lila pulled up the blind on Rosa's front window and stood looking across at her house. She had never seen her house from the perspective of Rosa Filipczak's window before. She had never seen what Rosa saw every day. Her house looked like a birthday cake, she thought, startled by the realization. The hanging planters of fuchsia geranium ivy on the second-floor deck made it look as if sugar rosettes had been stuck to each corner of it. The stark white trim of the house against pale blue looked fussy, she thought, and so did the windows, each one displaying, dead centre, a hanging plant, a piece of stained glass, or a sun-catcher. The sun was beginning its slide down behind the church steeple at the top of the street and her front flower beds were cast into deep shadows. All day long cars had driven past in the street, drivers honking in irritation or support. "Call the CBC, CTV, MTM!" the burly man would shout, or thump the roof of the car and shove a pamphlet in through the window. "Call the newspaper!" he'd plead. But, so far, the media had failed to attend the demonstration of the demonstrators, as Lila had come to think of them; people making a display of themselves. Spectators had stopped to chat with the squatters, among them a young man in a pale green suit and white shoes who had joined the demonstrators for a while to pray for them, he'd said, and bring them a "word of encouragement," from the Lord.

She began to feel uneasy, as though there was someone in the room behind her watching the way she was looking at the demonstrators, at the man stepping out of the comfort station and zipping up his fly, at Rosa sitting out on the lawn chair, a Thermos of coffee set on the TV tray at her side, her meaty shoulders encased in a brown sweater, and though the day had been hot, the flowered head-scarf was still tightly knotted beneath her whiskered chin. Her smile had been in place most of the day; the brightness of it Lila had found tiring. She turned from the window and her eyes met the solemn eyes of the Black Madonna. Solemn or sleepy-looking? Lila wondered. Or eyes that had bottled up something unspeakably sad that was threatening now to leak out. It's only a picture, Lila told herself, and yet she felt caught by the saint's gaze, and judged. She heard the *whirrt!* sound of the tailor's sewing machine start up once again. She turned back to the window in time to see an extension cord uncoil in the air as it flew across the back fence. "All right!" the woman with the orange tabby shouted as she caught the electrical cord and plugged in a television set sitting on a box in the centre of the yard. "Not too shabby," she said.

"You could stay with me for the night," Rosa said as she pulled a plastic bag off a bowl filled with potato salad and a plate of cold chicken, setting them down on the TV tray between them.

"Oh no, no, I'm sure that won't be necessary," Lila said, and thought about her head meeting Rosa's head at the right angle the couches made and almost touching. The leg brace jiggling on the wall above her, the room smelling of burlap sacking, of age; foreign. Paint and wallpaper, Lila thought, air-fresheners, something to look forward to, that's what Rosa needed, a change.

"Call the CBC, CTV, MTM! Call the newspapers!" the silvery-skinned man from Z.T.O.H. yelled as a car swept by. His voice had grown hoarse and Lila noticed how he walked less apelike now, how his shoulders had dropped. She had stopped rehearsing what she would say to the television cameras, that she was the widow of a World War II veteran just getting by on their combined small pensions. How Jim had gone off, still in his teens, willingly, to serve his country, and without receiving any handouts had dug in and educated himself when he'd returned. They'd been wise enough to wait to marry until he had done so, had practised birth control, lived within their means, scrimped and saved and not gone on fancy vacations or bought a cottage at the lake or even owned a second car. It is people like us who have made this country what it is today, she was going to say. I have earned the right to live alone in my house. But the media, apparently, had deemed the event not news-worthy and she would not have her say, she was certain. The man from Z.T.O.H. swore violently, and smacked at a mosquito on his arm. The tents glowed softly with light, the people inside them sharp outlines, the people outside becoming silhouettes, too, as they sat on blankets in a semicircle in front the television set, its screen glowing with images. Lila could see the maroon-haired woman at the front bedroom window, pulling the tunic up and over her head, getting ready to go to bed, she realized.

"Here," Rosa said, and draped a woollen shawl about Lila's shoulders. "If you won't put on a sweater, then at least a scarf."

"Thank you, Rosa," Lila said, using the woman's Christian name for the first time. She looked down at her feet and the crumpled toes of the shoes Rosa had given her to wear. Rosa's garden shoes, spotted with clay, pinched a corn on Lila's foot. The patio doors on the deck slid open and the man with the long white ponytail stepped out onto it, carrying Jim's old acoustic guitar. They'd been on the third floor. Her chest squeezed. Had they sat on the fold-down couch, too, and smelled the faint tinge of pipe smoke in its woolly fabric, the vinegary smell of wet diapers? He sat down, stretched his legs out onto the chair in front of him, cradled the guitar and began to strum it lazily. Lila yawned suddenly, fighting the impulse to cry. She felt abandoned, felt that what she knew and had come to expect was, hour by hour, drifting further and further away.

They were the last of the old neighbourhood, Lila Sanders and Rosa Filipczak. When they went for walks they came across coloured chalk murals of strange-looking worlds on the sidewalks. Mud huts, palm trees, things called Ninja Turtles, people with knives sticking out of their throats. They saw the bright eyes of the children who streamed out of the day-care or from the after-school programs at the church at the top of the street, their faces painted garish colours. When they sat in Vimy Ridge Park talking, people spilled from the halfway house across from the shaded green space, people sat on stairways, on bicycles, on broken chairs and benches borrowed from the park. People sat outside many of the houses at all times of the day, sometimes looking sullen and falling silent when Lila passed by, their tired eyes accusing, or angry, or what, Lila didn't know. None of their anger or their sadness was her fault, she told herself. She would not allow herself to feel guilty. But sometimes she did.

"Come," Rosa said softly and patted Lila's hand. "Poppy-seed cake, herbatka, and then we sleep."

"Oh, I couldn't," Lila protested.

"We're neighbours," Rosa said. "Why, couldn't?"

Lila felt herself smile. Yes, she thought, we're neighbours and we were here first, and we should really stick together.

Lila couldn't sleep. It wasn't so much the sound of Rosa's gentle snoring or the sound of the tailor's sewing machine that was keeping her awake, or even the smell of leather and per-spiration emanating from the leg brace. "Rosa," she'd whispered in the darkness before the elderly woman had fallen asleep, "why have you hung a leg brace on the wall?"

"An offering," Rosa said, "of thanks."

"For what?" Lila asked.

"For a miracle," Rosa said.

"Oh," Lila said softly.

"Władek's miracle."

"I see," Lila whispered.

"If Władek had to keep wearing the brace, they wouldn't let us in this country."

"Oh, I see," Lila whispered once again. But she didn't under-stand.

"Good," Rosa said with a bit of impatience, speaking as though Lila was being a bothersome child, "now we sleep."

But Lila couldn't sleep now that the demonstrators had begun to sing. She lifted the candle from its holder and the Virgin's face wavered and disappeared into the darkness as Lila crossed Rosa's front room. All around, flowers bloomed in the flickering light of the candle. She had recognized the song they were singing, she'd sung it herself, her children had brought it home from summer camp. "*Someone's sleeping, lord, kum ba yah,*" they sang, "*someone's sleeping, lord, kum ba yah, oh, lord, won't you kum ba yah?*" The young woman cradled her baby in her lap, and Lila saw how, as she lifted her T-shirt, the light from the small fire they'd lit in a charcoal burner flickered against the woman's skin as she placed the child against her breast to nurse. What would it be like, Lila wondered, to have a child, people in the house again? To fill the rooms with healthy cooking odours, soups and stews and biscuits, activities, skirmishes. And she, the matronly centre of it all, seated at the dining-room table, parcelling out advice, wisdom. Or to be down on her hands and knees mopping up after spills, scrubbing a back or washing away mud stuck between toes, abandoned to the passion of selflessness. She watched as the bonfire flared briefly, snapping off sparks. She imagined the heat of a fire burning in her face, flames licking up her thighs, singeing hair, catching onto her clothing, herself becoming a human torch and burning herself out to save them.

"*Someone's crying, lord, kum ba yah, oh, lord, won't you kum ba yah?*" the woman with the orange tabby sang, her voice twangy and off key as she left the circle of demonstrators, went over to a front flower bed and squatted in it. Relieving herself, Lila realized in a rush of anger, and the comfort station only steps away. She felt the push of tears behind her eyes. Strays. The word came as her pulse began hammering at the base of her throat. They were nothing but a pack of strays that would come to expect three meals a day and then demand it as their right. And do their business in corners of the house as repayment, thank you very much. "*Oh, lord, won't you kum ba yah?*" they sang, ragged, pitifully dull.

She set the candle down and picked up the telephone sitting in the centre of the round doily on the table painted with tiny poppies, and dialled 911. "Help," Lila said, with the correct amount of panic in her voice. "Someone has lit a fire in my yard and I'm afraid that it could get out of control." Her heart pounded in her chest as she set the receiver back into its cradle, and heard in the distance the faint wail of a siren drawing closer and closer.

⊸⊷

The man and woman had left their shoes at the front door and not tracked dirt across her shiny hardwood floors, Lila was happy to note the following morning, but she frowned when she saw that their damp sock feet had left behind smudges that would have to be spritzed with cleaner and buffed away. "Look, we're sorry," the man with the ponytail had said, "we weren't part of the gig. We honestly thought you had rooms for rent." He was a filmmaker, he'd said, between projects, and the woman a visual artist, which explained the dabs of paint on the cutting board in the kitchen, the butterfly on her cheek.

Lila had gone through most of the rooms and, other than the broken windowpane and a chip in the pinwheel-crystal bowl, there was no real harm done. As she passed by the door to the Blue Room off the second-floor hallway, she stopped. The couple had brought magazines with them, and they were scattered randomly across the carpet. Lila knelt and began to stack them in a pile when her eye was drawn to a glossy image of a woman, sand, water, blue sky. "Enjoying a day at the beach," the caption read in blazing colour. It was a photograph of a young woman with her back turned to the camera, up on her knees in the sand. She wore a strange kind of bathing suit that was meant to be held together by snaps at the sides of it, but the snaps had been undone, and the front of the bathing suit had fallen loose and trailed from her crotch and lay on the sand between her legs. She stood on her knees, head and shoulder turned to the camera. Then Lila saw the woman's pink nipple and her tanned thumb grazing the tip of it. She'd placed her other hand at her crotch. Obviously. Obviously masturbating. For several moments Lila couldn't stop looking at the image. Enjoying a day at the beach. The thumb tweaking the stiff nipple, the strategic placement of the woman's other hand, the front of the drop-away bathing suit dangling between her legs. And the smile, Lila thought, the red shining mouth turned up at the corners, eyes looking into Lila's eyes, mocking. What does it mean? "What does this mean?" she said aloud. Then she snatched up the magazine and flung it across the room. "What does it mean?" She curled forward, pressing her face into her knees and began to weep. "I don't know, I don't know," Lila howled, "I don't know what it means. I don't know what anything means any more. I just don't know what it means."

# The Ballad of the Sargent Brothers

⁓⌇

A man awakened on a Saturday night to the battering of hail against his house. He went to the cellar and brought up a quart crock of liquor and sat in his farm kitchen drinking until the storm petered out to a rumbling far away on the other side of a ridge of hills. His dog stopped its yapping; the sun began to rise above the fence line, but he was in no hurry to go out and survey the ruin.

When he finally did go, leaving his silent wife at the stove stirring a boiler of washing, he wasn't surprised by the water thigh-deep on his fields, but by the fish. Thousands of carp glided through his wheat; water rippling, splashing, tail fins flipping against the surface. As he waded among the fish, they curled about his legs and one another, as though wanting to spawn, but it was the wrong season for that, unless the weather had confused the fish somehow. The creeks overflowing so suddenly like that, the fish swept into drainage ditches and onto the fields. He should have been cursing or crying, or both. What a caution, he said, and then let loose with a belly laugh. He couldn't help it, the incongruous fact of fish swimming among his wheat, his reflection and the clouds on the surface of water. It was as though the land was in its proper state. Gone back to being what it was meant to be. He waded to the road, water slopping in his boots as he thumped across the yard and hollered at the bedroom windows for his children to shake a leg, come see what was up. Don't bother putting on your duds either, he said. Come in your altogether or underwear.

The sun had already warmed the day by then, the water in the fields was tepid, the fish flopped and swerved, brushed against the bodies of the father and children as they swam among them. There was plenty of time for worrying; as long as it lasted, it would be a day for swimming with the fish.

His wife watched from the window. Watched her man playing with their children, leaping and throwing himself backwards in the water, his arms flailing outwards like sunburnt wings. It was as much fun as shooting fish in a barrel, he yelled across the yard to her. It gave him the idea then, and he sent a son to the barn for his rifle. For almost an hour she endured the air punctuated with the crack of gunfire as he chased down fish with the children, hunted them as they zigzagged through matted and flattened wheat, frenzied by the children's thrashing legs and fish blood unravelling like smoke through water.

When his wife saw his shoulders begin to droop, the effects of the liquor draining away, she came to him barefoot through the water, her skirt knotted at the waist. She brought grain sacks. Water had pooled on their side of the road, she told him. On the other side it had already subsided. The culvert was likely plugged. She stayed with the children for the remainder of the morning as they scooped up dead carp, enough for their evening meal, to be smoked later and canned.

It was the other fish the man would never forget. He went with a pole to the road to unplug the culvert so the water could drain back into the creek. When he shoved the rod inside it, it met something solid deep inside the pipe. So he went to the other end of it, lay on his side in the muck and stuck his arm into the culvert as far as it could go. He felt something soft and squishy with mud, stringy. He'd twined his hand through the stringy mess until he got a fist of it and then pulled and felt it give. He wormed down the ditch on his side, bracing himself against the gush of water, but he hadn't been prepared for its force smashing into him, sending him flat on his fanny. He managed to keep his head and shoulders above the current, fish darting all around him.

The drainage ditch widened downstream and the current lost some of its steam. He found his feet then. Whatever he had delivered from the culvert floated towards him, something opaque, flesh-coloured, and strangely shiny. At first he saw a leg in a rayon stocking, the garter attached to it; then blue silk, the skirt of a dress billowing, a cloth rosette on a shoulder. He concentrated on these things separately because he did not want to look at the face of the woman. And when he did, he saw that it was one of the Morrison twins.

⁓ ⁓

During the previous winter, in the early evening, the Sargent brothers had just sat down for their supper meal when Emily Morrison came calling.

The brothers sat in their places on either side of a window that was framed by a crust of frost. They preferred not to use the electric lights. The lights only turned the windows into black mirrors that startled them with wavy images as they walked across a room or peered out at the lane. They watched for lights of vehicles passing along the road, a lantern hanging on a wagon. A kerosene lamp set on a kitchen cabinet across the room glimmered, its wick turned low. Outside, banks of snow, blue animals, had crept across the yard during the day and up the side of the tool shed. The lane would be blown in by morning. Whoever had come calling had not come through the lane but across land and on foot. Alfred stared at Henry, his fork suspended midway to his mouth. It clattered against his plate as Alfred dropped it and fled and his brother went to open the door.

"I'm Emily," Emily Morrison said, meaning she was not Mary, her twin. She pushed a wool scarf from her mouth and chin and plucked a tam from her head as though she took for granted he was bound to ask her in. A mole, like a fleck of charcoal on the cusp where her lip turned up, moved with her smile. The Morrison twins were identical except for the mole, Henry had heard, but he'd never been close enough to see if it was true.

The Sargent brothers always thought of the Morrison twins as children. When their father, Francis Sargent, left the brothers the farm and moved with their mother, Masie, and sister, Grace, into nearby Silver Plains where he taught school, the Morrison twins were only three years old. What separated the Sargent and Morrison farm sites was half a mile and a shallow gully where meltwater and rain ran off the land, overgrown with willow and field berries. The girls were only spots of colour then, bobbing about the yard as they played. In

winter when the frozen bushes rattled, a light in a window at
the Morrison place might wink at the brothers through the
bare branches. Later, the girls became gliding blue figures
when, in the dwindling light at the end of a winter day, they
skated on a pond. They remained children throughout the
years, dwarfed by the size of their father's Clydesdale going
by on the road, to and from school, in and out of town. Some
winters the boxy shape of a wooden cab mounted on sleigh
runners moved silently along the horizon, horse's reins looping
up through the square window. It was enough to know that
the girls were inside, warmed by a scuttle full of embers. It
wasn't that the brothers watched for them. The girls were just
there, a way to know the time of day, like the sunsets that overwhelmed the sky. The brothers had grown accustomed to a
landscape with the Morrison twins a part of it.

She had come to take the census, Emily said. The popula-
tion of the country was being counted. Not a whole lot to count
here, Henry told her. It wasn't meant as a joke, but she took it
as one and laughed. There was more to it than that, she said.
Could she come in? He returned to his supper leaving the door
ajar. Heat rushed to meet the cold air, condensing in a white
cloud that shredded apart in the black night around her shoulders. She peered into the kitchen, looking for his brother,
Alfred. A floorboard creaked in the parlour, which had become
Alfred's bedroom when they'd closed off the upstairs rooms.
No good heating the outside, Henry told her. His voice
sounded to him like a dull saw blade jamming in raw wood.

She stepped into the kitchen and closed the door behind her.

She sat where Alfred had sat, pushed aside his plate, and set
her fur mitts and portfolio onto the oilcloth. She shrugged from

her coat, looping it over the chair back, and a sweet odour entered the kitchen. Henry watched her hand curl around a wooden pencil box, a finger move the length of the lid, a slight pressure burning the fingernail white as she drew the lid open, revealing several pencils. As she grasped one, he saw how her smallest finger curved like the handle of a china cup. They heard the sound of bedsprings sighing in Alfred's room.

When Henry went to turn up the lantern's wick, his legs felt heavy.

She glanced about the room as it brightened, at the range and the woodbox beside it, at the stain of soot on the wall around the stovepipe. At the sealer jars filled with rivets and burrs, machine bolts, cotter pins and washers lining a plate rail halfway up the wall, enamel and tin pots hanging on nails, a scrub board, their work clothes. A log burning in the stove crumbled and clinkers fell through the grate into the ashbox.

"It's a large kitchen," she said, smiling. Then she opened a booklet, her pencil hovering among columns of questions. He rested his arms on either side of his plate; fat congealed in the fried potatoes and side pork. His hands tingled with a peculiar stiffness, making him unable, he knew, to lift a fork, or to drink tea without slopping it, much less pour a cup of it for her.

"There's a batch of kittens in the barn," Henry said, as she drew near to the end of her questions. He'd said the first thing that came.

She looked up in surprise. "How did you know?" she asked. When he didn't reply she answered for him. He must have seen their cat, Patches, along the road. "It got hold of a poisoned rat," she said. She'd found its carcass only yesterday.

He wouldn't have known her cat from any of the others that

showed up from time to time. Those who had tangled with a rabid fox or slunk off to die after they had met with an accident. But she seemed to take it that he had known and, out of kindness, was offering a replacement.

Could she come tomorrow in daylight with her sister, Mary, and choose a kitten?

He thought of the kittens, all teeth and claws, caw-cawing at him from the manger with their little hinged jaws. She would never catch one, much less tame it. "It doesn't matter to me one way or the other," he said; but it did. He wanted the Morrison sisters to come. He wanted to see if it was true what was said about them being alike except for the mole. He wanted to see the twins side by side, as others saw him and Alfred. He wondered if they, too, shared their brains.

As she twisted in her chair to get her coat, her breasts moved behind the soft wool of her sweater, and Henry thought of his sister, Grace. Of startling her in one of the upstairs rooms bathing, one foot on a chair, the other in a bucket of water, a cloth moving between her legs, the slope of her breasts profiled perfectly in the light shining in through the window behind her.

When the Morrison twin had gone, he left the lantern's wick turned high, wanting his shadow up near the ceiling instead of following him about the room. It wasn't so much that he felt her absence as it was his awareness that he felt no energy. It was like the day long ago when a man trained as a classical musician had come to his father looking for farm work. Henry was struck dumb by the music coming from the man's fingers as he sat at the piano in the parlour. When the man finished playing, Henry had stood there, disgruntled. The music had lit the room only to prove it empty.

Alfred returned to the supper table and sat down, but leapt

immediately from the chair and flipped over the seat cushion. It was warm, he said. He fidgeted and stirred through the cold food on his plate. The room stank of toilet water, he said, it spoiled his appetite. He set the plate on the countertop and took a metal strongbox from the sugar bin and a two-dollar bill from it. Henry knew before he heard the horses in the yard that Alfred would be gone most of the night and that the Barclay woman would be two dollars the richer for it.

Henry set the kerosene lamp onto the kitchen table and looked at his reflection in the windowpane; a face made youthful by its roundness and the boyish wedge of straw-coloured hair across his forehead. He watched his lips part in a smile. For all his thirty-five years he looked no different from anyone else, he thought, the men who paid him at the end of the month for the ice and coal he delivered, the young bucks who had come calling for Gracie. He blew out the flame and his face vanished. The clouds had thinned and the snowbanks between the house and tool shed glittered. The wagon turned from the lane onto the road beyond; Alfred, a silhouette hunched against the cold, going off to buy a bit of warmth, as much as two dollars would afford. Twins share each other's brains, their mother, Masie, had said. It was why Alfred had not progressed as Henry had in school, and out of fairness, Henry had been kept behind with him. The stove's heat released the odour of barn from their work clothes hanging on the wall, machine oil, the perspiration in their boots, their passivity.


Henry now noticed that the girl, Emily, was often at the mailbox just as he happened by on the road. Soon a wave became a spoken greeting and then moments of conversation that he mulled over while he cut ice on the river. Her father had gone to Winnipeg. The Russians were buying an enormous number of horses from Canadians, some of them from Manitoba. Her father, along with several others, was looking to invest in horses. Or, she said she was haunting the mailbox; she and Mary were anxious for the arrival of a new sewing pattern, a frock to wear come summer to the dances at Berry Lake.

As Henry cut and hauled ice from the snow-packed river that winter, he thought more of Emily than of what she said. What happened in other places had no effect on him. But the things she told him gave him pictures. Pictures of her at the sewing machine, or in the parlour sitting in a chair beside a radio. He could not, however, picture her dancing in the hall at Berry Lake. Although his sister, Grace, had gone there and often talked about it, he couldn't call it to his imagination. When the snow fell, flakes as large as pennies floated gently all around him. If he looked up into it, it seemed the sky revolved and he had to lean on the grapple pole to keep from tipping.

One day when he had finished cutting and was drawing the blocks out of the black water, he was taken by how the ice held light. It glowed green from its centre. As he hooked one of the last pieces and clamped the tongs about it, he noticed this piece of ice looked different. As he pulled it up onto the frozen river, he saw that something dark lay inside it. He flipped the block on its side and saw the features of a black and white dog, its amber eyes staring out at him.

Henry ran to the sleigh for his splitting chisel, ice chips flying from his encrusted pants, legs refusing to bend at the knees. On the way back he dropped the rod, and cursed as the chisel shot across the ice and down into the open water.

It took several attempts to split the block with an axe and free the dog. Henry stood looking at it, mesmerized, panting. The collie lay on its side, its front paws curled as though caught in the act of running. As his panic gave way, Henry wondered how he could have thought, even for a moment, that it might be alive. He wondered how the dog had come to be caught. Whether some quirk of nature had trapped it when it was swimming. He thought of the animal suspended in the green ice, frozen between light passing through the surface and the dark water below. He rued the lost tool, his foolish hurrying. It would have been best to push the ice back into the water, but now that he'd freed the animal, he couldn't leave it like this.

How would he be able bury it with the ground frozen solid? Emily asked, when they met on the road and she saw the dog's frozen body on the wagon bed. She'd driven the horse and sleigh, taken her mother and Mary into Silver Plains to attend Ladies Aid. He would build a fire, he told her. Keep it going all night, and in the morning the ground would be soft enough for a shallow burial.

The next morning Emily came down the lane pulling a sleigh. She had brought a shovel, a jar of hot lemon tea. She had brought a tattered piece of quilt. He watched as she spread it down and rolled the dog onto it and folded the blanket around it, tucking the ends in firmly. To keep it warm? he wondered, and felt a bit of laughter coming. Bundling it, the way Gracie had done her little cloth dollies. He realized it didn't seem important to his sister or Emily that there had to be life in a body in order to warm it. What the girls looked for, what they needed, he thought, was the warming of themselves, inside.

Because of Masie, Henry's mother, it didn't seem unusual to him that a woman would want to help bury the animal, or that a woman might work as energetically as he. He didn't want Emily, like his mother had, to do a man's work. She would spoil her mitts, he said; besides, the job required a pickaxe, and he only had the one.

She stayed to watch as he chipped out the burial hole. When Alfred came from the house, she waved, but he appeared not to notice. When Henry finished, she unwrapped the jar of tea and offered it to him. He should take off his mitts, warm his hands on the glass, she said. He'd been up several times in the night to stoke the fire, had gone to work on an empty stomach. When he took the jar from her it was with both hands to keep it from shaking.

Come and have some hot tea, Emily shouted in the direction of the barn. Henry realized she knew as well as he did that Alfred was just inside the door, watching them.

During an early thaw near the end of winter, Henry came upon the Morrison twins collecting weeds that had wintered along the edge of a field across from his lane. The milkweed pods were large, open, still showing off their silvery tufts of hair, Mary said.

"And just look at the burdock, thicker than I've ever seen it. We're going to put it with dried aster and cornflowers," Emily said, taking up where Mary had left off.

"An arrangement for the church," Mary said.

"It's the Annunciation of the Blessed Virgin on Sunday," Emily finished.

The way their sentences bumped into one another, over-lapped, Henry could barely follow. When they had come in winter looking to choose a kitten to replace their cat, the kittens were gone, moved to another place by the mother. Mary's voice was stronger, he had noticed then, and her movements quicker. Other differences had become apparent. Emily's hair, for instance, looked finer, and the feathery down curling at her temples held strands of dark red hair. When she turned her head in the sunlight, he saw them glinting among the black. Her hands were smaller and she had a mole beside her lip so precisely round and dark that it looked as though she'd drawn it with black ink.

In spring a late snowfall covered the Sargent and Morrison lanes and the road beyond where their mailboxes sat on posts at the edge of a ditch among yellowed grasses. The snow, icing on a cake, Emily said, would be gone in days. Spring was her favourite season, she told Henry. Beyond the car window, clouds the colour of muddied water hung so low it seemed the rusty tree-tops might meet them.

When Henry came upon Emily beside the road that day, the snowfall drifted in bands, cutting her in two. She gratefully accepted his offer of a ride to her lane, but as they approached his, she asked him to stop, and he wondered if she didn't want to be seen coming home in his car. I just can't imagine not living here, she said, and went on to say that she meant the open country, the sky, the snow frosting covering the fields. This is where I want to be, she said. Then she told him that Mary was anxious to go away to nursing school the following autumn. If their father agreed, of course, she would go, too. Whatever the one did, the same was expected of the other.

Henry sat in the car listening to snow sleeting against it. Until now, he hadn't thought much beyond the next season and the work attached to it. When he thought about his life he realized it was a life unconsidered. It was like the predictable march of fenceposts, like the day, colourless, clouds matching the gritty snow on the fields, the trees black, and all of it, the sky, land, trees, farm buildings, washed the colour of lead. He was water, colourless; older than necessary. Emily sat beside him, her hands folded against her spruce-green coat, knuckles reddened from the icy wind. The odour of her black hair made him think of the pickling season and of Masie counting and labelling jars of bread and butter, beet and dill pickles at the end of the day.

"Your mailbox is full," Emily said, as though she had grown uncomfortable with the silence and needed to end it. She left the car and collected his mail and returned. There were several periodicals, a package from T. Eaton and Co., the books he had ordered. Henry Sargent, she said, reading the name on the package, and handed it to him.

When she said his name, he felt himself step away from Alfred. He felt his heart beating inside the name Henry.

"You know what I will remember the most?" Emily said, as though she had already settled in her mind that she would be leaving in autumn.

And already, Henry felt the loss.

"I won't forget the day I saw you coming home. You'd unhitched the plough and were walking the team back. I was bringing the wash in from the line. There you were, reins slung over your shoulders, carrying a bundle of wildflowers. Must've been sunflowers, you could see them a mile away."

He'd put them in a cream can on the back step the way Masie had done. Wind gusted, and sleet swirled across the road beyond. Twins should marry twins. The thought was a pinprick of light, a lens opening to the obvious. Caramel buttons on her coat moved with her breath. As she turned to clear frost from the car window, he saw the downy sweep of hair along her jaw. Whenever he tried to imagine how he had happened, what he pictured seemed ridiculous. His diminutive father, a squiggly earthworm, mounting his mother's considerable bulk, crawling over the ridges and valleys of fat to burrow and plant his seed. The Barclay woman was all dark whispers at the door, the fear of noise waking sleeping children, groping in the dark in a bed that smelled of a child's wetting; a small shudder of pleasure.

He studied his hands spread across his knees. Except for their inheriting his father's small hands, he and Alfred did not resemble him. Their father had a perfectly proportioned body and was smaller-boned and shorter than their sister, Grace. Before his father had reached forty, his hair and handlebar moustache had turned white. He looked suited for what he'd been, a schoolteacher. A scandal had brought him west from London, Ontario, where, it was rumoured, he'd disgraced himself and a young female student. Masie Coombs was a perfect match because she preferred working on the fields to the kitchen, and so he had hired a man to assist her and returned to his books. He gave elocution lessons and held yearly recitals in Silver Plains, always including in the program the recitation of the poems "Charge of the Light Brigade" and "The Wreck of the Hesperus." Tennyson was his favourite and he had, of course, named Alfred after the poet and Henry for Longfellow. He fancied himself a thespian and formed a drama club. When he'd staged the story of Cupid and Psyche, it troubled some that he had played the role of Cupid, had cavorted on stage in a cape and leotards among the young women. Henry had always caught the slight mockery in the lifting of a hat to his father when wagons passed on the road.

Henry and Alfred had refused to be drawn into their father's interests. While sums came easily, it seemed the arrangement of words on a page failed to make sense the way it did for most. Francis drilled them, pinned slips of paper with words onto objects, forced them to memorize long poems and passages of Scripture. But they seemed unable to make a connection between words they spoke and letters on a page. When it came to reading, the light would never dawn in Alfred's eyes, their father concluded. But he suspected, he often said, that it was obstinacy that stopped Henry.

When they turned thirteen, Masie was stricken with apoplexy, and their father returned to teaching, taking Grace to Silver Plains to help care for her. Their father believed the town had nothing to offer the boys. They were relieved when he decided to keep the farm and, when they came of age, had put the title in their names. The moment the door closed behind his father, Henry ordered the first of many reading materials, a booklet, *What a Farmer Can Do With Concrete.*

His hands, Henry thought, were of course broader than Emily's hands, but not much larger. He had heard it said, you could measure a man between the legs by the size of his hands. *What a Young Husband Ought to Know*, the title of a book in the catalogue, came to Henry's mind, when he heard a sharp crack against the side of the car. Emily was startled by it, but said nothing. Moments later there was another sound, like a stone hitting metal. A grey figure emerged from among the field berries in the gully, a rifle barrel resting against a shoulder. Alfred, Henry knew. He started the engine. The Hudson rocked along the road, the snow having hidden deep ruts, jolting Emily against his arm. He concentrated on guiding the wheels along the frozen ruts, the muscles in his jaw working.

He stopped at her mailbox, the lane beyond untrodden, a clean sheet that she would put her tiny bootprints in when she walked to the house.

"I thought it so, well, so nice," she said. "I never once saw a man carrying flowers," she said, as she closed the car door.

He waited until she had gone into the house and got out of the car. He ran his hand across the side of it, his fingers finding what he was looking for. The metal was dented deeply, up near the window, and lower, near the running board, but the .22 shell had not penetrated. Then Henry saw movement, a spurt of snow as a jackrabbit fled across the field beyond the car. While Henry couldn't hit the side of a barn, Alfred seldom missed what he was aiming for.

That summer, on a Saturday, when Henry and Alfred went to wash up, carrying pails of water from the kitchen to the tool shed, it was the time of day when the landscape seemed to light up as if illuminated from within with sunset. The crowns of basswood and oak trees beyond the barn beamed a fuchsia colour and the grain fields had become incandescent, the shade of a rosy ripe peach.

As children, the boys had tried to get inside that particular light of sunset. They walked long distances across tall-grass prairie hoping to gain it, but, of course, never came close. In the same way — although their schoolteacher father had explained the phenomenon to them — they had tried to stalk down rainbows. If there was a full moon, a flat-faced winter moon casting blue shadows across the snow, or a harvest moon, one or the other of them would be certain to draw attention to it. The moon's cycles, how the stars seem to rotate around the seasons, the ceremonies of commerce conducted behind frosted glass inside the polished interior of a bank, a school-room, library, or church confounded them. The light shining out of the landscape at the end of a day always made them feel stranded; made them feel that they were, for some reason, alien.

Alfred swung round to look at it before entering the tool shed, the water in the pails flashing like burnished coins. Henry followed his gaze, tugged at his bill cap, and nodded.

For Alfred's sake, Henry had rigged up a shower in the tool shed. When Alfred was a young boy, once a month it took three of them, Masie, Francis, and Henry, to put Alfred into a tub of water and keep him there long enough for Masie to scrub him. His screams were unnatural; he became like a wild animal clawing at them, left their arms scratched and his own arms and shoulders bruised from their holding him down. Alfred could be heard clear across to the Morrisons' and, when they once came to investigate, Masie had to explain to the young couple Alfred's fear, how, as a child, he'd once come near to drowning.

Henry had soldered a spigot to the base of one of their

mother's canning boilers, attached a length of rubber hose to
it and a brass shower head he'd come across recently in a hard-
ware store in Grand Forks, Minnesota. That, and a billiard table.
When he and Alfred had gone with the stoneboat to the train
station to bring the Brunswick home, several men had gathered
there. They wanted to settle their wagers over the rumour of
the table. The winners offered to help load and unload it. They
thought they'd put a chink in the brothers' wall of shyness and
gain an invitation to play. Henry did not offer one. The billiard table would occupy some of the time he and Alfred normally spent in the house. He knew from having a sister that
women considered men underfoot a nuisance. The shower
improved Alfred's body odour, more than a quick spit and
polish with a washcloth in a basin of water ever had. The trip
to Grand Forks took two days there and two days back in the
Hudson. The city of Winnipeg was less than half the distance,
but he feared coming upon a familiar face. What was Henry
Sargent up to in the Hudson's Bay store buying an eight-piece
setting of china dishes? He feared they might decipher his
longing, suspect that he dreamt of Emily and awoke some
mornings to find the bedding sticky with his discharge.

Henry racked the billiard balls and began shooting them into
pockets while Alfred stripped to his bones, stepped into a
washtub on the floor, and opened the tap on the boiler they'd
lifted onto a shelf. Although the brothers shared a birthday,
they were as day and night. Alfred was a beanpole, long-limbed
and caved in beneath his ribs, his skin the blue-white colour
of milkweed sap. Henry was more like Masie, his mother's side.
He was shorter than his twin, with golden skin and hair. He
had a solid trunk and was thick in the limbs and, it was thought,

would sooner kick a dog than tell it to get out of the way.

Water dribbled into the washtub as Alfred directed the strings of water across his body, careful to avoid his neck and face. New Homespun suits hung from the rafters beside the dress shirts Henry had bought in Grand Forks. The shirts looked like ghosts hovering among the leather harnesses, chain hoists, the snowshoes, leg traps they had used as young boys to catch small animals. Billiard balls clicked on the table as Henry moved around it.

The brothers were more familiar with the sound of traces jingling, the sweep of grass beneath a wagon bed, than with one another's voices. They had worked together almost twenty years and lived together longer but didn't speak unless it was necessary. Commands, instructions, questions; they seldom conversed for the sake of it. Except for two teams of horses, they had no livestock; the chickens had been butchered when Masie left and the coop was empty. There was no need for a dog and so they were often surprised by children from neighbouring farms peering in windows at them. They spied on the Sargent twins for eccentricities or unnatural behaviour.

How was it possible, likely, even, they were going to accompany the Morrison twins to the dance hall at Berry Lake that night?

Alfred dropped the hose and the showerhead trailed over the rim of the washtub. "It's plain tomfoolery," he said. He got out of the washtub and left the tool shed.

Henry stared at the pool of water widening on the earthen floor, the specks of sawdust and straw swimming in it, then out the window at his brother, his body luminescent, a slippery-looking fish swimming away through foxtail.

Henry felt the blow in his elbows, saw a red stripe rising across Alfred's buttocks before he realized he'd gone after him with the cue.

"You're daft," Alfred said, his mouth white and quivering. The beating was proof of it. "What do you think the girl's coming round for? What do you suppose she's after? This?" he said and roughly cupped Henry's crotch. He jerked his head in the direction of the fields, the gully of bushes, and the Morrison farm site beyond. "It's the old man put a bee in her bonnet," he said. "And I, for christly one, ain't about to lose a single parcel of this place."

For a terrifying moment Henry was struck with indecision, grief that she might be making a fool of him. The father had come calling, twice now. Looking to borrow. Wanting to know if they had extra teeth for the harrow until his order arrived, wanting to use the grinding stone.

Alfred's eyes swerved from Henry's, and his stomach convulsed. He shuddered and hugged himself. "I ain't a-going," he said. He doubled over and vomited into the grass. Not for the first time Henry rued the day he'd chanced upon Alfred upended in a rain barrel and had rescued him.

By the time they arrived in Silver Plains and at their father's house, the dome of the sky had already begun to turn purple with the shadow of nightfall. Blankets strung across windows on either side of Masie's bed shut out the final blaze of sunset and left the room in semidarkness, so that the brothers could barely make out her features; her skin had become as white as the pillow she lay on. It seemed to them that the heat in town was always heavier, the cooling influence of intermittent breezes less apparent. Because Masie wanted to touch him, Alfred knelt beside her bed while her fingers roamed through his hair. An axe thumped against wood out in the yard: their father at the chopping block, keeping busy and staying away. They could hear Grace working in the kitchen, clearing up after the evening meal, the sounds of voices of people walking past the house, a car passing, the jingle of traces, and the room seemed to close in around them.

"He would've liked to have killed me," Alfred said.

"He darn near did kill *me*," Henry said from the doorway. "Tried to get me with the rifle back in spring."

"If I wanted to, I would have."

"Jealousy," Masie said. "From the start, men been killing men for that."

Two cats, yellow mounds, crouched in the crook of Masie's legs. One rose in a humpbacked stretch, settled again, and blinked at Henry where he stood in the doorway. He hated cats, and when the animals were in his mother's room would not come past the doorway.

"It's jealousy, isn't it?" she asked Alfred. "Say, if it isn't so."

"The other one only agreed to go because her sister begged," he said.

"One won't go without the other," Henry explained.

"You boys oughtn't fight."

"Twins should be marrying twins," Henry said.

The bed shook with Masie's laughter. Saliva welled from a corner of her mouth, threatening to break loose, and Alfred dabbed it away.

"With the rate Gracie's going, I never thought I'd be a

grandmaw," she said. "I never thought it likely to come from you boys either."

"It still ain't likely," Alfred said.

"I'm not going it alone any more," Henry said. "He can. Bugger if I will." His voice was thick, clogged with his pain.

"You boys always stuck together and you always will. So you just face up to it," she told Alfred. "Get on home, and get on going. . . . Here, kitty, kitty, kitty," Masie crooned, her fingers tickling Alfred's scalp, tired, gone off in her mind, mistaking him for a cat.

That night at Berry Lake, what looked like a range of navy blue hills rose from the lake and overcame the sky, bringing gusts of cold wind that swayed the tops of poplar on the shoreline. Frayed patches of clouds the colour of mustard raced towards land. In the woods, candles lined a path where lovers had gone down to the lakefront, flames shivering inside paper sleeves. Henry and Alfred and the Morrison twins had gone down to the lakefront too but, unlike others around them, they hadn't left the crowded dance floor expecting cuddling. They had arrived late, when the dance was almost finished, and hadn't been inside the hall yet. The band's music worried Alfred; Henry noticed the jerk of his Adam's apple and a faint skunky odour of fear emanating from his body when they got out of the car. The girls had pointed out the candles burning among the trees.

The couples around the four of them were silhouettes on benches, dark outlines strolling arm in arm along the pier. Now and again heads or mouths would meet, there would be a fragmented bit of laughter, or a woman's cheek illuminated suddenly by the flare of a match. Emily and Mary had said nothing about the brothers' late arrival at the farm, were congenial, chattering about this and that, as they steered Henry and Alfred away from the spooning couples. They stood at the farthest end of the pier, legs braced against the wash of waves rising beneath it. Henry barely followed what the girls were saying. A dog named Trixie had had another litter, it seemed. Under the porch steps. They had recently been to Chautauqua. A comet, Pons-Winnecke it was called, a comet without a tail, had come near to the earth.

The rain moved in swiftly then and Japanese lanterns strung around the pavilion beside the dance hall began swinging wildly, their coloured globes darkening instantly as wet tissue clotted around the hot bulbs. Then the bulbs began to pop, small explosions that sounded like gunfire on the other side of the lake. Women ran, shrieking, drenched immediately as they made for the shelter of the dance hall. Their hair became the colour of winter straw, a burnished chestnut. Emily's hair was like coal glistening, strands of it coming loose and pasting against her forehead and neck. Henry struggled from his jacket, made clumsy in his desire to shield her. She laughed, her mouth dripping with rain. She took the jacket from him and made a tent of it for both of them. As they sprinted through the trees, the paper lanterns along the path, though weighted with sand, tipped and quickly became clumps of fire tumbling among the undergrowth of wild fern. Henry's and Emily's cheeks touched, an instant of warm pressure, a softness that made Henry stumble on the path.

The soaked couples straggled into the hall, shivering, some whooping with exhilaration. The cavern above the hall's rafters rolled with the swooning sound of band music, clarinets dominating as the Blue Serenaders played "Goodnight Irene," what was to be the final song. Dancers swayed in place, faces turned to the dark hollow above the rafters, stilled by the hard sound of hail against the roof.

Emily and Mary realized the brothers' unwillingness to go any farther inside the dance hall, and stayed with them near the entrance. They plucked at their soaked dresses, aware that their breasts and stomachs were too apparent beneath the canton silk. Emily's little movements, a pressure on the inside of Henry's arm, made him think of holding a small fish and feeling its life force flipping against his palms. It was dark where they stood. His cheek still buzzed where they had touched. When the band gave up playing they listened to the crack of hailstones against the roof, outside, the sound of it like hooves beating against the ground. There were few who weren't thinking about their crops being flattened, but Henry thought how the sound of the storm enclosed them in the heat of their bodies, the smell of damp hair, wool, wild roses. He felt like a boy contemplating a climb to a perilous height, to drop towards earth; indecision, and then fear itself propelling him to test his courage. He wound his arm about Emily's waist, felt her surprise and the soft resistance of her flesh, felt it give way under his hand as he drew her into his side.

The usually taciturn Henry Sargent looked quietly smug that night as though he had just proved something. Alfred had been stiff as a new pair of shoes, comical almost, in a suit and tie; except that he looked wounded. His grey eyes were flat, stunned as an animal that had just been struck between the eyes.

Henry stared into the tunnel the headlights carved out of the darkness, at the flutter of insects rushing towards the windshield, listening. What had been a dull shushing sound for moments, the sound of a steady wind in poplar trees, grew louder as the car crested an incline in the road. As it began its descent to where a narrow wood bridge spanned an almost dry creek bed, Henry saw the bridge had been swept away. A river, black and as thick-looking as oil, rushed by, its current swift, carrying bobbing debris swept off the land. Henry braked the car and it slid sideways on the greasy clay. He turned off the engine and the headlights darkened. He stepped from the car and Alfred followed. The girls came up beside them.

The landscape became like quicksilver in the moonlight, the black trees along the road, purple now, dripped with it. They had to shout to be heard above the roar of the tumbling water, the girls' voices sharp with fear and excitement. They shivered beneath the brothers' jackets as they walked down the road to investigate.

They had waited out the worst of the storm in the car at the dance hall, until the spheres of ice like mothballs lying thick among the trees melted, and then, because Mary was impatient to leave, ventured the trip home. The car had slid this way and that, too precariously near the ditches swollen with water, and so the girls had preferred to walk behind the car. They held hands, Emily laughing and walking an exaggerated old woman's hobble as her patent-leather shoes became caked with mud.

He could somehow manoeuvre the car, turn it around, and return home another way, a longer route, and eventually meet up with a gravel road, Henry assured them. Not yet, Emily said, and linked her arm through his. The storm gave them reason to stay away longer. He hadn't expected cuddling, but as they had walked among shadows to the car earlier she'd asked with a joking exasperation if he wasn't going to kiss her. The heat of his embarrassment was displaced quickly by her heat, her hand on his, at her breast. An uprooted tree swept past them; a log pulled along by the current.

Lightning winked in the sky to the west where the storm had passed over a ridge of hills. "Look," Mary said, her voice crackling with excitement. "Fish!" She could see hundreds of fish, all at once, their silvery bodies shooting along like arrows just beneath the surface of the rushing water.

Don't. Henry wanted to caution Mary to come away, but he didn't think he had the right to say it. Just then, as Henry feared, near to where Mary stood, a chunk of earth broke away and dropped into the current. Emily stepped up behind Mary and began coaxing her to come away.

"Look! Look!" Mary cried and pointed out the fish to Alfred, who stared, mesmerized, an arm rising stiffly across his body as though to fend off the sight of the tumbling, roaring water. Mary grabbed at his raised arm to pull him nearer to the edge and Alfred recoiled. His mouth opened as though he might shout but no sound came as he lunged, pushing at Mary, tearing free from her grasp.

"Emily!" Mary cried, surprised to find herself falling backwards. She fought to gain her balance on the slippery grass, arms teetering, and hands grabbing for something to hold onto finding a ribbon dangling from the girdle of Emily's dress. As she toppled into the river, she took Emily with her.

Henry looked on, stunned at how their bodies were swallowed instantly by the streaming current. He yelled for Alfred as he began to run, but as Alfred fled, he knew it was up to him. He went after the girls, not feeling the strike of cold water against his body. Their arms flailed, as though waving for him to follow. Then, suddenly, one grabbed at an overhanging branch and clung to it. As Henry, drawn swiftly along by the current, drew nearer, he fought to see through eyes blurred by water which one she was. He wanted to go to her, to put his hands on her, push her up further onto the branch where its thickness would be sure to hold her safe. He wanted to go after the other whose head bobbed midstream like a shiny black ball, dipping beneath the frothing water and rising up again. He heard this one cry out, faint, a small voice, he thought, so he struck out after her, leaving the other clinging onto the branch. But the current proved too fast, strong, and the girl's weight far too much for the spindly branch, and it bent, broke, and released her into the river. As Henry went off after her sister, she sank beneath the water without crying out, without rising.

When Henry pulled the other onto the land, she was heaving water, crying, but alive. Henry turned her to him, cradled her head in his lap, searched for the mole beside her mouth. It wasn't there.

᭙᭜

There is something out there on the fields the Sargent brothers once farmed. It's like a breath withheld, moving through sage and buffalo grass, past chokecherry bushes growing through a wagon bed, bleached animal bones scattered beside its wheel.

When children come to prowl about they feel something out there on the land. It moves in to circle them as they emerge from the lane into a clearing. If they turn quickly to catch sight of whatever it is, it flits off and out the edge of their vision. It could be *muscal volintantes*, flying flies, cell fragments floating across their irises. As they approach the house where Alfred Sargent lived and left suddenly after Henry died, they see its gutted interior spilling out the back door and into the yard.

Where the Sargent brothers lived is overgrown and caving in. Their farmyard is a weaving of weeds, dog mustard, Russian pigweed bound up with morning glory, prickly lettuce, its leaf margins rotating to the glare of the high sun. The old bachelors were like the prickly lettuce, on edge to the hot eye of scrutiny while they had lived there; spiky leaves turned broadside to the horizontal plane of sunrise and sundown where the light is softer, the curvature of the horizon more apparent. The brothers, it is said, were recluses and spectators only to other worlds rising and going away from them.

There is a gully not far from the Sargent farm site that is reedy and wet, and often at the beginning and end of the day mist rises from it and rolls onto the yard. The refraction of light casts muted shadows then; a tilting tool shed, its weathered siding becomes the colour of dove, the texture of brushed suede; the tall farmhouse, a ship sailing through fog; a cinderblock building Henry built and lived in after Emily died becomes obliterated.

Beside the cinder-block building, in a clearing Henry hacked out of a stand of oak and cottonwood, is his garden. It is revealed suddenly, the whole of it, Henry's garden of concrete sculptures. When prowling children come upon it, it brings to their minds a commune of ghosts caught holding a meeting, or people dancing in white nightdresses, turned to stone at the appearance of the intruder. There are near to twenty sculptures in all, made in the years following Emily's death. A dragon towers over women reclining in the grass among deer, a lion; Pegasus keeps watch at the entrance of the garden. Satan and Eve are there too, and monkeys squat in the grass. In the centre of the garden Jonah erupts from the mouth of a whale and shakes a hammer at the evening sky. A naked woman sprawls, a lascivious smile, a finger pointing out a message scratched in a concrete tablet. *After spending three days and three nights in the whale, Jonah started to build a house inside. The whale did not tolerate that and threw him out.*

Because Alfred left his house suddenly, years ago, after he found Henry hanging from the rafters in the barn, there is more to see inside it. He left the furniture, blankets on a narrow cot in the kitchen, and food still in a cabinet. Jars of apple jelly; dill pickles gone soft and milky. Articles of clothing are strewn among a litter of broken crockery and chunks of gyprock, trampled underfoot and stinking of rodent faeces. Vandals have punched holes in the walls, searching for money. They have ripped the cloth on a billiard table in the tool shed, hacked its legs off with an axe, pulled down the ceiling. They have started in on the sculpture garden, and as children walk among the silent figures they notice a new ruin each time. Satan's horns have gone missing, an arm has been broken off, one of Pegasus' wings is shattered, a woman's nose, breast smashed. Each sculpture soon becomes incomplete in some way.

Except for one. It stands apart from the others among white birch, the figure of a sightless man looking skyward, his mouth open like a bird forever waiting to be fed. A single tablet sits at the edge of the sculpture garden, its words, faintly drawn, are almost obliterated by the elements. Where the Sargent brothers lived is, after all, a place where the course of life can still be changed by the elements.

*Forgive me*, the letters on the tablet say, *H. Sargent*.

# Acknowledgements

The author wishes to thank the Manitoba Arts Council, the Canada Council, and the Saskatoon Public Library Writer In Residency Program, for their assistance during the writing of these stories. Thanks to Susan Rempel Letkemann for her careful reading of the story "The Man from Mars." A special thanks to Ellen Seligman.

Some of these stories have appeared elsewhere in slightly different form. "The Midnight Hour" was published in *The New Quarterly* as "The Birthday Party." "A Necessary Treason" was published in *Prairie Fire* as "A Mother Sitting on a Chair." "I Used to Play Bass in a Band" was also published in *Prairie Fire*. "Rooms for Rent" appeared in the magazine *Border Crossings*, and was nominated for a National Magazine Award. "Phantom Limbs" appeared in *Heart's Wild*, an anthology of stories published by Turnstone Press. A small portion of "The Two-Headed Calf" was published as "Eleanore, Remembering" in an anthology of stories, *Due West*. "I Used to Play Bass in a Band" was the title of a shorter piece published in *More Than Words Can Say* (1990), an anthology of essays and thoughts on literacy. "Disappearances" was published in *Saturday Night*.